THROUGH SOFT AIR

THROUGH SOFT AIR

LEE BATTERSBY

PRIME BOOKS

THROUGH SOFT AIR.
Copyright © 2006 by **Lee Battersby**.
Cover art copyright © 2006 by **Ian Field-Richards**.
Cover design copyright © 2006 by **Garry Nurrish**.

Prime Books
www.prime-books.com

To Erin, who gave me a reason not to die,
And to Lyn, who gives me reason to live

Thanks are due: First and foremost, my darling wife Lyn—lover, editor, critic, fan; my wonderful children, both born and Bonus—Aiden who-will-grow-up-to-be-one-of-us, Blake the mosquito conversationalist, "Darth Barbie" Cassi the fighting Princess, Erin Jane Butterfly and Connor Bonner; Geoffrey Maloney, who badgered me to get off my ass and submit this thing to Prime. Without whom, and all that jazz: Sean Wallace, and a single word—Sold!; The editors who bought my stories and worked to make me better, in particular Sarah Endacott, Keith Stevenson, and the committees at Borderlands and ASIM who seem so fond of my stuff; the mighty Sunday Night Crew for enduring mood swings that would put a bear to shame—Chesh, Calli, Mynxii, Splanky, PRK, Tori, Martin, Dr Izz, and Sheldon; and lastly, those writers above me in the food-chain who have treated me like a peer when I am not fit to lace their drinks—most especially Stephen Dedman and Dave Luckett, but also the likes of Kate Forsyth, Simon Brown, KA Bedford, Kim Wilkins, Sean Williams, Terry Dowling, Rob Hood, Chris Lawson, and Tim Powers. I am humbled, guys.

CONTENTS

Introduction: Solid Air, by Geoffrey Maloney 9
Father Muerte & the Theft 13
Silk 28
Carrying The God 39
Pass The Parcel 53
Through The Window Merrilee Dances 60
Elyse 69
The Divergence Tree 79
Jaracara's Kiss 90
The Hobbyist 107
Mikal 119
Letters To Josie 128
A Stone To Mark My Passing 137
Vortle 146
Ecdysis 154
A Very Good Lawyer 173
Goodfellow 178
Stalag Hollywood 185
Brillig 196

continued

His Calliope 207
Father Renoir's Hands. 214
Through Soft Air. 222
Dark Ages 236
Tales of Nireym. 245
Father Muerte & The Rain 256
Pater Familias 277

SOLID AIR: AN INTRODUCTION
GEOFFREY MALONEY

When asked to write an introduction for Lee Battersby's very first collection of stories, I was immediately reminded of the song "Solid Air" that English folkie, John Martyn, wrote for his mate, another English folkie, the legendary Nick Drake. I'm not John Martyn and Lee's not Nick Drake, but as an Australian writer I'm happy to count Lee as one of my mates, a colleague of grand fantastical literary pursuits and a writer who has a style, sensibility and approach that resonates deeply.

Our friendship grew out of a mutual respect for each other's writing. Simple as that. We didn't belong to the same writer's workshop, we didn't meet each other at any of the conventions that seem to be the place to make *the* connections, and we didn't grow up in the same city. We live on the opposite sides of our vast opposing continent. I'm east coast. He's west coast. There's a great big desert in-between. I don't travel much. Lee travels a bit more. But only twice have we met in person. We didn't become friends, or realise that we had anything in common, until we'd read each other's work in the various Aussie magazines, and both saw something in what the other had written that we admired. I like to think we both asked ourselves, "How does he do that?"

I've known Lee for few years now, read just about everything that he's written and, for me, that's a question I still can't answer very well. But I'll try.

Lee Battersby's writing is Solid Air. I can't think of two words that describe his work better than that. There is dark grit and substance to his writing, something that is so substantial and solid that, when you read his stuff, you can feel it in your hands. All the darkness of the earth is there, the sense there are things dwelling under the floorboards of the house you've just bought that you don't wish to know about, and even further down, if you dig deep enough, you'll find your own personal hell.

Just about everybody in Lee's stories finds that hell. Some joyfully create it, as the gentleman detective in 'The Hobbyist" and relish in that joy. Others, like the rotten priest in 'Father Renoir's Hands' and Doctor Robards in "Carrying the God" joyfully create it and are astonished at the reckoning that it brings. And still others, like the lost driver in "A Stone to Mark My Passing" or the young homemakers in "Silk" find it unwittingly.

But Lee Battersby is not all darkness. Let me cough here for a moment. No, he does occasionally, let you come up for some air—and gives you a chance to breathe again. And that air, when he gives it to you, is delightful, full of humanity and spirit, the occasional rainbow and the odd double sunrise—on a nice day.

The Father Muerte tales in this collection, while holding many dark undercurrents, dazzle with their wit and humour, and their sense of a history untold. Father Muerte understands evil like none of Lee's other characters do. There is no chance luck about this. Lee makes his other characters suffer or overcome as the muse instructs him, but with Father Muerte, Lee has given him the power to understand and control the dark and evil, and the light and the air too, and in doing so has created a classic literary figure. Father Muerte has been there, done the evil stuff ,and now he tries to bring some peace and tranquillity to the world he inhabits. We love Father Muerte, but how much do we wish to know of his past? When you read the stories, you'll find out what a big question that is. There's a novel in there at least, if the whole story should be known.

Finally, I can't resist mentioning the sheer delight to be found in stories such as "Goodfellow," "Pass the Parcel," and "Through the Window, Merrilee Dances." In these stories we get a glimpse of the softer air. Love, life, romance and magic. Stories that are like pure oxygen. Sometimes there are happy endings—well, kind of—and I think Lee, despite his dark sensibility, understands this better than most of us do.

Lee Battersby's stories are all born from a fantastic imagination, imbued with a wonderful sense of history and an occasional doff of the hat to popular culture. They are stories which resonate with life and the sweet dark mystery it is—stories of solid air.

Geoffrey Maloney
Brisbane, Australia
May 2005

FATHER MUERTE & THE THEFT

Mama Casson showed me along the mosaic-covered corridor and into the little room at the end. I'd have found it without her. In the narrow hallways of the Hotel Quixote any sound is magnified. I could have followed the loudest of the echoing sobs to its source. However, it is Mama's hotel, and she does like to feel a part of things. I pressed a fifty peso note into her fat hand and took off my hat.

"Bueno, Mama." It's good to keep people in this town lubricated. Costa Satanas is an unusual place. Distractions are always to be found. A healthy band of informants ensures I have the pick of the most inviting cases. I coughed discreetly. The young woman doing the crying got up from her chair and wiped fingers across her damp eyes.

"Signori Muerte?"

"Not Signori, Senorita." I replied, taking her outstretched hand and giving it a gentle squeeze. "The locals occasionally ask me to perform some priestly functions so they call me that for convenience, but it has been a long time since I shared conversations with God. I'm more of a, how would you say, investigator of unusual happenings. A jack of no trades, perhaps." I manufactured a small, sympathetic smile. "Which may be more use to you than an ordinary priest." I nodded past her, to the bed she had been sitting beside. A muscular young man lay on it. "Your husband?"

"Yes. We were on our honeymoon . . . " She started her crying again.

I patted her shoulders. "May I?"

She signaled assent. I bent down to examine him. I guessed him to be around the same age as his wife, in that vague way the young have of being ageless. He was good looking, I suppose, if you like that sort of thing. I ran fingers lightly over him, but could detect, neither visually or by touch, any marks, scratches, or puncture wounds. He made no response to my contact. His bare chest rose and fell with solemn grace.

"Are there any unusual marks or discolourations?" I asked, gesturing towards his denim shorts.

The girl shook her head. "No. Why?"

"It may have indicated some poisoning, perhaps. There are a few little nasties of the fish and spider variety hereabout."

"We haven't been to the country or anything. We haven't even been to the beach yet."

"Hmm." I looked into his eyes. They were open, and stared through me as I bent over. I pulled a penlight from my jacket pocket and shined its beam into first one, then the other. They made no movement. Not even the irises shrank in the sudden light. I reached out and placed a fingertip on one, ignoring the shocked gasp behind me. The eyeball was dry. If and when he came out of his fugue, this fellow was going to be photosensitive for a few days. I motioned to his wife to bring my Gladstone bag from where I had laid it near the door. She did so. I opened it and pulled out some favourite implements. She looked at me nervously.

"What are you going to do?"

"Nothing out of the ordinary," I told her. "Just a few standard tests to check reflexes, see if I can detect any sort of unconscious conditioning operating." For the next few minutes I buried myself in tapping his knees, pricking the inside of his elbows, opening his mouth and poking the tongue, and a few other tests the reasons for which I chose not to share with the young woman beside me. I received no reaction for my efforts. Finally, I took blood and saliva samples and placed the test tubes into the bag.

"Has he voided at all?" I asked.

"Uh, no." She shook her head.

"Any excess sweating, nose running, drooling even?"

"No, nothing," she replied. "He's just been lying there, just lying . . . " She started her crying once more. I offered her a tissue, which she used to blow her nose.

"And you say he's been like this for—"

"Th . . . three days," she managed between sniffles. "But he started to get tired and clumsy a couple of days beforehand. It was like he just . . . just slowed down and stopped." She hid her nose in the tissue again.

"Hmm. When exactly was the first time you noticed a change in his behaviour?"

There was a stool in front of the tiny washstand. She sat down. Her prettyish face lined itself with thought. I folded my hands and gazed through the window toward where Carlos bullied his crew on the deck of *The Seagull*; the only fishing boat left in the harbour this late in the morning. Carlos is an idiot, and one day I shall do something about him. Presently the young wife made a small noise, and I turned to her again.

"It was about a week ago, I think." she began. "We had gone into town to get some fresh air and buy food. We'd only been here a few days and . . . " She crinkled one corner of her lips and shrugged.

I nodded. "I understand. A honeymoon, after all."

She blushed and continued. "We were sitting at a little café when a man approached us. He was taking photographs of people, and he asked us if we'd like one. Only, when he gave it to us . . . "

"Yes?"

"I—I have it somewhere." There was an open suitcase on the floor at the end of the bed, overflowing with crumpled clothes. She plunged her hands into the pile and rummaged around, drawing out a small square of paper and handing it to me. "See?"

I looked at it. The photograph showed her sitting at one of the tables outside a café I recognised as Benito's, one of the nicer establishments along the seafront. She was smiling and squinting in the morning sun, happy and pretty and slightly sunburnt. There was another chair at the table. It was empty. I looked up at her.

"He said it must be a fault in the film, that he wouldn't charge us for it. I wanted to give him something anyway, but he simply said he had what he wanted and walked off."

"And after that, your husband began to act strangely?"

"Yes." She looked at his supine form and used the back of her hand to stifle a small sob. "He complained about being tired that afternoon, so we had an early night. After that he was just more and more tired all the time, until . . . " She started crying yet again. I looked out the window. *The Seagull* was finally chugging out of the harbour. The sun shone brightly, high in a cloudless sky. I stood and walked to the door.

"I have a number of enquiries to make regarding this matter, but I shouldn't worry too much. These things often end up being solved in the simplest manner." I made my exit, stopping at Mama Casson's room to pay my respects and leave some instructions for the care of the young woman. Before she came to our little town, Mama had been persecuted in her native country for her talents with potions and brews. I was confident she could make sure her charge got some sleep.

Costa Satanas is an unusual place, on any number of levels. Its street plan for example, were you able to draw it accurately, forms a perfect tessaract. This is good news for an experienced resident. Nothing is very far away from anything else if you know the right way to get there. Within moments of leaving the hotel, I was knocking on the door of Benito's, a mile away at the opposite end of the beach. Through the glass I could see Benito shuffling toward me, his face coloured with the fury that always rests just beneath its surface. He was about to shake a fat finger toward the opening times painted on the window when I allowed him to see me. His immediately adopted a more obsequious pose, and rushed to open the door.

"Signori Muerte. Forgive me. I did not realise it was you, or I would have been much quicker."

"No, it is I who should ask forgiveness, Benito. Were this matter not so urgent, I would not have prevailed upon you to open so early in the afternoon when I know you and Manuela are busy with your stocktaking."

A small cloud flushed Benito's greasy skin. He considers himself a careful man. His wife remains unaware of the way he and his young assistant count stock. Occasionally, I like to let him see that I do know. It kills him to wonder how I find out such things.

"Yes, well, a proprietor of an establishment such as this is always busy, Signori." He opened the door further and ushered me inside. "Manuela," he bellowed, taking two seats from the top of a table, "bring some Madeira for myself and the Father. The one we keep for visitors."

The good stuff, eh? I thought, and made a mental note to find out later why he assumed he was in trouble. We sat down.

"Thank you, Benito, but not for me. I do not drink—wine."

He waved his hand. "Of course. Some coffee instead, perhaps?"

I sighed and nodded. One day, when I have tracked down a print of sufficient quality, I will introduce the people of this place to Bela Lugosi. I may even introduce them to the concept of irony. While the fat man shouted the new order to Manuela, I pulled the photograph from my pocket.

"Benito," I said, pushing it across the tabletop. "Do you remember this woman? Say, a week or so ago?"

He looked at the photo, taking note of the background, looking up to compare it to the view out of his front window. Eventually he sighed and passed it back to me.

"I am sorry, Signori. She is not familiar. We get so many here and . . ." He shrugged. *She is too pale and blonde for my tastes. I wouldn't have paid her any attention* the shrug said. "I hope she is not in any trouble?"

You fat gossip, I thought, but merely replied, "Her? No, my friend, not this one. She simply wishes to contact the person who took this photo so she can order another print for her poor dear grandmother. Tell me, would you know of any photographers working hereabouts?"

Manuela arrived with our wine and coffee. I waited while Benito watched his mistress retreat to the kitchen. He poured drinks for us both.

"Cream?"

"No, thank you," I replied. "Dark as the Devil and twice as sweet."

He smiled at the old saying. I drank. It was as good as always. There are many things wrong with this world, but Benito D'Amico's coffee is not one of them. He considered my question while I sat and let the warm, sugary liquid flow through my bones.

At *Benito's* the service is quick and friendly. This has nothing to do with the owner, who took his own time thinking over my question. It wasn't until I was on my second cup, and he on his third glass, that he spoke.

"There are any number of photographers around here each day, Signori, but there has been one . . . "

"Yes?"

"Well, he is a new face, that is all. I remember him because he only wants to photograph foreigners, and because he has such an unusual camera. It caught my eye, you see. But other than that . . . " He turned his hands upward and shrugged.

"If I give you a pen and paper," I said, pulling them from a jacket pocket, "could you draw him?"

A minute's stroll from *Benito's* along the right streets and I was on the outskirts of town, comfortably ensconced within my house. It looks no different from the other buildings crouched along the small street leading out into the hills. However, it is built in such a way, and at such an angle in relation to the world around it, that I have unlimited views of the little universe that is my home. From here, should I choose, I can look over the length and breadth of the entire town, watching those whose lives I make my business.

For now, however, my view was cast inward. Seating myself at the kitchen table, I pulled Benito's picture from a jacket pocket, smoothed a line or two, and laid it on a cutting board. I fixed each corner with a pin made of pure silver. Benito had been an artist in a previous life, and much of his talent remained. He had produced no ordinary ballpoint cartoon. The face on the square of paper danced with hidden life. It was perfect for my needs.

I spent ten minutes gathering the ingredients I needed, and finding the right book from amongst the jumbled library I keep crammed in one of the kitchen cupboards. I have some powers, thanks to the manner of my birth. For everything else, there are books. Chanting the words of the required spell, I sprinkled pinches of the assembled herbs across the paper. Some Jimson Weed, a little hex-grass, garlic to taste . . . .

"Hey!"

I stopped chanting and looked down. The picture stared up at me with a sneer.

"You wanna watch it with the fairy dust, champ?"

Typical. I always get the rude ones. "Dreadfully sorry," I said, brushing some of the herbs onto the table. "Is that better? Shall we begin?"

"Whatever. It's your dime." Charming. And this was only the essence of the man I sought, the shadow of identity captured within his image. I couldn't wait to meet the real article.

"Okay." I leaned forward and looked into his blue-inked eyes. "It's simple, really. I just want to know your name and where you live."

"Oh, please." The picture rolled its eyes. "You know the rules, pal. I don't have to do nothing to betray myself to the likes of you. Non-harmful advice, that's all I'm giving."

"Betray? What makes you think you'd be betraying yourself?"

"What am I, an idiot? I'm not as thick as these pen lines, buddy. I know who you are. You ain't trying to find me so you can give me a big bunch of flowers."

"No, you're right there. Still, you *will* tell me what I need to know." I picked a box of matches up from the table. I took a match out and struck it, holding it so the flickering flame filled my captive's vision. He watched it fearfully, but still managed to offer some resistance.

"You wouldn't have the balls."

"No?" I touched the flame to the lower corner of the paper. We both watched it blacken and curl, chewing the page and forcing the ink head further and further into the opposite corner. As the ruined edge of paper drew closer to him he began to shout.

"All right, all right. I'll tell you. Just put it out, okay? Put it out!"

I licked my thumb and used it to tamp out the flame. When I was finished, barely a quarter of the sheet remained, held in place by a single pin.

"Well?"

"Anglomar. My name is Henri Anglomar." He looked to where his feet would be had Benito drawn a body. "Over on the Avenue of Artists, between the churches of Saint Genesius and Nicholas of Tolentino."

"Thank you." I lit another match and applied it to the paper. When the flames had fully disposed of my informant, I scraped the ashes into my hand and left the house.

Around me the day hung still and tired. Tourists like this sort of heat, so I'm told. A few suitable gestures and incantations, and a wind sprang from the harbour and raced lightly through the streets towards where I stood. As it passed, I opened my fist and let it snatch the ashes.

A long time ago, a woman whose name the world has forgotten taught me how to read the weather. I didn't just feel the wind that surrounded me, I could see it. I saw the patterns it formed in the sky, traced the paths it followed and the trails it left behind. I watched the ashes rise, learning their destination from the way they skittered and jumped across the heavens. Still imbued with Anglomar's essence, they headed straight for his residence, their only wish to become one with him again. I smiled. I had been right not to trust the picture. They weren't moving towards the Avenue of Artists. They were heading for the Corpus.

It has been said, and indeed it is what attracts many people to the place, that each person who comes to Costa Satanas sees only what they want to in the surroundings the town provides them. Some parts of town have many names, and wear as many faces as they have visitors. Others, however, have such a strong identity that they impose only a single reality upon everyone. The Corpus is one of these places.

It is a remarkable thing: a swift flowing river charges through a cleft in the ninety-foot cliffs upon which the upper village is situated, before pouring down towards the beach which circles the town's rear end. Years ago, when The Baron still ran joy-flights over the bay, a vacationing doctor had looked down upon the circular town, with its mazes of streets and alleyways and proclaimed that it looked like nothing so much as a giant brain. As the river bisected the town, he called it the Corpus Callosum, and the name, shortened to "The Corpus," stuck.

I had no need to catch the wind to get there, so I was in place long before the tattered ashes crested the edge of the cliff and floated across the river. They headed towards apartments carved into the wall opposite my vantage point. They soon swooped down to flutter helplessly against a door on the second tier of walkways.

Back when Costa Satanas was first allowed to attract outsiders, some enterprising soul had the bright idea of using the cliffs to provide cheap housing for the anticipated flood of backpackers and tourists. Overnight, and I mean literally overnight, balconies appeared along the sheer wall faces. Doors were erected, leading to spacious rooms hollowed out from the rock. Lights, and water, and fittings were installed, and a trickle of sunburnt strangers began to take up residence. A week after work began the Corpus was a place, not just a fancy name dreamed up by a temporary foreigner. Now it was home to all manner of residents—some temporary; some more permanent—each of whom found the crashing of the river on the rocks below to their liking. This Anglomar was unknown to me, which meant he was either a newcomer or a tourist. How I dealt with him would largely depend upon which.

I did not have to wait long before I spied a figure descending the steps from the clifftop and moving along the walkway. It was Anglomar. Judging by his weary stoop, and the camera that dangled from the strap over his shoulder, his day's work was complete. He opened his door and went inside. I smiled as the gust from the closing door blew the ashes over the edge of the walkway to the river below. I muttered a few words and let the Corpus fall into evening. Some things are better achieved in the dark. Stepping from my perch, I floated down to stand in front of Anglomar's door. It was locked, but when I am in the mood, that is no impediment.

Nothing magical, I'm just good at picking locks. Within seconds, I stepped inside. I found my prey in the tiny dining room, hunched over a table, watching a tray of anonymous lumps rotating in the kitchenette's microwave oven. At my entrance, he leaped to his feet.

"What the hell?"

"Sit down." I waved a hand and watched him sink into the chair, his face reflecting his struggle to stop his muscles from betraying him.

"Now," I said, sitting on the chair at the opposite side of the table, "where is it?"

"Where is what?" Sheer physical strength enabled him to push the question out past the location his lips were trying to reveal to me.

"Please don't annoy me, Henri." The microwave rang the end of its cooking cycle. I removed the tray and placed it on the table. From a jacket pocket I took the coltello d'amore knife I once received from a Borgia sister, and began to eat. The meal was chicken. Allegedly. Anglomar's eyes never left the knife. When I was finished I cleared away the table and laid the coltello in front of me, the blade pointing directly toward his heart. His eyes widened but did not move from its shining point.

"Henri." His eyes dragged themselves upwards. "I am not in the mood to be played with. You have caused a lot of trouble to a young couple who expected to enjoy themselves in my town. This upsets me. Where is it?"

This time, his strength was not enough. His arm flung outwards, pointing towards an unkempt sofa bed that spread itself across the far corner of the room.

"Under—sheets."

"Be so good as to get it for me." Fighting my command with every step, he walked over and retrieved his camera. I examined it as he placed it on the table before me. It looked slightly old fashioned, perhaps bulky compared to the compact units favoured by photographers these days, although it was not so huge as to appear archaic. To the casual eye, it would resemble something handed down by a grandfather, or bought in one of those crowded old antique shops that hide in the town's alleys. There was a clasp along one side. I undid it, swinging the box open to reveal its inner workings. I laughed when I saw what was inside.

"Well, well, well. That I did *not* expect. Come on, out you come!" I drew a large pair of tweezers from a jacket pocket and used them to reach in amongst the gearwheels and levers and snare the tiny creature that crouched there. I pulled him out, ignoring his curses and complaints, and held him up in front of my face.

"Hello, Bauer." I smiled, then dropped him on the table. The little demon brushed himself off and stood up.

"You turd! You've bruised my wing." He flexed the appendage, wincing. "What the hell are you doing here?" His tiny face curled into a snarl. He spat onto the table, and a wisp of smoke rose from where the spittle began to burn through the cheap Formica.

"Now, now. Show some respect to your betters." I poked him in the chest, causing him to fall backwards and roll toward the edge of the table. He managed to stop himself in time and sat up.

"What the hell is going on here?" Bauer and I turned to where, unnoticed by us both, Anglomar had backed against the wall and was now viewing us with a terrified expression. I summoned him forward, and his body walked jerkily across to the table. I stared past his eyes, then laughed and turned to Bauer.

"You clever little sod. He has no idea, does he?"

Bauer shrugged in a way that said, *but of course*. "I needed someone who was going to be here for a long time, and this one was *so* full of plans." He smiled a truly unpleasant smile. I turned back to Anglomar. Reaching into my jacket, I extracted one of my business cards and put it in his unresisting hand.

"Henri, listen to me closely. On Jongleur Street is a small shop. The owner, Mr Gull, lives above it. Use my name as a credit marker and buy a lease. It will make a perfect studio. Do not come back for at least three hours. You will retain no memory of these events. Go now." He left the apartment. I returned my attention once more to the demon and his camera. While he made threats against me, I bent to the case and examined its workings.

"Very clever, Bauer. Does Mister Babbage know you're using his machine this way?"

"Babbage was an idiot. It was no challenge to harvest him."

"Not like Crowley, eh?" I smiled at him. "He wasn't too pleased to discover you weren't quite the Lord of the Pain Spheres he was expecting, was he?"

The discomfort of memory crossed his ugly little maw, and he snapped, "What are you doing here anyway, Shadow? What do you want?"

I reached out and gripped his jaw between thumb and forefinger. "Do not ever presume to call me that again so long as you exist. Now, give me what I require."

"You have no power over me," he managed to strangle out. "I answer to our Master, not to one of his cast-off shades."

"Really?" I twisted my hand so he was encased in a fist, with only his head sticking above. With the other hand, I reached into the camera and drew out three vials, each filled with a pearl-coloured liquid. I stood them before him.

"Which one is the young foreigner's soul?"

The demon smiled at me, a fanged grin full with malice.

"Which one are you, puppet? When the Lord fell and the fire burned away all his useless, human aspects, which one did you become, hmm? You want to give the meat-sack his soul back, you decide which one it should be." He threw his head back and shrieked in laughter. "The Lord giving a soul back. That's rich, that's really rich."

I increased the pressure of my grip until pain made him gasp. I slid the tip of my thumb up under his chin until his head was tilted back hard against the top of my index finger.

"I have not been part of your Lord for a long time, ugly little beast. I will not see harm come to those under my care. Now,"—I tilted my hand until he could see the vials again—"which one is the soul of the foreigner?"

"Forget it."

I shrugged and examined the vials. As I expected, there was nothing to distinguish one from the others. The soul has no physical aspect, no volume or dimensions. The vials contained a liquid known only in a few select circles. It will absorb a soul, but the soul will not change the liquid in any way. It would be impossible to find by any means of which I was aware. I heard Bauer laughing.

"Give up, Shadow? There's no way you'll find it. Only I know. Only me. And I'm not telling you for anything."

"You won't?" I looked at the way I was holding the little demon, his horny head emerging from my closed fist like a cartoon worm peeking from his hole. Something about that image gave me pause. I followed the thought, letting it lead my subconscious until it turned over the answer to my problem. Bauer saw me smile, and frowned.

"What?"

"Worms." I said. "Planarian worms."

"Planary what?"

"Teach a planarian worm to run a maze, then chop it up and feed it to a bunch of other planarian worms that have never even seen the maze. What do you think happens?"

"They get sick? I don't care. What has that got to do wi—" He choked as I squeezed my fist.

"Shush. The new worms can run the maze, that's what happens, even though they've never been inside it. As if they've absorbed the knowledge at the cellular level, below any conscious thought."

"So what? That has . . ." he stopped and stared at me as the thread of my thoughts became apparent to him. "You wouldn't."

"I wouldn't?" Now my smile was filled with malice. "Knowledge below consciousness. Race memory, osmosis, tapes that teach while you sleep. Chop up a worm and it still retains knowledge. Give a stupid little demon a secret and let it settle deep inside, right to the cellular level, way down into every atom of its ugly little body . . ." I increased the pressure of my thumb under his chin. "So if you won't consciously tell me which one holds the boy's soul, maybe I'll just see whether your cells will oblige me."

"I'll tell him where you are," he gulped. "He'll destroy you."

I sighed. "He already knows."

I flicked my thumb forward like someone tossing a coin. Bauer's head sailed up, and across, and knocked over one of the vials.

"You bastard!" he screamed. I picked up the other vials and emptied them into the sink. I dropped Bauer's body into one, then grasped his cursing head between finger and thumb and dropped it in the other.

"Thank you, you've been very helpful." I sealed both tubes and placed them in a jacket pocket. I could hear the little demon's head continuing to curse through the fabric. I closed the camera and picked it up, placed the vial containing the young husband's soul into another pocket, retrieved my knife, and made my exit.

Mama Casson and I stood at the end of the pier and watched as the muscular young man loaded suitcases into the back of the small flying boat. His wife chattered away, constantly touching and hugging him as she talked. He smiled at her gaiety, only pausing in his work to readjust the sunglasses that shielded his eyes. The black gentleman helping them straightened from his crouch, slapped the man on the back, and hustled the young couple together for one last photograph. Then the husband waved to us and climbed into the plane. Together the young bride and the photographer walked towards us.

"All set," the smiling woman announced. "Henri has our address and he's promised to send us a full set of prints as soon as they're developed."

"Absolutely," Anglomar said. "I'll get stuck into them straight away. Mama, Father." He nodded his good-byes to us, waved towards the plane, and walked away down the pier. We watched him go. The young bride turned to us.

"Thank you both so much. I don't know how I can ever repay—"

"Watching you enjoy yourselves these last two weeks has been payment enough," I said with as much cavalier grace as I could manage. One day, I shall introduce Douglas Fairbanks Junior to this town as well. Tears welled in the wife's eyes. I feared she was going to start her crying again, but instead she stood on tiptoes and threw her arms around my neck. I allowed her to kiss my cheek and whisper, "Thank you" in my ear. Behind her, the pilot started his engines.

She disengaged herself from me and ran to the aircraft. We waved. The door closed and the plane taxied out into the bay and took off. I smiled as it roared just over the top of *The Seagull* returning late again, causing Carlos to throw himself onto the deck of the little boat. One good deed deserves another: as the aircraft rose, I allowed rainbows to break out and follow it out of the bay. After it passed out of sight, Mama Casson and I began the walk back up the pier toward town. At the end of it, we turned to go our separate ways. Mama reached up to pat my arm and smile at me.

"You are a good man, Father. A good man."

"Not yet, Mama," I said, "but I'm learning."

AFTERWORD

Every now and again, I write a story that ends up being a "kitchen-sinker": all my current fascinations, odd bits of research and weird little bits of trivia I've stored up get spurted out onto the page and then assembled into some sort of rough order. This was the first time it happened, and it dominated something like three months of writing time—until I finished this story, I could concentrate on nothing else. It was worth it: the story made Datlow & Windling's Recommended Reading List, and spawned (to date) three sequels. I don't like to do it too often, because I'm a bit of a magpie when it comes to writing and have a bunch of projects on the go at once, but such complete immersion in a story is a frightening and wonderful place to be.

SILK

The worst house in the best street, that's what Dad always told me.

"You can renovate a house, but you can't improve a neighbourhood unless you leave it," he'd say, signalling my step-mum for another beer.

The house we bought was a rundown afterthought, planted firmly at the end of the road like a gatecrasher who can't quite believe his luck. Dad walked in, nodded his approval, and put his arm around Susan with a familial warmth neither of us were entirely comfortable with.

"You'll be all right here," he said with an undercurrent of envy. "You'd be surprised what these old houses can do, once you start digging away. I was born in one just like this, a couple of months after the War started. Bomb-proof, they are." He punched a wall with an affectionate fist. "You'd be surprised."

And surprised we were. I've never been one for hard graft, but once we got stuck into the task it became addictive. The joy of finding *just* that right tint of paint, or the perfect paper, to recreate the feeling of the house's original days was like the thrill of the hunt. We became a dog pack of two, running down wrought iron railings and shellac, lead-free fillers and wood stains, until we could separate our chosen prey from the herd and bring it down with a howl, credit cards raised in feral triumph. The day we found a working radio from the '40s I was like an ancestor who'd single-handedly brought down a mastodon. Only the veneer of civilisation stopped me from pulling Susan to the ground and having her right there in the carpark.

We worked our way from back to front, starting with those rooms we could not live without, and leaving the casual rooms until last. The kitchen and bathroom were early successes, as was the master bedroom, where pride of place was accorded the ceiling rose Dad had gifted us once he'd seen the job we were doing. The house was almost complete by the time we were ready to tackle the living room. Only this last space, and the patio area, remained to be conquered. Susan and I stood at the door and surveyed our objectives.

"I call the floor," she shouted, an all-important half second before me.

"You did the last one."

"Quick or dead, my friend," she laughed, striding into the room and picking up the crowbar. "You should know by now."

I snorted in return and made my way to where the paper stripper leaned against the wall, waiting. "You won't be so quick when you're looking at the bricks outside."

She raised her eyebrows in amusement, grabbed the metal bar, and began quartering the floor, tapping and poking at the floorboards. Every now and again she would bend down and make a mark with a stick of carpenter's chalk, delineating spots where timber putty, or outright replacement, was merited. I watched her, my own task forgotten, lost in the movement of her lithe body and the childlike frown that always adorned her face whenever she was deep in concentration. She was halfway across the room when the crowbar thunked down on a board and went through without pausing.

"Crap!" Susan jumped back in shock, then pulled the jemmy out. "Oh hell, that whole section's going to need . . . hey, what's that?"

She knelt, and peered into the opening the accident had created. "David, check this out."

"What?" I dropped down next to her. "I can't see. Where did we put the torch?"

"Watch yourself." The crowbar slid past my face and back into the hole. Susan grunted. A six-inch section of floor whipped up and spun away.

"Shit!"

"Told you to watch yourself." She bent her head once more . "Now, what is this?"

Before I could warn her about holes and the things that live in them, she reached in and pulled something out, looking at it in wonderment.

"It's silk."

"What?"

"It's silk. Loads of it. It's crammed in there, David. I can see tons of the stuff." She started pulling at the material, dragging it from its confinement. "Help me."

I grabbed the crowbar and used it to lever up the surrounding floorboards. Soon we had a gap large enough to pull up armfuls of grubby fabric. It lay heaped around us, filling the living room in drifts almost to our knees. We looked at each other across a snowfield of dirty grey material.

"Well," I said eventually. "What now?"

"Let's get it outside. I think this is all one piece. If we spread it out on the lawn we might be able to see what it is."

We managed to drag the massive pile of silk into the front yard, then around to the back where we could open it out without attracting the attention of neighbours and passers by. Our backyard is huge, nearly twenty metres to a side. It was one of the reasons we bought the house: room to grow, room for a garden, room for children to play, one day. We covered almost every inch of it. The more we grabbed handfuls and walked in opposite directions, the more of the stuff there seemed to be. Finally, after nearly an hour of sweating and straining, we stood hand in hand on the patio and surveyed our handiwork.

"It's a balloon," I said in bemusement, finally seeing the full shape of the thing for the first time.

"It's a barrage balloon."

"How did you work that out?"

She smiled. "They're called books, David. You really should try them sometimes."

"Oh, ha ha. So what the hell is it doing under my floor?"

She frowned. "I don't know. The house was built in the 30s, but I don't think there were any balloons in Perth during the War. Maybe some Londoner owned the place and brought it with them, used it as insulation under *our* floor."

"Insulation? We should put it back then."

"Are you kidding?" She put her hand on my arm to stop me from gathering up the material, and looked at me with that look which says she's working through an opportunity and needs just one minute more to figure out how to start making it pay.

"Uh oh. What are you thinking?"

"Do you know how much this stuff is worth? That's parachute grade silk, not the flimsy Chinese stuff. Dressmakers will pay a bundle for it. We've got to have, what, seven or eight hundred square metres?"

"It's filthy." I indicated the grey-brown surface. "Who's going to clean that up? Not me."

Susan shrugged. "We're not using the yard at the moment. Leave it out here. It's going to rain tonight. We can just hose off whatever's left in the morning, see how it looks."

That's my Susan. Always has a plan, even if the rest of us can't see it. She turned and went back inside, the problem solved in her mind, no longer miraculous or even terribly interesting. I stayed behind for a few minutes longer, eyeing the lake of silk, until the smell of burnt toast and Susan's cry of "Lunch" drew me back inside.

It did rain that night, a vicious attack of drops that had us lying under the covers, giggling like little children and listening to the thunderclaps overhead. I drifted off to sleep late, lulled by the warmth of Susan's body against mine and the smell of our lovemaking.

When I woke I was alone, and the house was silent. I found Susan out on the back patio, standing stiff and cold in the early morning light. She jumped when I came up behind her and put my arms about her waist.

"Someone's been fucking about," she said in a tight, frightened little voice.

"What?"

I looked past her into the garden. Empty grass stared back. The silk was gone. Someone had stolen our balloon! To make it worse, they had dumped a monstrous concrete block in its place, an ugly grey edifice the height of my shoulder, sitting in the middle of our lawn, like a gravestone marking the death of our avaricious dreams. I walked toward it on unsteady legs.

"How the hell . . . ?"

"No way," I heard Susan behind me. "No way could they have got it in here without us hearing."

I paused, remembering the sounds of the storm, and of Susan screaming my name and urging me along. Then something about the block caught my notice. A cable rose from the far side, disappearing into the sky. I rounded the mass, and saw the winch attached to its far side. I tilted my head, following the cable's ascent. A black shape hung far above me, as if weightless. I shaded my eyes with my hands, and squinted. It was our balloon, no longer flat and lifeless but bulbous and pregnant, straining against its tether as if seeking escape beyond horizons only it could see.

"Susan . . ."

"I see it." Her voice came from just behind my shoulder, where she had come while I stood staring. "But how?"

"I don't know. What do we do now?"

She looked up, her hands raised in imitation of my own. "I've no idea."

"We can't just leave it there."

"No, I know." She lowered her hands. "Let's go inside. I'm hungry, and maybe you'd better put something on before the police get here and tell us to stop blocking the flight path."

She looked me up and down, and I realised I was still naked. I smiled sheepishly, and we turned back into the house. I went into the bedroom to get dressed, and open the curtains upon the day. What I saw made me swear.

"What's the matter?" Susan called from the kitchen.

"The trees! Some bastard's painted the trees!"

"What?" She came into the bedroom, two plates of toast in her hands.

"Look." I pointed outside. "Some bastard's painted the trees in the front yard black."

"Son of a bitch." She placed the plates on the bed and pressed up against our window. "It's not just us, look. Across the road's is the same, and Mrs Henderson's. Unbelievable."

"This is too much. First our balloon and now this. I thought this was supposed to be a good neighbourhood?"

"It is."

"Prove it."

Munching our breakfast, we headed onto the front lawn and scanned the street. Blacked-up trees ran its full length. Susan saw Mrs Henderson in her front yard, so we headed over to say hello.

"Terrible, isn't it?" Susan said to her, nodding toward a formerly-beautiful jacaranda which dominated the old lady's garden. "Have you ever seen such a thing?"

"What's that, dear?" Mrs Henderson replied, squinting through brick-thick glasses in the direction of Susan's pointing finger.

"The trees. To paint them like that. It's such a blatant act of vandalism."

"Really? Oh dear, that would be awful. Just like the War."

Susan and I looked at each other.

"Why do you say that, Mrs H?"

"They used to paint trees during the Blitz, you know," our neighbour replied, peering up at us. My Susan is a petite girl, barely five foot three in her stilettos, but next to the old lady even she stood tall. "Helped with the blackout or something, I suppose. I was only a young girl then, up in Coventry."

"The Blitz? Hey, you wouldn't know anything about barrage balloons, would you?" I asked. "You don't know how anyone could have brought one here with them?"

She blinked at me in surprise. "That's an odd question. Why do you ask?"

"Well," I said, gesturing to where our dressmaking fortune floated five thousand feet above us. "Look what we found."

Mrs Henderson peered into the sky. "I'm sorry, dear. What is it you wanted me to see?"

I followed her gaze. The balloon hung heavy and obvious before us, its comic-cigar shape bright against the blue sky. Even with her myopia, our old neighbour couldn't have missed it. It would be like failing to see the full moon on a clear night.

"There, Mrs H. Right there."

She favoured me with the patronising smile I have never liked from teachers and parents, never mind casual acquaintances.

"Yes, dear. I'm sure there's something very nice there. Must be my eyes. Will you excuse me? I think I hear the kettle whistling."

She shuffled away from us, retreating into the dim recesses of her house.

"Humph. Typical. Can't see a giant balloon, but the old biddy's got the hearing of a bat if she can hear a kettle from this distance."

Susan smiled. "Poor baby. Still don't recognise an excuse when you hear one."

"Very funny." We walked back toward our house. "Still, you'd think she'd see it. It's hardly unnoticeable."

"No, no it isn't." We reached the front door and Susan preceded me inside. "Still, she *is* old, and . . . "

She stopped so suddenly I banged into her.

"What's the . . . "

"The living room. David . . . "

I looked into a room I had never seen. Before we had left the house, it was an empty space with a broken hole in the floor. Now it was . . . well, it was a living room. A wallpapered, painted, furnished living room. Our newly-bought radio, in need of sanding back and varnishing, and with two knobs missing, dominated the view. It stood between two armchairs; near the fireplace we didn't have twenty minutes ago; dark wood shining, knobs gleaming. There was the sound of static, and then it burst into life.

"This is the BBC Home Service . . . "

"That's John Snagge." I spoke in quiet shock, recognising his voice from numerous guest spots on my collection of Goon Show LPs. "But he died in the mid-nineties."

"Maybe it's a tape recording." Susan sounded dreamy, disconnected. I felt the same. This wasn't real, couldn't be real. Weeks of work confronted us, possibly months. There was no way someone could sneak into our house and do it while we chatted to our neighbour in full view of our entrance. Not to mention there was absolutely no reason *why*.

"But... but he stopped reading the news... just after the War..."

"David, this is getting freaky." Susan was frightened. I did my best to hold down my own rising fear.

"I think we should go outside. Now."

We back-pedalled out of the front door, our eyes fixed on the alien room. When we reached the patio we stopped, and turned around.

"David?"

"I see them."

A cable rose from beyond a house at the other end of the street, a barrage balloon floating serenely at its upper reach. Beyond that hung another, and another, the sky a dark backdrop to a legion of globular white shapes, spread out to the horizon. Through the black-painted trees I saw cars in the driveways around us, upright shapes I'd only ever seen in movies, with running boards and external headlights like bug eyes. Directly across from us, three houses had disappeared, including Mrs Henderson's. In their place lay a wasteland of rubble and ruin. I stared at it in horror. I wished very much to see the enormous jacaranda I had stood beneath less than half an hour ago.

Susan's hand flitted against mine. I opened my clenched fingers to grasp it, reassuring each other that we stood as real and solid as always. People passed in the street, their hairstyles and dress relics of a time our *parents* were only just able to remember. One doffed his hat to a lady in a WAC uniform, then looked over in our direction.

"Hey! Turn that bloody light out!"

Without thinking, I reached behind me to the door and pulled it shut, blocking the early evening gloom from the hallway's glare. I had not even noticed the changing of time, nor wondered why the day had so suddenly disappeared before us. We had just finished breakfast, yet we now stood at the beginning of night. The light failed before our eyes. The foreign world slipped into darkness while we watched, our hands entwined, too afraid to look at each other lest the illusion be complete. I didn't want to see the paint-stained and tattered t-shirts and jeans we loved so much replaced by garb indistinguishable from the passers-by who glanced up at the sky and hurried away.

When the day deserted us completely, and we stood engulfed in shadows, Susan slipped her hand from mine.

"What now?" she whispered.

"I'm afraid."

"Me too."

I turned my head then, and regarded the front door. "We can't stay out here."

"I know."

"We have to go in."

"I know."

"Maybe we'll wake up in the morning and this will all have been an hallucination. A dream."

"Yes. Too much paint stripper, or something."

"Yes."

"Yes."

I pushed open the door open. The hallway stretched out before us; resplendent in the old-time fashions we had taken so much pride in recreating. Our bedroom stood shut to our left, and to our right, the terrible and awful living room mocked our gaze. We stepped inside, and shut the door behind us.

"You still have your clothes on."

I looked at her.

"So do you."

She smiled at me then, a small and brave thing that crept onto her face and disappeared just as quickly.

"I'm not hungry."

"Neither am I."

I opened the bedroom door and made to reach for the light switch.

"Don't."

I stopped my hand. Susan moved past me and into the room.

"I don't want to see. I don't want to find the room changed. Not our bedroom. Not here."

I left the light off. We undressed in the dark, on opposite sides of the bed, then climbed under the thin, scratchy blankets that lay in place of our duvet. We made no mention of it to each other, simply drew the harsh fabric around ourselves and reached out arms that shivered, although not from cold. Her head found the crook of my arm, and we turned toward each other.

"An hallucination."

"A bad dream."

We lay awake in the dark, listening to the wind through black-painted trees, and the distant drone of engines.

I began crying when the first bombs fell.

AFTERWORD

When the guidelines for the Wheatland Press anthology *All-Star Zeppelin Adventure* stories were announced I was immediately dared, in public, to write a story to fit. Double dared, so, you know, I had to! Seems my predilection for unsaleable ideas preceded me. Nobody I trusted thought I should write for this one: after all, if I failed to place the story, the central idea was too narrow to sell anywhere else. But it was zeppelins. Science fiction zeppelins! For eight months I stared at an empty page. Then, with the submission period closing on Friday, I woke up on Monday morning with the entire story in my mind, the result of an early morning dream. The only thing not present was the black-painted trees, the result of five minutes search on the web. Give me these kind of dreams any day.

CARRYING THE GOD

Bugh was excited, and a little nervous. He had passed his age only a few days ago, and already it was his turn to carry the God. Excited, because there was no greater honour in all the family, and there was always the chance he would be the chosen carrier when the God allowed the rains to begin. Nervous, because it was still fresh in everybody's memory what had happened the day Geff had stumbled and dropped the God. One of its fingers had broken off. The family had stopped, in fright and shock, their breaths held in anticipation of a mighty vengeance. Then Da had noticed how the finger lay in the sand, pointing its blame at Grama. Even though it had been Geff who dropped the idol, the message was clear: the God blamed Grama for the catastrophe. Their course was clear. They took it quickly, and savagely. The God must have been satisfied: nothing further happened to them.

   Bugh moved to the centre of the family group, and accepted the God and its harness from his older brother, Ler. He was surprised to find it much lighter than he had expected. Like a thing of sticks and bark it lay in its harness, made from strips of cloth the family had torn from their own clothing, and stared up at him with empty eyes. Suppressing a shudder, lest the God should see him and be displeased, Bugh hefted his burden. He turned into the wind, squinting against the inevitable spray of sand. He waited for the God to speak to him, to show him which way the family should shuffle and plod in the search for food or salvation. Nothing happened. No divine voice came whispering through the layers of thin rags that covered his head; no strange, ephemeral tug was felt in his bones to point him in the right direction. The family started to stir, restless at standing still in the searing heat and whipping, stinging wind. Finally, Bugh decided that this must be some sort of test. The God must be watching, waiting to see if the lessons Bugh had learned by trotting alongside Da, and Granda, and Geff and all the other carriers had been absorbed. Picking a course that looked like any other, except for the fact that they had not been walking towards it, Bugh pointed.

"That way," he said. The group moved off in the appointed direction. Bugh held his breath. Nothing happened. He must have passed the God's first test, he decided. Breathing a sigh of relief, he moved after the family.

"Right this way please." Dr Robards opened the door into yet another aseptic white room. The large attendant, whose name Robards had never been permitted to know, pushed forward the wheelchair containing the immobile statue that was Mister Douglas Black. A large machine of arcane shape dominated the room. Part capsule, part still, part who-knows-what, it crouched in the centre of the space like a giant alien arachnid. Chrome perfection glinted in the overhead lights, whilst various tubes pulsed with the liquids that ceaselessly ebbed and flowed through them.

"This is where Mr. Black will be staying." Robards could not keep the patina of satisfaction from glazing his words. "It's been a long time, and taken a lot of money . . . "

"Mr. Black is aware of how much time and money he has invested in this project." The large man spoke without inflection, his voice a flat blade that sliced along Robards' self-congratulation and killed it immediately. "What Mr. Black wishes to know is whether or not it will work. That is all you need to tell him"

"It . . . . Yes, it will work." Robards suppressed a shudder as he looked at the two men. Nobody knew how they had achieved the strange symbiosis that enabled the hulking, nameless man to know what his employer was thinking, and to translate it so quickly into speech. What little Robards had learnt was enough to persuade him to shutup, accept the pay cheques, and not think of anything other than the task he had been employed to perform. "We have used the apparatus upon a number of smaller animals. Only this morning we brought back a chimpanzee from an anhydro sleep of over six weeks."

"Mr. Black is not a chimpanzee."

"No, no, I know that, of course. But a chimpanzee is as close as we can get to a human being without actually using one. We share over ninety eight percent of the same genetic structure, you see, so it really is almost the perfect test subject." When no response was forthcoming, Robards went on. "It seems like cryogenics to a lot of people, you know, but cryogenics has one small problem. It doesn't work." He laughed a small laugh. "Cryogenics involves freezing a subject, and of course, once you freeze a liquid, it expands. Cells are mostly liquid, so you freeze one, and ppph," he made a small exploding motion with one hand, "the cell liquid expands, the cell ruptures, and what you're left with is little more than . . . meat." He risked a look at Mr. Black, but if his remark made any impact upon the billionaire, the cold visage reflected no awareness.

"Mr. Black is aware of the faults of cryogenic freezing. That was why Mr. Black commissioned you to build this . . . device." The attendant almost kept the sneer from his voice. "What Mister Black wishes to know is whether your process has circumvented those problems and whether it will result in a successful regeneration after the process is complete."

"Yes." Robards brought his eyes up to meet the cold liquid of his employer's thousand-yard stare. "Yes, it will."

That evening the family feasted, and Bugh sat in the centre of the group, drawing in their awe like warmth. Late that afternoon, a Slither had crossed the family's path, almost as if it had planned to meet them. They had trapped and killed it with ease. Never before had the family been led to such a bounty on the first day of a new Carrier. Tonight he was the first to fill his belly, the one to rest while the others gathered sticks and brush, and the one to sit closest to the tiny fire they made. Bugh luxuriated in the warmth, not wishing to stir even though he could feel his skin scalding, for fear that would signal an end to the wonderful evening. Without a thing having been said, a subtle shift in power had occurred within the family. The God had ordained him. From now on, as long as he continued to steer them in the right direction, the God would ensure that he was the beneficiary of its gifts.

Robards' hand held steady as the scalpel descended and shaved the merest flake of skin from the inside of Douglas Black's elbow. Three times the blade dipped. Three times a wafer-thin slice of the billionaire was placed onto a slide and consigned to a small, airtight box.

"We'll need to run some tests," he explained as he worked, "to determine the correct set of parameters for anhydrogenic procedure. After all," he allowed himself a slight loosening at one corner of the mouth, "we certainly wouldn't want anything to go wrong, would we?"

"You assured Mr. Black that the process was perfected. How can something go wrong? Are your assurances premature?" The flat voice held just a hint of the danger the attendant's bulk promised.

"Go wrong? This is a major medical procedure, not to mention quite revolutionary in its application. If the correct procedures aren't strictly followed, if everything isn't followed to the absolute letter, then you allow for the possibility of unknown variables entering the equation. And if that happens," he shook the stiffness from his wrist, "your employer could find himself a very rich, dead man." Annoyed with himself for allowing the argument to compromise his air of professional reserve, he carried the boxes over to a complicated array of tubes and measuring devices that sat on a nearby bench.

"That tube there," he pointed almost at random, "contains sodium azide. That one," another stab of a fleshy finger, "a trehalose-sucrose solution." Stab. "Light microscope." Stab. "Water loss." Stab. "Narrowing of skin annulation." Stab. "Hyaline loss." The doctor's voice grew more confident as he catalogued each item. "Each factor needs to be measured, quantified. Each component has a different optimum quotient for every individual subject. There are hundreds of variables, each of which needs to be faultless, and each of which necessitates hours in front of the terminal." He pointed to a small computer, almost forgotten amongst a cluster of exotic paraphernalia. "Only once every factor is in perfect, and I mean perfect, alignment can Mr. Black be desiccated..."

"Can he what?"

"Sorry, anhydrobiotically engaged," Robards let a small measure of sarcasm creep into his voice, secure in his intellectual superiority now the conversation was within his area of expertise, "without fear of anything going wrong. He can be revived whenever a cure for his condition is found, be treated, and go on to enjoy the rest of a long and fruitful life. But if any one of these many factors is off-beam, then ppph," again the small exploding motion of the hand, "well, we've thrown away enough mistakes to know he won't be coming back."

Burgh lay down his burden and looked closely into its wizened face for a sign. The family had not eaten for three days. Unless he had success soon it would be time to pass the God onto another, and wait for his next turn. Already Geff was moving forward, his head tilted in enquiry. Bugh inspected the God, looking for something, anything that could prompt him to confidently announce the next path to follow. Only blankness greeted him. Geff now stood at his shoulder. Bugh looked up at his brother, then back at the crumbling relic. Finally, he reached a decision. Ignoring his brother's outstretched hand he stood up, hefting the God onto his back.

"This way," he pointed randomly into the distance, "this way."

Robards smiled confidently as he faced his employer. He'd spent hours collecting his thoughts, ordering them as he would roll out a catalogue of exhibits to impress adoring students. This was the pinnacle of his career. For too many years he had toiled in obscurity, without formal recognition, without reward. His failures had been too numerous to mention, his setbacks legion. The pioneers whose footsteps he had initially followed had given up, moved on, or broken their wills against the walls of chemistry which he, and only he, had been able to breach. This was the greatest moment his life would ever contain. He wanted it to be perfect. Behind him, the dimly lit sarcophagus glinted, its opaque surface only helping to increase his sense of drama. Keeping his voice as calm as possible, he addressed the wheelchair-bound figure.

"I thought you might like to see this."

At his gesture, the lights in the room rose sharply. There, lying within the glass capsule, arms raised as if in prayer or supplication, lay the shriveled, shrunken figure of what had once been a man.

"His name isn't important. Until a few weeks ago he was nothing more than a poor homeless bum, willing to be part of a medical test for fifty dollars a day and a clean bed. But," Robards paused to brush at an imaginary crease in his shirt, "he's the first human to be successfully anhydrobated and bought back."

"The first?"

"That's correct." Robards' voice was abrupt. Black's demeanour didn't change, but the look of shock and incredulity on the face of his manservant bought a surge of pleasure to the doctor.

"Then . . . "

"Yes, yes, yes, It can be done. We've leaped the final two percent between chimps and humans at last."

There was a long, long pause. To Robards it seemed as if the giant attendant was struggling to control a flow of complex emotions. He made careful to conceal his disgust at the sight. Finally, the servant spoke once more.

"Mr. Black wishes to know how you know this . . . " he gestured at the sarcophagus, "can be successfully reanimated."

"Because we've already done it. I did say we had brought him back." Robards walked to a nearby door, opened it, and held it wide. "This is a medical procedure. We need to establish a margin for error before we can pronounce the experimental phase complete. The subject in that machine has been successfully anhydrobated and rehydrated eleven times, with no recordable physical ill effects. In fact," he looked at his watch, "we're just about to start procedure number twelve. I though you might wish to observe."

Silently, the giant wheeled his master through the door.

Two days later, with no end in sight to the sands that stretched before them, the family watched as Geff moved forward to take up the God from where Bugh had laid him. After a moment spent running fingers across the God's dried and flaked skin, he pointed in a direction tangential to that which they'd been travelling.

"That way."

Bugh wandered alone to the back of the group. After a few minutes, Granda fell in beside him. Presently he spoke.

"Five days, young one. You must have received a lot of signs."

Bugh said nothing, merely kicked at the sand, head bowed. Granda chuckled, a low hoarse cough that held neither warmth nor joy.

"I take it you understand our little secret now, eh?"

"But why, Granda? I don't . . . ."

"You are of age now. This is what it means, to share this secret with all the other men. The females and the children trust us."

"But . . ."

"It has been this way for generations, before you or I were born. It is all we know."

"But why . . . why do we go on like this?" Bugh waved a despairing arm at the featureless horizon. "Why do we keep pretending?"

Granda looked at him for long moments, then began to move toward the front of the group. As he left Bugh, he said, "Wait a few days. I shall take us somewhere and you shall see, and hear a story, too."

At the next change, something unusual happened. After a whispered exchange with Da, it was Granda who took the God from Geff, not Ler as should have happened. Ler knew better than to protest, but for hours trooped sullenly behind the family, kicking sprays of sand into the air with petty viciousness. After Granda, it was Da who shouldered the God, leading them without pronouncement along exactly the same path Granda had been following. This alone was enough for the rest of the group to engage in excited conversation. A change of carrier always presaged a change of direction. For the next few days the family moved along in a buzz of expectation. All but Bugh, who kept his silence, and studied Da and Granda intently as they walked.

"Incredible." The manservant spoke in a hushed whisper. Before him, on a hospital bed, lay a man of indeterminate age; his face screwed up in recognition of a bones-deep pain. "Can I . . . talk to him?"

"Go ahead." Robards stood back. "You'll find he's completely responsive. There's been no loss of function in any way."

The big man wheeled his master to the bed, until his masque-like face was no more than inches from the nameless test subject. In the silence of the room, the rasping of the bum's breath drew loud scratches down Robards' skin.

"You there."

Slowly the man turned his head. His eyes focussed carefully on Black, then past him at the looming ebony frame behind. He licked his cracked lips.

"Yes?" His voice was little more than a dry croak. The giant also licked his lips. To Robards it was as if he were anticipating a particularly good meal. He looked away.

"What's it like?"

The bed-ridden man looked up, eyes still struggling to keep focus.

"Like?"

"The procedure. The drying, the . . . anhydro procedure."

"The pro . . . pain. There's so much pain. All my muscles cramping and burning. It never ends. I can feel my eyes dry up. Oh . . . " He broke into tears. Robards coughed discreetly, attracting the ear of the massive manservant.

"Mr. Black will be given the benefit of painkillers for the procedure proper. To ensure no variations in the test results we could not afford to apply them to this subject."

His employer, not having been moved, could make no reaction. The glare that passed through the eyes of his assistant, however, made Robards step backwards. Once more the assistant spoke to the wretched figure on the bed.

"What do you feel like now? Do you feel well? Are you still . . . capable?"

A weak cough racked the man's body. "I'm so weak . . . I . . . I need to sleep now." Almost immediately he fell into a deep slumber. At this, Robards once again spoke up.

"The weakness is merely a result of the time taken to rehydrate the body. From this point Mr. Black could expect another three weeks of physical therapy to bring the muscles back to full working order. Psychologically, a subject with the benefits of painkillers will suffer absolutely no ill effects from the process whatsoever. By the end of the physical therapy, a rehydrated subject will be in no worse condition than when he entered the tank. In fact," he risked looking straight into his employer's eyes, "in Mr. Black's case, we would be expecting a complete recovery from whatever curative procedure prompted his rehydration, and that he would be able to walk from the clinic under his own aegis."

If he had expected any reaction to this pronouncement, Robards was to be disappointed. Saying simply, "Mr. Black expects to be called when the procedure is ready to be performed," the giant pushed his employer past the doctor and out of the room, leaving him alone with his sleeping guinea pig.

For three days the family travelled in the wake of Da's determined stride, always in a straight line. At night they chewed upon the few strips of dried slither they had saved from their last meal, and lay quiet, no-one wanting to speak, each alone with their thoughts. An air of trepidation covered the group, a feeling that something momentous was about to occur. In such a circumstance, the normal range of muttered conversation fell by the wayside.

Then, on the fourth morning, they crested a large sand-drift, and the object of their journey became apparent. There before them, rising from the eternal sands, lay the first interruption to a world which in Bugh's experience had consisted only of an endless sea of dirty yellow. They had reached the ruins.

In the darkened room, the form of Douglas Black lay without moving. The unknown disease that had caused his paralysis prevented him from turning his head to see who had opened his door and approached his bed. His manservant, motionless on his bed at the other side of the room, did not stir. A hot breath brushed the billionaire's ear.

"I have to tell you."

Black could not acknowledge the voice. It was impossible to tell whether he indeed even heard the words, the words that poured unbidden from the hidden speaker, tumbling and rolling over each other in their bid to escape.

"You can feel it when it happens. They don't tell you that, but you can. You can feel yourself drying up. It's like they rip the flesh from your body and replace it with something made of old leaves and sand. And it hurts, it hurts so much . . . but you'll be doped up, won't you? He won't want to harm you, not his little cash cow. He doesn't care about you. As soon as you're a shrivelled little ball of wood he'll be onto the talk shows, and the speaking circuit, showing pictures of you like a sideshow freak. But I know who you are. I know why you want to do this. I'd do the same if I were you. But I know something he doesn't, something he can't measure, something I wouldn't tell him even if he'd thought to ask. I'm just a lab rat to him, just a rabbit with shampoo in his eyes. So I've been saving it for you. Because who are you going to tell, eh? Since I first saw you and realised why he was doing this to me. I saved this little nugget. I only want you to know. You may not feel pain when you change, but you won't be sleeping. *You're still aware!*"

There is a pause, as if the unseen voice expected a reaction. When none was forthcoming, it continued. "I don't get how he missed it. Maybe because he can't measure it when you can't move or something, but you stay aware the whole time. Oh, they understand that you feel what's happening to you while they suck your moisture out and fill you up like you're some sponge they're using to wipe the floor. I've seen that bastard smiling. Don't think he won't enjoy watching you shrivel and warp. But he doesn't know what happens while you're lying there like a dead man, all dried up and being measured with his scales and calipers. Your thoughts won't go away. You're going to lie there like a piece of driftwood, just trapped inside your mind with your thoughts going round and round and round while you wait for them to bring you back." A spray of spittle hits Black on the side of the face and runs down towards the pillow. "You think you hate being the freak you are now, Mister Billionaire? How do you think you'll like being aware of what you are for a hundred years? Two hundred? A thousand? How long do you think your thought will echo then?"

Douglas Black lay helpless as the poor mad bum leaned over and gently pressed warm lips against his forehead, unable to respond to a kiss that may be curse, or benediction, or both.

That night, huddled round a fire made from the few sticks and scraps they had managed to gather, the males listened, barely daring to breathe, as Da, his voice trance-like as he repeated the words taught to him by his father, told them of the Gods. Behind Bugh, the temple crouched, scarred and pitted from countless eons exposed to the winds, yet still bearing their likeness in its form. Bugh squatted against its warm belly, understanding few of the words but much of the tone, as Da spoke.

"And there came a time when the Gods outreached their power, and spread across the world like grains of sand, some high in power and some low, some with bellies full and sagging, and others with no bellies at all, with Families on the ground and in the sky, even on Face-In-The-Night. And there came a God with rags on his head, who rose in the East and laid claim over the power that dwells deep within the Earth. And the Gods did split in two, half before and half beside, and mightily did they wage war upon each other, fang and claw until the world was covered in their blood, and great bites were taken from Face-In-The-Night. And the Rag-headed God drew on his last great source of power, and brought down balls of fire from the sky so that the world glowed like the face of Fire-Of-Day, and all who walked or flew or slithered, all bar a few who became our ancestors, were swept away like ashes in the morning, and the world lay cold and dark and silent, and the Gods were no more."

Then Granda, who had taught the tale to Da, but could never resist a chance to show off for the youngsters, spoke up.

"But if everything was dead, where did we come from?" He rolled his eyes, so that Bugh had to stifle a giggle as Da glared at him and continued.

"To all things come a time, and life does not ever truly end. Only lives are short. In time the world yawned and woke, and felt the heat from Fire-Of-Day, and from holes and crevices and cracks we came. We, who had been beneath the Gods as the merest grain of sand is under the mountain, we came forth to find the world empty, and ours alone. And we came to this place," he gestured to the crumbling walls around him, "and we cleared away the ashes and dust which covered it, and we explored the empty corridors. And in a room, far below the ground, we found a temple. A temple of the Gods, strange and beautiful and terrible, as much like us as a God, and yet as beyond our knowing as a God. And as time passed, and our people grew and changed to fit this world, so we gained the strength to draw this temple from below and bring it out to bask in the light of the world once more, and we came back and back to this temple that was shaped like us and yet not like us, until one of our number thought to touch it in a way it had not been touched before, and it opened like a crackseed and inside . . ."

"The God!" Ler's whisper echoed, breaking the thrall.

"Yes, The God." Da pointed to where the battered relic leaned against a wall. "And since that day we have carried it with us. Through times when we numbered as many as the footsteps we have walked, through the great hunger and the time of dying. And now, when we lie scattered and few, and only this small family still seeks guidance and does not cavort like animals, we have carried the God as a symbol, a beacon to point to the way to our survival."

"But . . ." Bugh began, then fell silent, as if he had unconsciously uttered some great blasphemy.

"It doesn't mean anything? It doesn't really show us the way?" Granda smiled. "We just pick a direction and tell the others it was the God?" He touched Bugh's shoulder and gestured to where the world waited just outside the shelter of the walls. "In all your life boy, what have you seen beside this place?"

"Nothing. Just sand and slithers and sometimes a plant or a mad stranger or bones."

"Exactly. The world is large and empty, is it not?"

"Yes, but . . . "

"So would you walk around in circles your whole life looking for who knows what just because I or your Da told you that you must?"

"No. That would be . . . "

"Mad? Pointless? Exactly. Yet there is a point, youngster. The whole world is sand and slithers. We must find some point to surviving, something to stop us from just lying down and dying. The care of the women and the children, the provision of a reason for them to keep going until we find that which will give our struggle a purpose. That is our responsibility. There may be an answer, hmm? But we have to give them a reason to find it. And Gods make easier masters than fathers."

There was little more talk that night. One by one the young males fell asleep, Bugh amongst them, curled up against the body of the temple that had spawned his God. The next morning, as Fire-Of-Day clawed his swollen red bulk into the sky to hang, spreading his tepid warmth through the dust layer and across the world, Bugh found himself at the outer rim of the ruins, crouched upon the crest of a dune with the God and Granda. Behind him, he could hear the women and children making their way up the rise to join the men. Granda smiled down at him.

"Ready?"

Bugh stared into the blank eye sockets of the God, searching for something to connect him to this ancient race of alien beings. The ancient husk stared back, revealing nothing of the awareness that had haunted the decaying corridors of its body for countless millennia. No cry for release echoed back from a world that had lost the knowledge necessary to answer. Bugh shrugged, and using all four arms, hefted his burden. Shading his eye clusters, he looked off into the distance.

"That way."

The family, bearing no resemblance to their arachnid ancestors, walk towards the morning horizon.

Doctor Robards picked his way through gloom-laden corridors towards the sanctuary of the anhydro chamber, cursing the memory of that bastard cripple Black with every step. Famous, he should have been famous. The Einstein or Pasteur of his day, feted and heralded for what he'd achieved. Instead he'd been forced to scrabble about in the semi-darkness, conserving power from the generators and money from the dwindling investments he'd been smart enough to accumulate. Ever since the morning that frozen freak had witnessed the rehydration. Robards had come in the next morning to find his staff gone, the building closed down. And when he'd finally met with his employer, that black son-of-a-bitch who pushed him around had simply announced that the project had been closed down due to 'unforeseen developments'. None of Robards' protests had been acknowledged, none of his calls answered. Twenty years of loyal service turned to dust in a moment.

Well it hadn't stopped him. It had taken the devil's time to organise, everything he'd owned, all the favours he'd farmed out to friends and colleagues over the years, but he'd got six months access to this place. For fully half a year he'd shuffled the corridors alone, like a half-forgotten ghost, muttering to himself as he'd placed wires in solution, made readings on instruments powered by emergency reserves of power from backup generators.

Now he stood in the centre of the anhydro chamber, a man alone with his beautiful creation. He made one last tour of the capsule, checking seals and instruments that had already undergone innumerable tests. All the tests had been performed. All the preparations had been completed. This is what he should have been working towards all along. At last, satisfied that everything was perfect, he made his way to the workbench and undressed, neatly folding each garment into a pile. He pulled away sticking plasters from the abrasions that bespoke his many hours of tests, and dropped them into a wastebasket.

As he climbed into the capsule he reflected on the work that had been necessary to carry him to this point. All the instructions had been written out by hand, for who knew whether computers would even be used so far in the future? The contract with a venerated and royally-appointed law firm to ensure the continuation of the building lease, the contingency plans, the investments made to keep enough money in the coffers (Wouldn't want to wake up a poor man, after all). All had presented special problems. After all, who in the world was used to dealing with someone who talked in decades, never mind the centuries he had wanted to discuss?

He lay back and pressed the button to begin the auto-start sequence. In two hundred and fifty years he would wake a rich man, and go out into the brave new future to announce himself to the world, to reap the acclaim and fame his monumental achievement deserved. As the first needle bit into his skin, and the painkillers began to course through him, he thought "The first thing I shall do is find the grave of Douglas Black, and spit upon it."

The painkillers began to grip him. Robards closed his eyes and smiled. He anticipated a long restful sleep, content in the knowledge that he had thought of everything. Nothing had been overlooked.

"A man from the past," he said to himself. "I'll be like some ancient God."

AFTERWORD

The second story I ever sold, the news coming half an hour after the first (that day was a *good* day). This story won third place in its quarter of the 'L. Ron Hubbard presents the Writers of The Future" competition, making me the first Western Australian, and sixth Australian, to do so. Not bad for a story written in two parts—I'd written the present day stuff first, realised it wasn't enough to carry the story, and bashed out the future-history sections to fill in the gaps. Strangely, reading it now, it's the future stuff I like better.

PASS THE PARCEL

"Mu-ummm!" Naomi's voice contained all the pain and sense of injury her fourteen year old frame could muster. Julie took the 'Teen Queen' magazine from the trolley and placed it back in the rack.

"I said no. I can't afford it."

"But Mummm . . ."

"No." She slammed the frozen chicken onto the checkout conveyor harder than she intended. The checkout girl glowered.

"Nimrod." David's mumble was just loud enough to be heard.

"Shutup!"

They began to slap at each other.

"Will you two stop it?" Julie reached into her purse and thrust money towards the sullen checkout girl's hand. "I'm sick to death of it. Just be quiet and stand over there until I'm finished." She pointed in a random direction away from the stares of the others in the queue. Her children slouched away, sliding insults at each other under their breath. Flustered at the unwanted attention, Julie loaded her bags into the trolley and began to move after them.

"Excuse me?" The voice behind her was calm.

"Yes?" She turned defensively, half-expecting a lecture from some do-gooder about the state of her parenting skills and 'just what those children need'.

"You forgot your change." The woman who spoke was well dressed, her hair brushed back into a ponytail, the makeup on her face smooth and unlined. Behind her, two children loaded items onto the conveyor in silence, moving around each other in concert. Julie swatted at her dishevelled hair and looked down at the twenty-dollar note in the woman's hand.

"Oh. Uh, thanks." She took the proffered bill and put it in her purse. It felt greasy to the touch. 'Too much hand cream' Julie thought.

"Not at all." The stranger smiled in sympathy. "Good luck." She nodded to where Julie's errant children waited. Julie said nothing, merely looked puzzled and moved away. She felt the woman watching as she took her offspring in tow and began the journey back to the carpark.

By the time Friday evening arrived, Julie had forgotten all about the shopping trip. David had been grounded for his role in the constant fighting all the way home that afternoon, and was taking it out on her by bringing her almost to the point of shouting before doing anything he was asked. After three attempts she'd managed to get him to bring the mail in. She heard the thump as he dropped it on the table.

"What is it?" she called from the kitchen. When she received no reply, she pulled her hands from the mixing bowl, wiped the clinging scraps of meatball mixture onto her apron, and stuck her head into the dining room. A parcel lay on the undistributed cutlery. Wiping her hands against the apron again she picked it up. Her name was on the address label. She looked at the handwriting but didn't recognise it. She wasn't expecting anything. Her birthday was months away, and she'd long since learnt not to expect anniversary presents. Even if the last one was only a week gone, it would be completely out of character for her husband Kevin to remember. With a shrug she opened the package. Inside, wrapped in bubble wrap, was a scrapbook, covered in floral paper. On the cover, written in gold ink, were the words 'Pass It On'.

Julie looked at the parcel again. There was no return address, no clue as to who may have sent it. She glanced at her watch. No time to read it now, she decided. Kevin would be home soon, and she still had to get dinner organised. She walked back into the kitchen, dropped the book onto the counter and the packaging into the bin, and bent again to her mixing bowl.

It was only later, once Kevin had slithered onto the couch with a couple of beers to watch the pre-season football match and the kids had disappeared into their bedrooms to block out the world with thumping stereos, that she was able to put the last of the dishes in the rack and turn once more to her mysterious scrapbook. Its gold-inked title still gave no clue as to its origin, or why it had been sent to her. She licked a fingertip and flicked through the first few pages. It appeared to be a cookbook of sorts. The first recipes, written in a spidery, old-looking hand, bore titles like 'True Love' and 'Self-Cleaning Floors'. Odd maybe, but certainly nothing that helped her divine its purpose. After half a dozen pages the handwriting changed, then changed again for each of a dozen sheets, as if the recipes had been added by different people. The last written page caught her attention.

Written in clipped cursive across the top of the page were the words 'Obedient Children'. Julie could feel her heart keep time with the beating from the distant stereos. A list of ingredients dominated the page. Some of them made her blink and read twice in surprise. And the instructions! Julie put the book down. This was some kind of joke, surely. It read like a spell. In this day and age! This was suburban Perth, for Pete's sake, a place of canteen rosters and oven-fried chips, not clay voodoo dolls and chicken blood. A stupid gag, initiated by David and his friends. He'd always had a cruel sense of humour. He's probably getting some sort of kick, calling her an old witch. Well, she wouldn't give him the satisfaction. Make snide comments about obedient children all he wanted, he was still grounded. No silly little prank was going to change that. She picked the book up and pushed it through the flip-top lid of the kitchen bin, then went to see if she'd been left enough hot water for a decent shower.

Next morning, Kevin left the house before she rose. A scribbled note lay on the table next to his breakfast dishes, telling her of a workmate's car and how he hoped to be back in time for dinner with any luck. Julie read it without picking it up. She was making her own breakfast when David and Naomi came out of their rooms. They were already fully dressed, and made for the front door without acknowledging her presence.

"Hey," she called to them, "what about breakfast?"

"Yeah, right," her son replied, "half a week cooped up with you and I'm not getting out as soon as possible? I'll get something with Josh."

"Don't eat breakfast," Naomi joined in, "don't you know that *yet*?"

Her scorn made Julie snap back. "Well, you should! How do you expect to maintain proper weight if you don't eat a good breakfast?"

"You should know," her daughter replied, "You eat enough for both of us."

Then they were gone, the security door crashing against the outside wall and then the doorframe as if to drown out any further response. Julie gazed at the spot where they had been, ignoring the cereal going soggy in the bowl beside her. Then very slowly, and very deliberately, she bent over and reached into the kitchen bin.

Julie had never felt so stupid. Standing naked on the back lawn, the luminous dial of her watch showing a few minutes to twelve, she was tempted to throw the whole thing in and run back into the house. If Kevin should wake up to find her not in bed, and come to find out where she was, or Mr. Whately next door decide to have a midnight snack and just happen to look out of his kitchen window . . . with a shake of her head she abandoned the thought. It had taken all day to gather the ingredients and prepare for this. If she stopped now it would seem, well, a waste really. Closing her eyes, she chanted the words she had spent the afternoon memorizing. She drew the steak knife along the back of the Steggles Number 15 (no need for a live chicken, the book had said. This is the 21st century. Convenience is everything). She'd made dolls from modelling clay. Now she placed them inside the chicken. It took ages to sew the cut closed with twine she'd made from hair rescued from the kids' hairbrushes. She dropped the chicken in the hole she'd dug at the back of the veggie garden. She'd lined it with one of David's old baby jumpsuits and Naomi's favorite t-shirt from kindergarten. Finally, she took a shovel and filled the hole in, before sneaking back into the house and slumping on the bed. She was asleep within moments.

She woke the next morning to clattering from the kitchen. She emerged from the bedroom to find David with his back to her, standing at the sink. A sink filled with dishes. David. Was doing. The dishes. She felt her jaw slide away from her face.

"Wha . . . what are you doing?"

"Morning Mum," he replied cheerfully, "hope I didn't wake you." He pulled his hands from the water, wiped them on the apron he was wearing, then approached her and kissed her on the cheek. "Dad's already out I'm afraid, but sit down and I'll fix you some breakfast."

"Huh?" Julie rubbed at her cheek. She hadn't noticed that Kevin wasn't in the bed with her. She sat at the table and watched as her son busied himself making her breakfast. She was still in shock when Naomi returned from her trip to get the Sunday paper. It took Julie twenty minutes to realize that her daughter was no longer wearing her nose ring. The rest of the day passed in a happy blur. While she sat and watched, the kids tidied their rooms, did their homework, even hung out the washing. David wrote a letter to his grandparents. Naomi went into the kitchen and made sweet and sour for dinner. The chicken was a bit undercooked, the sauce runny, and there was the occasional crunch hidden amongst the rice. Julie ate every last mouthful. When Kevin got home and flopped onto the couch she told him what had happened.

"So?" he replied, "Shouldn't you be doing that instead of making the kids do it for you?"

Julie made no reply, merely went into the kitchen and took her new book from the drawer.

A week later, and she stood once more in her backyard at midnight. There had been no spells to cure rotten husbands, so she'd had to cobble one together from bits of 'True Love', 'Obedient Children', 'Promises That Keep' and one or two others she thought might come in useful. It took more than an hour to complete the ritual, and she was sore all over by the time she crawled into bed and fell asleep. When the alarm went off the next morning, she rolled over and touched Kevin on the back.

"Hon, it's six. Time to get up for work." She shook him. Kevin grunted and twitched his shoulder. Julie lay back onto the pillow. Kevin mumbled and let go a semi-conscious fart.

"Oh well," she thought to herself, "back to the drawing board."

Julie sat at the table and listened to the sounds of a house in motion. She could hear David in the living room, vacuuming. Naomi was on the phone, accepting yet another baby-sitting job. From the front yard came the sound of Kevin mowing the lawn. Julie smiled. It had taken three weeks of constant experimentation, twenty consecutive midnight failures, but eventually she'd done it. She looked at the blank page in front of her, then slowly wrote 'Perfect Husband' across the top. She viewed the script with pride. A spell of her own. Her very own entry in the scrapbook. Judging her words with care, she wrote it down in a methodical hand. When she'd finished, she closed the book and looked at the golden words on the cover. 'Pass It On.'

"Okay," she said aloud, "how? And whom?"

She opened the book to look at her spell again, then paused, puzzled. There was something on the page, something she'd not noticed before. Between the words, underneath them, letters showed, like writing seen through the page. She turned to the next page. There it was again, still too faint to make out. Another page, and another. Julie flicked through the book, trying to decipher the strange new writing.

Six pages from the end, she found it. Half a dozen sheets of writing, in the same spidery hand as at the front, on pages that had been blank in all the time she'd possessed the book.

"Dear sister," she read out loud, "now that you have gained the knowledge you need, it is time to help another join us . . . "

As the sounds around her melted into the background, Julie settled down for one final read.

Kevin finished loading the shopping into the car and shut the trunk with a soft click. David took the trolley from his father and began to push it towards the trolley rack.

"Ready, dear." Kevin moved to the passenger door and opened it, waiting for Julie to walk over and seat herself. Julie nodded, her attention elsewhere. She was thinking of the twenty-dollar note in her purse, coated with a special substance that would, when she looked in her scrying pool, help her to find the address of whoever possessed it. She was also watching a family in the next row of cars. As her husband shouted at her, and her children pointed and laughed, an Indian woman tried to collect the tins that had spilled from a dropped shopping bag. Julie smiled and opened her purse.

"I'll be back in a minute."

She walked across to the family.

"Excuse me." She knelt down and touched the woman on the shoulder. "I think you dropped this."

Manjita Singh held the twenty-dollar note and watched the stranger walk back across to where her husband held the car door open for her. The money felt greasy to the touch.

"Too much hand cream," she thought to herself, and bent down to pick up the last of the tins.

AFTERWORD

This was the first of my stories to actually see print, appearing in the *Australian Woman's Day* in November of 2001. I attended my first ever science fiction convention nine days after it came out. It shouldn't have surprised me, with a first name like Lee, that the two people who had read the story were surprised to find I was a man.

THROUGH THE WINDOW MERRILEE DANCES

She twirls and spins; arms flung outwards as she moves in arcs around the empty ballroom. She is alone. Layers of silk and velvet encase her, shimmering in the light cast by chandeliers hanging constant as stars from the ceiling. The room is a dream, golden statues and rich red hangings wherever his eyes turn. She outshines them all. She is a Princess. She is the most beautiful treasure in a palace known the world over for its riches.

Every day, in the fifteen minutes between weeding the vegetable gardens and cleaning the pigsties, the boy comes to the window and watches her dance. He crouches outside, scarcely daring to breathe in case she should hear, and the noise cause her to take flight. He loves her with an intensity of gaze that would frighten him if he could see it. For fifteen minutes a day he takes all her beauty and folds it around him to give him warmth.

Gaizka checks his appearance in the mirror. He scowls. The collar of his cape is bent, the result of too little starch. It is the third time this week. Gaizka straightens the collar and sighs. The laundry boy will have to be punished, but this is not the source of Gaizka's dissatisfaction. There are greater problems to be conquered, greater events that must take place.

Gaizka suppresses a shiver. He dreads the sequence he must now set in motion. Still, he knew this day would come. The girl has been growing older.

He turns from his self-appraisal, and retrieves his staff from where it leans against the wall. The wall contains a mosaic, tiny tiles arranged to form a map of countries surrounding the Kingdom, all bar one connected to the nation at the centre by strips of different-coloured ribbon. Each ribbon represents years of careful negotiations, relationships nurtured by the man standing before them. Gaizka touches the Kingdom at the heart of the map, an area of colour only just larger than his hand. The facts are simple. Even should it mean war. There have been no suitors. Today the King's sole daughter will come of age, and not a single proposal has been received. It is hardly surprising, but Gaizka knows this will not mollify the King. It will take a light tread, and a careful one, to deal with the insult visited upon them by their neighbours. He shakes his head, puffs out his cheeks with a blow.

"Ah well," he says, "away we go."

Step, step, pirouette, step. Merrilee dances around her empty ballroom, eyes closed, moving in time to music that exists nowhere outside her mind. Gaizka stands in the doorway and watches. After a time he clears his throat.

"Princess."

Merrilee makes no response. She twirls and jumps, continuing her parade.

"Princess." A note of annoyance colours Gaizka's call. The dance does not slow. As Merrilee swings past him he reaches out and grabs her arms.

"Your Highness," he says in a sharp voice. "Your Father wishes to see you. Now."

Merrilee squints up at him. Gaizka sighs.

"Please. Daddy. Go now."

The Princess breaks into a little girl smile and hobbles from the room. Gaizka watches her go, his face a mask of pity. He senses a movement out of the corner of his eye and turns to look at one of the windows. The movement, if there was one, is not repeated.

The next day the boy comes back. He peers through the glass, clutching his forbidden prize. She is dancing again. He looks around in fear, then settles into a more comfortable position. He has never before dared to disobey the rules, never before thought to kneel before the plants he tends and remove a coloured trophy. He grips the flower in a sweaty hand. He has no idea how he could give it to her. The window through which he looks is heavy and dirty. He can see no hinge or clasp that would allow him to swing it open and present her with his gift. Even if he could do such a thing, the thought of it fills him with panic. She is a goddess, and he, he is less than the gardener, or even the swineherd. He is a worm. He is an insect. They have told him so on many an occasion.

Oblivious to his torment, the object of his ardour twists and floats in the dusty light. All too soon the time to return to his tasks is upon him. He pauses, lost in the desire to reach out, to knock his warped fingers against the glass and show her what he cannot give her. He hears his name being called. If he is late the swineherd will beat him. He places the stolen rose on the sill, where he hopes she may see it, and shuffles away.

Gaizka faces the King across the empty length of the throne room. The monarch sits staring into space, white-bearded chin impaled upon one huge, gnarled fist. Gaizka clears his throat.

"Sire?"

The King does not acknowledge him.

"Sire? I have made arrangements. I have sent messengers to our neighbours, reminding them of the services we do them, and the benefits to their welfare of an elder son becoming one with your family. We need to prepare for their arrival. Sire?"

The sovereign sighs, a pained shudder that engages his whole body. When he speaks his voice is softer and dustier than Gaizka had hoped for.

"When I was a young man, I travelled to seven kingdoms before my suit was accepted. It took four years of constant travel. Four years as a homeless wanderer, peddling my little claim from Princess to Princess like some sort of common tinker. It wasn't until I reached the eighth kingdom that I was accepted, and found a woman who would become my Queen. Did you ever meet the Queen?" He looks at Gaizka, and the advisor notes the sharpness that still floats beneath the watery eye.

"No, Sire. I came into your service shortly after the Princess was born. Sire, the messengers were sent to Endismorre, Taslingham, Scorby and Tal. We should expect the first arrival within a week."

"She was a wonderful wife. You would have liked her. The people saw how much she loved me. I think they loved her all the more for it. She was the first noble I ever met who even *liked* commoners. She changed this country because of it. When she died it nearly broke my heart. She was unique. Do you know what the exceptional thing about her was?"

"No, Sire."

"She was the ugliest woman I ever saw in my life." The King sighs another long sigh. "What happened to Princes who would make sacrifices to rule a kingdom, eh? Where did they all go?" He climbs from his perch, pain apparent in his movements. "Not a single suitor."

He limps past his advisor and into his antechamber, leaving Gaizka standing mute behind him.

The boy stands at the edge of the gardens, and stares at the horses gathered in the castle forecourt. He has never been allowed near the royal stables. He has never seen such regal and beautiful animals. He longs to go to them, to run his hands along their flanks and through the ribbons tied into their manes. He imagines it would feel soft and fresh. He imagines it would feel like the hair of his love, were he ever to run fingers against her. He makes no move to leave the confines of the gardens. He knows enough to understand that touching these beasts would mean his life. A short distance away from the horses stand a group of boys, more beautifully dressed than even their charges. Their clothes glow in the sunlight, vibrant reds and blues, brilliant yellows and greens. They are talking, laughing every now and then, making shuffling dances, and laughing again. He is too far away to hear what they are saying.

Without warning, the great wooden doors of the Keep bang open. A noble in bright colours storms out, accompanied by a man in a high-collared cape. He has seen this second man around the castle grounds, giving orders to people who run to obey them. As one, the boys cease their laughter and come to attention. One of them, dressed in colours to match the angry figure at the door, moves forward and grasps a horse's reigns. The noble is shouting. Some of his words blow to where the gardener's boy crouches in the garden. He hears 'insult' and 'war', 'freak' and 'retard'. He whimpers, hoping he is not in some kind of trouble: the gardener has used many of those words when he has done something bad and is being beaten. Making soft, mewling sounds of fright, he scuttles to the far corner of the garden in case the tall man should see him and come to punish him. He hides there the rest of the day, too afraid even to go to the window to watch his love dance.

Gaizka pauses before the throne room door, listening to the shouts and crashes coming from within. His hands move across his clothes, straightening edges, smoothing down creases. Now would not be the time to call down the King's rage because of shoddy dress. He glances at the guard standing to the door's side.

"Be careful, my Lord," the guard murmurs. "He has ordered two floggings already today. He had the drink slave beaten for not filling his glass full enough."

Gaizka makes a slow nod in reply, takes a deep breath, and opens the door. The sight that greets his eyes makes him consider calling the guard inside. The throne room is in ruin. Tapestries lie torn and shredded upon the floor. Priceless statues and vases, some from as far as the Spine Isles, are scattered and smashed beyond salvation. Many lie underneath the overturned pedestals that once bore them. Gold and bronze weapons that adorned the walls now lie bent and broken. Gaizka raises a hand to his throat.

"You!"

The advisor turns to face the voice. It is the King; clothes hung in disarray upon him, face red and twisted. In his hands he holds the Sceptre of Mistrithal, a gift received hundreds of years ago from a Kingdom which has long since sunk beneath the waves. As Gaizka watches, his master smashes the priceless relic against the arm of his throne and tosses it aside. He levels a finger at his counsellor.

"You! You caused this. This insult! This humiliation! You called them here. You let them see her, let them call her those . . . . those names. You've forced me to war with these people. Four countries! You destroyer, you traitor!"

Gaizka forces himself to breathe in rhythm, to ignore the King's fury. He remembers his plan, and that there are more steps to be taken. He returns the sovereign's gaze and speaks very clearly.

"What rubbish."

The King stops his tirade, blinking in shock.

"What?"

"What rot. Traitor indeed."

"You dare . . . ?"

"I most certainly do." He strides into the room. "War is it? Just like that? Good God, Sire, can you not understand an advantage when you have one?"

The King eyes him warily. "What do you mean?"

Gaizka picks up the Sceptre of Mistrithal, eyes its ruined head, and drops it again with a sigh.

"Four nations sent you their firstborn Princes because they were reminded of the benefits that remaining in our good view afforded them. Each of the Princes they sent offered you the gravest insult."

"And now I have no recourse but to avenge that insult."

"Stay your arm for a moment and listen to me, my Lord. Four Princes, out of all the countries that surround us. You said yourself that you visited at least seven before you came here. Did you not wonder why I sent for only those four?"

He points to a mosaic that dominates one wall of the throne room. It is a larger brother to the map in his own quarters, although it lacks the complex interweaving of ribbons. The King looks at it with a frown.

"Go on."

Gaizka points to various spots on the map.

"Endismorre, who rely on us for crops. Taslingham, who would be overcome by rebels if not for our mercenaries. Scorby, who buy more textiles from us than anywhere else. Tal, whose elite are educated at our University. All of whom will be well aware of the debt they shall owe you, Sire, for overlooking the insults delivered by their unthinking sons and heirs."

"How does that change the situation with . . ." he nods toward a door at the far end of the room.

"Look again at the map. Four nations. All have common ties with one country. Here." Gaizka slaps his hand against a country at the far left of the map. "A country in which we have had great difficulty establishing a commercial foothold. One King may resist the financial pressures of another. But can he resist five?" Gaizka rests his hand against the small area of coloured tile. It is cool beneath his touch. "It is a country, Majesty, with a single Prince."

There is a pause during which Gaizka cannot dare to breathe. Then the King begins to smile.

He stands outside the window and peeks at the collection of flowers on the sill. Beyond them his love twirls and twists, as if the room holds an orchestra playing for her pleasure. The boy stands transfixed. He watches her elegant, graceful movements until he hears the swineherd calling his name and threatening to feed him what he should be sweeping. As he stumbles away the idea strikes him. It is her dance that he knows best. He will learn it, learn to glide and fly the steps that she performs with such grace. Once he has mastered it he will knock on the window. She will press her face to the glass, and he will dance for her. He will express all his love, and she will return it with her own movements. They will dance together, forever and always. As he enters the first sty and grasps his shovel he makes his resolve clear: tomorrow he begins to dance.

Gaizka stands on the Keep steps, and allows himself a small smile. The sun shines as befits a Royal wedding. He runs his fingers along his collar, nodding in satisfaction at the stiffness beneath his touch. All the preparations are complete. The bride has been dressed and is no doubt alone in her favourite room. The King sits upon his refurbished throne, awaiting the entrance of the Prince and the beginning of the ceremony. Gaizka has met this Prince, and briefed him on his role in the affair. The young noble is not the happiest of men. Gaizka can perhaps even sympathise, but he is sure that inheriting a Kingdom will one day take the edge off the young man's disappointment.

The Lord Bishop will arrive soon, and the wedding can begin. Gaizka decides to take one last turn around the gardens before he greets the priest. It is a beautiful day; it would be a shame not to take a few extra minutes to appreciate it. He sets off at a leisurely stroll for the corner of the Keep.

He is halfway along the side of the building when he sees the gardener's cripple. The boy reels this way and that, throwing his misshapen body to and fro as if drunk. From time to time he looks toward the building, as if making sure someone inside is watching. The dance is unmistakable. Gaizka has watched it many times before. He feels his face growing pale.

"Guards! Guards!"

At his first cry the cripple freezes and stares toward him, his malformed face contorted with terror. He begins to run, but his scurry is no match for the guards who round the corner and overtake him. Within a few strides he is apprehended and dragged before the furious Counsellor.

"You dare?" he hisses. "You mock her? Today of all days you insult her in this way?"

The cripple sees the rage on Gaizka's face and shrinks away. He begins to cry, sounds falling over his lips in an insensible rush. Gaizka looks down at him in disgust.

"I will have no ridicule of her Highness on her wedding day. Take him away. Make sure I never find him."

The guards drag the screaming wretch around the corner of the building. Gaizka turns toward the object of his attention, and sees a window. On its outer ledge he finds a pile of rotting flowers. A daisy has been laid on top. Gaizka uses the back of his hand to brush it off, and peers through the glass. Behind the thick dust, a white-robed figure shuffles and turns, the movements under her wedding dress an obscene parody of those made by someone with a whole mind or body. Gaizka watches, his face an impassive mask. Only his eyes show pity, and a great sadness. Then he turns from the sight and goes to meet the Bishop.

Through the window, oblivious to all that has happened, Merrilee dances.

AFTERWORD

An anti-phantasy story, the result of too much time spent at a science fiction writing group where everybody was working on a traditional Phat Phantasy trilogy and nobody had any idea of research (or realism) outside the pages of a Jordan novel. So this is my attempt to do for soft-focus fantasy what Terry Gilliam did to the Middle Ages in Jabberwocky. It's funny how everyone wants to be descended from King Arthur and nobody wants ancestors from the Dirt-Shagger Cult of Skara Brae, isn't it?

ELYSE

Elyse was working in her garden when the strangers arrived. She knelt amongst the tomato plants, picking weeds out of the mulch, casually eating the tough stalks rather than find a basket in which to dispose of them. Sunny days were likely to be few and far between now the Big Snow was approaching. Elyse was caught up in plans to survive the half-yearly winter, plans which died as soon as the intrusion began. A clatter of hooves sounded on the stone path behind her, the sudden cacophony shattering months of solitude. Elyse looked up in shock. What she saw triggered a lifetime's instinct. She froze, doing her best to become invisible against the broken background of the garden.

There were four of them. They were all male. They tied their horses to the little fence she had built to edge the short path, and looked around. Elyse became very aware of the neatly arranged rows of vegetables, and of what they signified.

"Inhabited, definitely," the largest of the invaders said. "This is the first sign of order we've seen in days."

"There."

The shortest one pointed at Elyse, crouching in the middle of the vegetable beds. She rose slowly, leaving her little tools on the ground lest they be mistaken for weapons. The strangers drew guns and moved slowly into the garden, fanning out and scanning the surrounding area, barrels following their turning heads. The short one, Elyse saw, was hardly more than a boy, eleven or twelve years old at most. Like the others he carried his rifle as if he would have no hesitation in using it.

"You!" the large man snapped at her. "How many here?"

Elyse made no answer. He moved closer, raising his firearm and sighting down it toward her. "Answer me. How many beside you?"

"Dad," the boy spoke. He pointed at Elyse. The man's gaze followed the finger.

"Jesus," he said. "Where's your mouth?"

"A freak. She's a stinking freak."

The thick cords of muscle around Elyse's neck prevented her from turning her head to see which of the others was speaking. Before she could swivel her body, something hard and heavy caught the edge of her temple and knocked her into darkness.

When she woke, Elyse found herself lying in a discarded heap on her kitchen floor. Rough stones that had taken months to collect dug into her side. Her head was jammed against the front of the wood stove, her legs curled around it, arms tucked underneath her body and pressed painfully into the uneven ground. Elyse had built the shack around the stove, the only remnant of the building which once stood on the site. Now it served to shield her movements as she raised her hand to the hem of her dress. She breathed a slow, careful sigh of relief. The simple cotton shift had barely moved, riding only as far as her thighs. Behind her the strangers were talking. Elyse lay still and listened.

". . . ievable. How the hell has it gotten away with this?" a gravelly voice was asking.

A deeper voice laughed. She recognised it as the man the boy had called 'Dad'.

"Easy. It chose well. Ephraim!"

"Yes, Dad?"

"See if there's anything more to eat."

"Yes, Dad." Elyse heard footsteps moving across the kitchen. There was a swish as the boy pulled aside the blanket separating the room from her sleeping and bathing areas. The first voice spoke again.

"What do you mean 'it chose well'?"

"Think about it. We're four days ride from the regular trails, and hard riding too. There probably hasn't been anyone past here in years."

"So how did it get here?"

"Who knows? It's been twenty years since this part of the State was abandoned. It could have wandered out here at any time. Takes work to put together a nest like this. Hell, there are rebuilt places in some of the cities aren't half as cosy. It's probably had the pick of wherever it wants for junk to build with."

"Yeah, well, I don't care. As long as Dover and his crew don't come out this way."

"They won't. We might have taken a lot of money for three road builders, but it's small change for a man like Dover. He won't risk his bailiffs chasing us out here, not with the Big Snow coming on. Once he's seen six months of ice he'll have other problems on his mind. There are advantages to being easily replaced. He'll assume we're long dead once the Snow sets in. Ephraim! Where the hell is that boy?"

A chair scraped back and heavy footsteps left the room. Elyse lay still, hoping the remaining invader would fail to notice her. She was not lucky. Seconds after the voice's exit something wet slapped against the front of the stove, inches from her head. It slid down and dropped onto the side of her face. A trickle of pulpy liquid ran along her cheek. Elyse squinted at it. It was a tomato.

"Hey, freak." A missile exploded against her. "Freak!" Another burst against her nerve-dead back, then another. "Get up, monster."

Eyes averted, Elyse rose to her knees then stood, hands holding the edge of her shift hard against her legs. Two men sat at the table, tomatoes in their hands. Elyse recognised them as the ones who had stood behind her in the garden. One had undoubtedly struck her. The bowl lay empty before them.

"What do you grow this shit for, eh?" the man with the gravelly voice asked. He bit into the fruit, dribbling flesh and juice down his dirty chin. "What do you do with it, huh? You ain't eating it with no mouth, are you?" He held out the half-eaten tomato. "You want to eat this? Do you?"

The other man giggled. Elyse saw that his eyes were crossed. A white scar ran across the top of his head from just above his right eye deep into his lank black hair.

"Yeah, come on, freak. Eat it," he said in a thick, stupid voice.

The first man threw his tomato, hard. Elyse raised both hands to catch it before it could hit her face. The fruit spattered against her broken, twisted palms. She stood with eyes focused upon the floor, letting the juice drip unheeded against the front of her shift. The stupid man drew a revolver from his belt and pointed it at her.

"Eat it."

Elyse looked at the gun. Then she turned away and lifted the front of her dress. When she turned back to the men the tomato was gone.

"What the hell?"

The two invaders exchanged looks, then stood and moved towards her along opposite sides of the table. Elyse backed away until the coarse wood of the wall stopped her retreat. The raiders kept advancing. She tried to run, but the bigger man caught her arm. She raised a clawed hand to scratch, and the other grabbed her wrist. She kicked out both legs, tried to butt with her head, but both men pulled her backwards until she lost balance and fell against the table. The cross-eyed attacker took both wrists and held them straight above her head. The other took two handfuls of her shift and tore it away in one quick movement.

"Oh, dear God." He fell back, one hand over his mouth, eyes staring. "Oh, my God."

Elyse twisted out of her assailant's grasp and dived for the remnants of her dress.

"Isaiah! Isaiah!" the big man shouted in his stupid voice, eyes locked on hers in fright and revulsion. Elyse ran for the door. Her escape ended before it began, the hard chest of the outlaw leader blocking her flight and forcing her back into the room.

"What is it?" Ephraim strove against his father's restraining hand, trying to squirm past and get a better look at the thing spread across Elyse's naked torso. A surface of translucent grey skin lay where her abdomen should be, puckered tissue tying it to her normal flesh like a scar. Gelatinous slime covered the mutation, glistening in the light that came through the gaps in the walls.

"I don't know." Isaiah replied. "You say it ate the tomato with that thing?"

"That's right," the gravel-voiced attacker said. "Just shoved it up under its dress and it disappeared."

"Hmm." Isaiah held a chunk of the crude bread Ephraim had found in her food store. He offered it to Elyse. "Eat this." He needed no gun to command her. She took the bread from the leader's heavy hand and held it against her chest. Bubbles of froth appeared around the edges of the food, climbing over and around the coarse fibre of the bread until it disappeared beneath the sticky surface. The men stood transfixed, watching the food dissolve into Elyse's chest cavity. Soon, only a film of spume covered where it had been ingested. Dark specks floated beneath the surface for a moment, then they too were gone.

"God damn," Isaiah said in a soft voice, his eyes fixed on Elyse's face. She stared back. Choking noises came from where the big stupid one was being sick in the far corner. "I saw something like this once. A book I found in a big old pre-war library I was cleaning out, back in Denver when we were rebuilding. It's like some slugs and stuff; they have their stomachs on the outside instead of the inside. God damn." He leaned forward, made as if to poke her in the chest then thought better of it. "Where were you, I wonder? Los Angeles? Houston? They only dropped the gene-scramblers on the big cities."

He stared at her for long moments, then straightened. "Well it *is* weird, but it doesn't change our plans. I reckon we've got about three weeks until the Big Snow closes in. This is a better place to ride it out than anywhere else I can imagine out here. Nobody's coming so far this late in the year. We'll rest up good and easy and see if we can't build up some fat. You," he looked down at Elyse. "It's no matter to me if you're dead or alive, so if you'd rather live you'll cover that thing of yours and get some decent food ready to eat by nightfall."

Elyse matched his gaze for a few short seconds before dropping her eyes. She picked up her tattered dress and draped it clumsily across herself, then took the bowl from the table and went out into the garden.

From that day the pattern of Elyse's life changed. The strangers appropriated her few pieces of furniture for sleeping, consigning her to the kitchen floor. She rescued one of the larger baskets she used for collecting vegetables, stuffing it with leaves and grass to provide some barrier between her and the stones. The invaders had suffered numerous tears in their clothing and riding tack during their flight, and she was soon put to work repairing them. She managed to save a few scraps here and there, and used them to patch the rips in her shift. When Isaiah saw her efforts he laughed.

"Wearing our colours are you? You must be part of our crew now, eh?" He clipped her across the cheek with the back of his hand. "Thieve from us again and we won't even bother to bury you."

After they finished eating they would toss whatever scraps were left into her basket. She would gather them up and scurry outside, soon having learnt the penalty for ingesting in front of the men. Only Ephraim occasionally saved her any real food. He would bring it to her on a plate once the others had gone into the sleeping area. Elyse would eat gratefully, listening through the thin wall as the men continued their never-ending discussion of post-Snow plans. Then one night Isaiah came into the kitchen and caught the boy handing her his leftovers. He beat him, and after that none of them showed her any care at all.

As the Big Snow drew closer she started to save some of the fruit and vegetables, pickling them in jars she had collected over the years. On her first day of this new activity, the stupid man came up behind her and grabbed her wrists.

"Spoiler!" he shouted, throwing her to the ground and kicking her, careful not to let his boots touch her chest, as if afraid she would absorb the blow and his foot at the same time. "Food spoiler!"

Elyse curled around the blows, doing her best to twist so they fell against the unfeeling flesh of her back and shoulders. She saw Isaiah come into the kitchen and pause, appraising the situation before walking over and calmly pushing her attacker out of the way.

"You're an idiot, Chad," he said. "You want to starve? That stuff's going to get us through the Snow. The creature's saving it, not spoiling it. You know how to do that?"

Chad reluctantly shook his head, looking at Elyse with lethal intent as she rose from the floor.

"No. So why don't you go out and chop some wood and let it get on with things? Go on."

Chad left, murderous eyes fixed on Elyse. When he was gone Isaiah turned and slapped her, sending her back to the hard stone at his feet.

"And you'd better not be stealing any of this. If I find you've been screwing with our food you'll be lying on the snow waiting for the wolves to finish you off. Now get on with it."

Elyse focussed through her pain and waited for him to leave. Seconds later she heard the blanket swish again, and lighter footsteps come across the floor. Small hands lifted her to her feet.

"Are you all right?" Ephraim asked. "Chad's a thug. He's too stupid to do nothing for himself, but he took a bullet for Dad once so Dad keeps him around. And he's still a good shot too. You shouldn't worry about Dad. I know he hits people sometimes, but he's just worried 'cause he doesn't know about plants and stuff, and he's afraid you won't have enough to keep us going. I told him you done good so far. You just got to promise to keep the food coming and you'll be all right, okay?" He gave her a worried look. "You will do that, won't you? "

Elyse made no response. Ephraim moved his hands in small helpless circles.

"Okay. Okay then. You just, uh, just remember, okay?" He shuffled backwards through the blanket. Elyse took no notice. She had found a memory in the boy's words.

Elyse's hands moved over the hare, pulling and teasing the skin away from the flesh. She had watched the invaders as they fashioned snares at the table, but had not really believed they would work until the men stamped into the kitchen bearing the dead animal and demanding it be cooked for dinner. She was still surprised they had been able to get to it. Wolves had taken to living near the house, now the smell of stabled horses reached them across the crisp snow-clean air. Few catches survived their attention. She was glad the snares worked. A means of getting meat next winter would be a blessing.

Skilfully she finished skinning the hare, and put aside the empty pelt to be cured later. She picked up a cleaver and separated head from torso, then used a knife to open the belly and disgorge the innards into another bowl. Two quick strikes of the cleaver split the body into four even parts. Elyse washed them in a basin filled with melted snow, then set one quarter aside and laid the remaining three pieces on the section of smoothed wood she used as a chopping board.

She shuffled into the new pantry the men had built, and spent some time among the jars and bottles within, choosing the remaining ingredients for the evening meal. When they were assembled on the table she made one last trip into the store cupboard. She reached to the back of a shelf and pulled out a large baking dish, half-filled with greenish liquid. Within the liquid floated a dozen sprigs, taken from a bush at the back of the garden; a plant she had known about for years, but never had cause to visit until reminded of it by Ephraim's words. Elyse took the dish into the kitchen, opened it, and dropped the three cuts of hare inside.

Elyse had the house ready by the time the men returned that evening. She heard them outside the newly-erected kitchen door, stamping the snow from their boots and shedding their jackets. They stepped inside. Isaiah dropped a brace of hares into a basket near the door. Elyse had a fire going in the wood stove, radiating heat onto clothes hanging from a line in front. The men stripped out of their wet attire and threw them in a corner, then put on the dry garments and sat at the table.

Elyse already had plates in front of their places, and a bowl of pickled salad in the centre. As they passed it between them she opened the oven door and pulled out the large baking dish. She removed three pieces of hare and gently dropped one onto each of the adult's plates. Then she took out a smaller dish, pulled out the single cut of meat it contained, and gave that to the boy. As they started to eat she retreated to her basket, now occupying a space on the pantry floor, and settled down to watch.

When they finished she stood up and cleared the table. The men settled back to discuss their plans for the following day. The Big Snow would end soon. Isaiah was eager to continue their ride. There were places to the East where the money they had been sitting on for half a year could be spent. Elyse placed the dishes in a bowl of water ready for cleaning.

From behind her the flow of voices was interrupted by the sound of choking. Elyse turned around. All three of the adults: Isaiah, Chad, and the gravel-voiced one whose name she had never learnt were grasping at their throats, eyes bulging in fear and agony. Isaiah began to vomit uncontrollably. The others followed, crying with pain as convulsions shook them. They lost control of their bowels. Elyse watched dispassionately as they collapsed to the floor in shaking, shit-stained heaps. Ephraim jumped from his seat, terrified eyes fixed upon his dying father. Elyse moved to a nearby shelf and picked up the heavy iron skillet that was all she had rescued from her childhood home. She walked to the screaming boy. As he stared at his father's final convulsions she brought the skillet down as hard as she could upon the back of Ephraim's head.

The oleander completed its work in less than ten minutes. Elyse moved amongst the corpses, carefully stripping them of their clothes. Tomorrow would signal the start of a busy period. She would spend that first day disposing of the bodies; using her cleaver to chop them into easily-carried pieces and then taking them up above the tree-line to be fed upon by wolves. They would in turn be poisoned, and would serve to scare off any surviving predators. The men's clothing and belongings she would pick apart and put to good use around the house. The horses would provide much meat, but would take time to slaughter and hang to dry. Only the gold coins in the saddlebags were useless.

But all that would begin tomorrow. Elyse had a more immediate need. She looked at the rabbits in their basket. She was hungry after so long on a near-starvation diet, and the rabbits would fill a hole, but she knew what she needed to satisfy her craving. She laid Ephraim full-length on the floor, and laboriously stripped him of his clothes. When he was naked she removed her dress, knelt down, and cradled his unpoisoned body against her chest.

Surrounded by the silent house, Elyse began to feed.

AFTERWORD

You can learn something from anyone. This story went through seven drafts, was read by a bunch of seasoned writers and editors, and not one of us could work out why it just didn't sit right. Then my brother, who doesn't read that much, and really doesn't give a damn about science fiction, read it while he was over one day, and said "Why would she eat the dead guy when she's got two rabbits in the basket?" Shit shit shit shit. One line, that's all it took, and suddenly the motivation all made sense. Of course, by then, we were looking for material for the book . . .

THE DIVERGENCE TREE

I saw myself at a bus stop today. Three of me, standing in line between oblivious commuters. One of me looked as if I'd been hit by a car. As soon as I walked out of the Post Office they began calling to me in high, pre-pubescent voices, telling me their stories, demanding I acknowledge my good fortune and their tragedy. Their yelling attracted more of me, each one wanting me to know where their path had differed from mine. They homed in, crowding me, barging and fighting amongst themselves to be the one nearest my ear, the one to enforce their misery and pain onto my thoughts. By the time I reached the sanctuary of home, there were seventeen trailing in my wake. They won't come inside the house. It's the only place they leave me alone. I still haven't figured out why. There's a lot I haven't figured out. The most important being 'Why *me?*' I'm nothing special. I'm just an accountant. Or more accurately, in this life I'm an accountant. But then, it's not this life that's the problem.

He first appeared in the most unlikely of places. I was standing in line for the chair-ride at the Royal Show when he arrived. I saw a flash, and there he was, lying on the ground with arms and legs outflung, a wreath of smoke rising from his body and dissipating in the night air. There was a fresh breeze that night, but the smoke rose straight into the sky. I would have gone over to him, but my turn came to climb aboard a chair and I was motioned forward and on to it. I kept trying to crane around to see him, but was forced to stop. My rocking caused my fellow passenger to enquire whether I was going to jump, or wanted throwing off. By the time the ride finished and I made my way back across the showgrounds, he was gone. I turned my attentions to where the ride attendant sat on a stool at the head of the queue, face buried in a motorcycling magazine.

"Excuse me?"

He looked at me with barely concealed disinterest. "Yeah?"

"Can you tell me, did you see a man lying on the ground there about fifteen minutes ago?" His eyes moved to the point I indicated.

"Nuh."

"But there was a flash. He just appeared. You didn't see that?"

"No, I didn't. You going on the ride or what?" He pointed a dirty finger at the line.

"No, I've already been. How can you not have seen it? I mean, there was this flash. A big one. He was lying on the ground, with all this smoke. He could have been hurt. You didn't see anything?"

"Look, mate." He put down the magazine and stood up. "I didn't see nothing, all right? Now if you want to go on the ride get to the back of the line, and if you don't, piss off would you?" He turned his back and began ushering people onto newly arriving seats. I thought about making one last attempt, but he was an awfully large man, and I had only caught a glimpse of my mysterious stranger. Perhaps I was wrong. There could have been any number of explanations for what I saw, if in fact I had really seen it. There's always something going on at the Show, performances and magicians and so on. That was probably it, a magic trick for passing children. I shrugged, and moved away, resolving to put it out of my mind and enjoy the rest of my evening.

It was two hours later, as I sat on a toilet regretting an evening's diet of undercooked hot dogs and watered down soft drink, that he found me. There was no polite knock on the door, however. He simply came through the front wall of the cubicle.

As I stared at him in shock, he asked me in a voice laced with confusion and panic, "What is this place?"

"Wha . . . . . it's the dunny! How did you do that?" I pointed at the solid door through which he'd just passed. He ignored my question.

"No, no. This place, outside? This . . . fun fair?"

"It's the Royal Show. What do you mean what is it? And how did you do that?" This time I knocked on the wooden door for emphasis. Again he ignored my question.

"Showgrounds? Then . . . this isn't the technology centre?"

"Does it look like a technology centre to you? Look, I don't know what you've been smoking, but you should get back to whatever magic show you learnt your little trick from, and leave me . . . "

"Never mind," he interrupted. "I must have done it. I must have pierced the barrier. I have to show you something." He turned and walked back through the door. I finished my business and followed him. I found him standing outside the cubicle, staring down at his body.

"How did I do that?"

I didn't hear his question. I was seeing something I had failed to notice in the cubicle. Opposite us stood a mirror, filling the wall above the hand basins. I had been too shocked by his sudden appearance to look at his face, but now I caught my first real sight of him. His reflection, next to my own. We were identical. This stranger and I, side by side in the mirror, for all the world like twin brothers. Perhaps my hair was a little more advanced in its retreat, perhaps he was a little heavier around the jowls, but these were moot points. For all intents and purposes, we could have come from the same litter.

"How did I just walk through that door? How did I . . . ?"

Still staring at our reflection, I reached out to tap him on the shoulder, and draw his attention away from his self-examination. My hand, instead of touching his shirt, passed through it. I yelped in surprise. Only then did he raise his head.

"Oh dear." He saw our reflection, with my hand located approximately where his lung should be. "I don't think this has worked out quite the way I intended."

The Royal Show has a couple of bars. I made liberal use of one. We spent the next hour or so trying to work out what had happened, with no success. I did, however, find out quite a bit about my double.

"Multiple universes," he said as I nursed a plastic cup of warm, watery beer.

"Like on Doctor Who?"

"Sorry, don't know it."

He'd been a physicist, he told me, working on what he called an 'Interspatial Wave Indexer', something that recorded and catalogued variations in time waves. He wasn't a twin. He was me, me from another dimension. Somewhere along the line, when I'd been a kid, the fascination I'd had with science had led him into the field of physics, whereas in this world I'd become bored with it and taken up something else.

"Each time a variation occurred in the wave index it would create new variations in the time periods deeper into the past, queering those we'd already recorded," he said as I gingerly sipped from my cup. I don't often drink, and this beer was helping to remind me why.

"Don't you mean nearer the present, or the future, or further... I don't get it."

"Just take my word for it, okay?" Not for the first time he looked disappointed that I'd turned out not to be the scientist he'd hoped he'd contact. He'd muttered something about not realising universes could differ that much when I'd told him what I did for a living. He seemed shocked to think that there would be versions of him that would not become scientists.

"So you decided to build something to do more than record these different pathways."

He shrugged. "The technology was already there. All I had to do was bridge the knowledge gap, and get it in the right configuration."

"Transmit instead of receive."

"Exactly." He looked around him. "So many differences. I just wish I knew how far across the Divergence Tree I've come."

"The what tree?"

"Divergence. It's how we map changes in time waves." He started drawing imaginary lines in the air. "Every decision is a yes-no binary, right? So, at each divergence point, the graph splits into two new paths, which split, and split again . . ."

My eyes began to ache as I tried to follow his waving finger.

"Like a family tree?"

"Yes, sort of like a family tree. Only it records universes instead of children."

"Right. I get it, I think." I didn't. "But what about . . . ?"

I pointed to where his elbows rested a couple of centimetres below the level of the table.

"I don't know. Maybe it's a synch thing, or a misalignment of planetary position between my universe and yours."

"At least you've got something to work on while you're here."

"Yes." He looked around the pub, and sighed. "A fun fair. Herod wept."

I got up and made my way to the bar, motioning to the bartender for a refill. He smiled and shook his head.

"I think you've had enough, mate."

"Sorry?"

He nodded back towards our table. "Enjoying your conversation?"

"What's that got to do with anything? Why can't I get another beer?"

He leaned forward and took my cup from the damp bar rug.

"Listen mate, anybody starts having conversations with their invisible friend has probably had enough for one day, know what I mean?" He pointed to where a sign listed all the reasons why an inebriated patron would not be served. "I've got laws I got to obey. You've had your fill."

Slowly I turned back to the table. The other me still sat there with a puzzled expression. I looked again at the bartender.

"You don't see anyone there?"

"Geez," he laughed, "you, mate, have definitely had enough." He moved off to serve another patron. I turned again. My twin still sat at the table. An awful realisation hit me. I motioned to him, and began to walk from the bar. He got up and fell into step beside me as I exited.

"What's the matter? What happened?"

"I think I know what's happened to you. But you're not going to like it."

"Ghost? What the hell do you mean ghost?"

I started the engine and pulled the car out of the parking bay.

"Exactly that. Look, it all adds up, doesn't it? No-one can see you, you can't touch anything, you even walk through walls for Christ's sake. And the way you suddenly sprang into existence . . . "

"I did not 'suddenly spring into existence'. I've existed for thirty-seven years thank you very much! And if I'm a ghost, how can I sit in a moving car, huh?"

I glanced to where he perched a centimetre below the surface of the passenger seat. "I don't know. Maybe you know what's supposed to happen when you sit in a car, so your body subconsciously moves with it or something. Anyway, I'm no ghost expert. I just had the idea, didn't I? And you've only lived thirty-seven years in your universe. In my world you've only existed since you threw the switch on your Waving Indexy Discombobulator and the lights went out."

"I didn't say they went out. I said they flared and blew. The power rise in the generator drew off some wattage from the lighting system and blew the bulb, that's all." He stopped speaking, and stared out of the window.

"What?"

"Sssh." He waved me to silence. I shrugged, and concentrated on my driving. I know what I'm like when I'm in one of these moods. Presently he spoke again. This time he seemed uncertain, and his voice wavered in the way mine does when I'm really upset.

"It wasn't a bulb. I was facing the ceiling. I'd have seen it. I would have. I was in the travel capsule. I was looking at the HUD, but I could see the ceiling through it. It must have been the coolant tank, or the oxygen valve or . . . or . . . Oh God, I'm really dead, aren't I? I really am dead."

"But then how did your ghost, I mean how did *you*, end up here?"

"I . . . I don't know." He punched at the dashboard in frustration. His hand went into it up to the wrist. He made a small noise. We drove on in silence. As I pulled into my driveway he spoke again.

"I don't think I'll come in. I'm not ready to see what your life looks like. I need to do a bit of wandering, a bit of thinking. I'll . . . I'll just see you later, okay?"

"Um, sure. Are you certain you'll be all right?"

He didn't reply, just stood up. His head vanished through the ceiling of the car, he stepped through the closed passenger side door, and walked away into the night.

I didn't see him again until I was leaving work on Monday afternoon. My weekend had been ruined, worrying about him and trying to figure out what had happened and whether we could put it all back together again. When I saw him waiting by my car I hurried over.

"Where have you been? Are you all right? What have you been doing?"

He waved away my questions. "Don't worry about that just at the moment. I think I've figured out what's happened. Are you ready to hear this?" He didn't look happy.

"What? Are you kidding? Of course, I am."

"Come with me. But I warn you, I don't think you're going to like this. Just promise not to freak out, okay?"

"Freak out? What is it? What's happened?"

Ignoring my questions, he walked off towards the far side of the carpark. There was a spare block, thick with untamed bush, but he walked through it without pause, leaving me to scramble after him. Each bush bore a variety of spikes, suckers, and fangs. They all seemed to be pointing in my direction. After twenty metres or so of this Black Forest we entered a small clearing. I stopped dead in my tracks, gaping at the sight that greeted me. Three men stood before me, dressed in garb that verged on the surreal. Each one stared back at me from a face that mirrored my own.

"More?" I managed to strangle out. My original double gave forth with a small, embarrassed cough.

"David, this is Dawfydd, Devi and Taffy. They've, uh, arrived in the same way I have."

"You mean they're . . . "

"Yes. Scientists." He waved a hand towards the one wearing the cape and conical hat. "In their own way, anyway. They were all working toward the same goal as me, though they have different processes and names for it."

"But how . . . .here . . . .?"

"Uh, look, maybe you'd best sit down." One of them, dressed in a suit that looked wrong in some way I couldn't put my finger on, made way. He'd been perching just below the surface of a large flat rock. I slumped down onto it in his place. "We've been talking, and we think we may have nutted out what happened."

"Dave," I looked around the faces. It was like being in a hall of mirrors. "Why are they here?"

He kneeled in front of me. At his direction, I drew what looked like a family tree in the dirt.

"The divergence tree."

"You remember I talked about wondering how far I'd come across it?" I nodded. "Well, based upon what we all know about our individual worlds, and what I know of this one, we've been doing some triangulation and, well . . . ." At the bottom of the tree he'd had me draw what seemed a lot of lines. Now he bade me run my finger across them all, connecting them with a single crossways stroke. I stared at it for long moments.

"So far?"

"Near as we can reckon without getting to our labs or Dawfydd's sanctorum. That's not really the extent of the problem, though."

"What?" I looked up again. Solemn and grave, my own face stared back, four times.

"I said we were all working on the same thing. Do you remember what that was?"

"Measuring variations in the time stream."

"Yes, at first. But it became more than that, remember? Multiple universes. Travelling across multiple universes." He kneeled down again, moved his finger along the tracks of the divergence tree. "We've punched a hole through the skins of all these separate time streams. We've created a path that crosses all of these divergent realities. Once we realised the common factor in how we came to be here, and how that relates to events further up the tree, we were able to ascertain what else is going to happen."

"What else is going to . . . .what do you mean, Dave?"

"Devi died about a day before I did, near as we can figure, chronologically speaking. And Dawfydd before him, and Taffy just before him." His finger stabbed down at various spots on the lower half of his diagram. "Exactly the opposite order in which we arrived. Every change in the time stream causes changes further up the Divergence Tree. So every you that ever existed along this whole area of the divergence tree is going to make their way down the tree to the path we've created. And one by one, they're going to arrive in this world. All those dead Davids and Daves and Tevis and Taffys and on and on." He gazed at us all, and there was great sadness in his eyes. "And the record runs backwards."

"I don't understand."

"Multiple universes. Every time you ran across the road and didn't get hit by a car, somewhere across the tree you did. When we were five and got measles, well, some of us didn't get better. When we got pulled out in that rip and a lifesaver rescued us, a lot of us drowned."

"Oh, God."

"Every decision we've ever made, every path we've ever taken, has paths leading from it, and those paths have paths that have paths . . ." His voice broke into a sob. One of the others, the one who looked like he came from an army camp, spoke. His voice was strangely croaky.

"How many decisions does one of us make in thirty seven years? How many decisions do we all make?"

I'm alone now, for the first time today. They don't come into the house. I don't know why. I'm in the bathroom. The mirror feels cool against my forehead. I can't bear to look into it anymore. I can't stand what I see. I haven't shaven in days.

This morning I choked on my breakfast. Just a coughing fit, that's all. Just some coughing. For me. But in how many worlds, what else? In how many worlds did I lie there, blue and choking, grabbing at the table, the chair, finally the carpet as the breath refused to come and my life strangled and ended? When do they come to see me, my blue and bloated ghosts? How many changes do they create further up the tree? I have a bottle of sleeping pills. The doctor gave them to me a few days ago.

There was a child sitting on his desk as he filled out the prescription. He looked just like me when I was seven. I remember seeing Superman on TV, and jumping off the roof, trying to fly. I broke my wrist. He broke his neck.

That's the thing, see? That's what Dave was trying to tell me. The time-stream, the variations. The record runs backwards. Less and less often do I see adults, or teenagers. All the dead reflections of myself, all my broken and bent ghosts, they're almost always children now. There are a lot of pills in the bottle. I could swallow them, all at once. But I remember the divergence tree, all those paths on paths on paths. If I put the bottle down, there will be worlds where I swallow them and die, and those poor bastards will be waiting for me when I open the front door tomorrow.

And if I do it, if I take the top of the bottle and swallow all those pills, if I put an end to it, what then? There will be worlds, won't there, where I will hold this bottle and decide against it, where I will put it down unopened, and live. And if I die in this world, do I arrive in one of those worlds? Do I join the queue to haunt some desperate, maddened wreck that wears my face? Do I visit this plague of me onto some other innocent soul?

What do I do? What do I do?

AFTERWORD

The first story I sold. I'm fascinated by the concept of multiple universes, and especially the notion of multiple selves meeting. What would I say if I met me, or what would they say to me? Probably "Get a haircut". And there are a whole bunch of points in my life where I could take myself in hand and say "No, do it this way." The question is, as always, what would you lose? Which is pretty much the core of all my writing. Not one for happy endings, me.

JARACARA'S KISS

These days, in winter, the mail truck only comes through town once a month, and nobody bothers braving the mountain roads to visit. So there is more than a little surprise when it pulls up outside the general store and an old man falls out of the rear door, landing face-first in the mud that passes for a main street. He lies in the filth, scarcely moving, his moaning just audible over the sounds of the mailman unloading his cargo. Then the driver climbs back in and the truck rolls away, depositing a fresh layer of muck over the form of its recent passenger. The old man rolls onto his back, and turns his mud-caked face to the sky.

"Are you all right, mister?"

The newcomer cracks open an eye. A young man of no more than seventeen or eighteen years is peering down at him, concern colouring his unlined face. Behind him a small crowd has gathered, muttering amongst themselves and doing their best not to stare.

"Wat is je naam?"

"Um, I'm sorry, mister. I don't get what you're saying." The young man looks around for assistance, but nobody else seems to understand the words.

"Your name," the stranger croaks. "What is your name?"

"Bram, sir. Bram Shelby."

The newcomer laughs, a pained gasp that brings his knees up to his chest and forces a stream of dirty white bile over his chin and into the mud.

"Your church," he manages, when the wracking coughs have left him. "Take me to your church."

He wakes under clean white sheets. Opening his eyes causes another coughing attack. A hand cups the back of his head and draws him upright. Cold porcelain presses against his lips.

"Here. Drink this," a voice commands. The old man opens his mouth and lets the icy water salve his tongue and throat. The hand lays him back onto the pillow.

"Thank you."

"My pleasure."

The old man turns his head towards the voice. A stranger sits beside the bed, as broad and strong in features as his hand had felt against the back of the visitor's aching skull.

"Where am I?"

"Where you asked to be. Our church. My name is Hitchens, Graeme Hitchens. I'm the Pastor here."

"I . . . call me Abraham."

"That's quite a wound you have there, Abraham."

The visitor reaches a hand up to cover an area of damage at the corner of neck and shoulder.

"A bite. An old one. There was some . . . business. Someone . . . something bit me. It was . . . infected. Please, tell me. What year is this?"

"The year?" The Pastor smiles in surprise. "1925, last time I passed the calendar."

Abraham stares at him, his face a mask of horror. "Twenty years?" he whispers. "Twenty years?"

"Are you all right?"

"Please. Where am I?"

"I told you. You're in our church. This is the rectory."

"But where? Where?"

"Colburg. Tennessee."

"America?" Abraham sinks back into his pillow and closes his eyes. He seems to shrink slightly, as if something vital has left him. "Good God. Where have I *been*?"

Two days later, Abraham appears in his doorway as the Pastor arrives to bring him more water. Hitchens puts down his tray and takes the old man's weight against his arms.

"Are you all right?"

"Your church," his patient replies. "I must see your Church."

"Can you walk?"

Abraham smiles wanly. "I may need some guidance."

The chapel stands alone on the defile marking the cleared boundary of the town, like a sentinel, warning of the approach of wilderness. The two men make their way toward it, stopping a number of times to allow Abraham to catch his breath. When they reach the door, he stands for a moment, hand pressed against the rough wooden entrance.

"Wait."

"What is it?"

The old man gathers himself, and raises his head to view the simple cross carved into the door.

"Please," he says to the image, "this time, please."

He pushes open the door and limps inside, collapsing into a pew halfway down the short room. Hitchens stands back, busying himself with small matters of neatness to allow his visitor the space he desires.

Abraham sits for half the day, mumbling in languages the Pastor does not recognise. Every half hour or so he stops, then begins chanting again in a new tongue, tears streaming over his sunken cheeks.

Eventually, Hitchens moves toward him and lays a hand upon his shoulder.

"Abraham. I'm due back at the house. We should go."

The old man lowers his head into his hands and weeps.

"He does not answer," Hitchens hears him say. "He has turned away."

That night, Abraham has dinner with the Pastor, a simple meal in the younger man's kitchen. Despite not having eaten in the days of his delirium he tastes no more than a few fresh vegetables and a small portion of cooked meat, which brings a grimace of distaste to his features. He soon pushes his plate to one side.

"Is it not to your liking?" the Pastor asks, seeing his expression. "I can have my wife prepare something else if you'd prefer."

"No, no, it is fine. It is just, I do not eat as much as I used to."

"Something to drink perhaps?" Hitchens reaches for a small bottle of wine that sits on the nearby draining board.

"No, thank you. I do not drink . . . wine."

"You've no objection if I do?"

"Please, go ahead."

The Pastor pours. Abraham stares at the stream of red liquid as if transfixed, only breaking out of his reverie once the glass is full and the bottle returned to its resting place. Hitchens has lifted the glass and taken his first sip before the older man speaks again.

"Father. Your next mass. I wonder?"

"You'd like to attend? Of course." Hitchens leans back in his chair. "You're a God-fearing man, Abraham?"

"Oh, yes." The older man raises a hand to the crease between neck and shoulder. "I fear God very much."

"Then you'll be more than welcome. The day after tomorrow is Sunday. I'll be at the Church before dawn, but I'll send someone to fetch you. Although I should say . . . "

Abraham looks up with such intensity that the Pastor is taken aback for a moment. He regathers himself and matches the older man's gaze.

"This is Tennessee, Abraham. You may find our services a bit different than those you're used to."

Abraham says nothing, merely searches Hitchens' face with his red eyes. Hitchens shifts in discomfort, taken by the notion that the older man is looking for some excuse to strike. Abraham settles back in his seat and the feeling passes.

"It has been a long time," the old man says mildly. "I am no longer used to much of anything."

Abraham slinks into the church and sits in the pew nearest the exit. The tiny chapel is full. Everyone in the town appears to be here, crammed into the hot, dark space shoulder to shoulder in Sunday-Best of varying quality. Abraham sucks the air in through bared teeth and hunches down into his small portion of pew, body angled away from contact with the heavy dowager filling more than her share of space next to him.

He has barely settled into some semblance of comfort when a light is turned on near the front of the room. Pastor Hitchens strides to the open space before the townspeople.

"My friends," he shouts, his hands raised so that Abraham is unsure whether the gesture is merely meant to draw the people together under his gaze, or whether Hitchens has designed an eerie parallel with the wooden Christ pinned like a butterfly to the wall behind him. "Do you believe in Jesus Christ, the Lord Almighty?"

"Yuzzah!" the crowd shouts in unison. The woman next to Abraham pumps her arms, nearly knocking the old man from his perilous roost.

"And are you the tools of the Lord?"

"Yuzzah!"

"Do you believe in the Word and the Spirit? Do you live in sight of the blessed realm and all its holy glories?"

"Yuzzah! Yuzzah!"

Abraham looks around him in shock. The quiet and respectful townspeople have gone, replaced by hypnotised creatures that wave their hands and punch the air at each communal outcry. Audience members are jumping to their feet, raising their arms in imitation of their holy man and his carven effigy. Abraham grabs the back of the pew in front of him, fingers biting into the wood, the prick of splinters a pain to anchor him in the face of his mounting panic.

"Do you claim dominion over the beasts that walk and crawl and fly? Do you claim dominion over the beast within *you*?"

Abraham falls back into his seat, eyes wide, shaking his head. The Pastor seems to be staring straight at him over the heads of the swaying and cheering parishioners, eyes steady and measured despite the rising fervour in his voice.

"Show me your glory!" he cries. "Show me your faith!"

At his words two young men move into the light. Each man carries a burlap sack that shifts and writhes in the uneven illumination. They upend the bags at the Pastor's feet. A welter of snakes pours onto the dirt, a cascade of browns, blacks, greens, and greys that spreads out like liquid to fill the space provided. Hitchens bends over and plunges his hands into the writhing mass. He rises, his fists clutching a dozen serpents that roil and curl around his arms in an effort to escape his grip. As the congregation watches the Pastor lifts up his arms and lays his catch over his shoulders and head.

"No!"

Abraham leaps to his feet, arms outstretched toward the priest. All noise in the church stops, save the rustling of cloth as heads turn to study the wild-eyed old man who has interrupted their devotions. The Pastor lowers his arms and looks at him from between spirals of flesh.

"It's all right, Abraham," he says. "This is what we do." He faces the crowd. "These signs will accompany those who believe," he says in a soft voice. "They will cast out demons."

"They will speak in new tongues," the townspeople answer, eyes still fixed upon the intruder in their midst.

"They will pick up serpents, and if they drink any deadly thing it will not hurt them."

"They will lay their hands on the sick, and they will recover."

"Do you see?" Hitchens asks, taking a step toward him. "Do you understand?"

Abraham has not moved since his outcry. Now he stumbles backwards, towards the door. His shoulders thump against the rough wood. His hand scrabbles for the handle. He stares at the snake-clad preacher in terror.

"You cannot..." he whispers." The serpent... I have seen the serpent! I..."

"Look!" The cry comes from somewhere in the audience.

"My God! Abraham!"

The old man locks eyes with the Pastor, then follows his finger. The snakes are travelling, moving in silent collusion away from the holy man toward a single spot on the floor. They gather around the intruder. Already more than twenty lie before him, silent and still as if drugged, heads turned so that his eyes cannot escape their gaze. More join them. Hitchens speaks with great calm.

"Reach down, my friend. Reach down and take control of the serpent. Let the Lord embrace and protect you. Reach down."

Abraham sinks to his knees before the slithering gallery. A hand slides up to stifle the moan that escapes unbidden. He closes his eyes, and turns his face away from the reptiles surrounding him. One snake coils demurely up his body and over his shoulder, laying its head upon his pale arm. He feels its tongue kiss the hairs, calming him like the soft stroking of a child's head.

"Look, Abraham," Hitchens calls. "Look at what the Lord has presented you."

Abraham opens his eyes. The snake gazes back at him, matching his stare without so much as a blink.

"What . . . ?"

No earth-coloured native, clad in dull camouflage, embraces him. Multi-coloured rings clothe this serpent. Bands of crimson, yellow, and white pulse across a backing of purest jet, moving like liquid against his flesh, hypnotising him.

"A coral snake," the Pastor whispers, his voice carrying clear as air to the old man. "They don't exist in this region. It takes a week to collect the snakes from the hills around us, and I didn't see anything like it, Abraham. So where? Where but the Lord could such a gift come from?"

Abraham cannot answer. His eyes refuse to leave the glittering reptile. It stares back at him, its tongue emerging every few seconds to repeat its lover's kiss upon the upturned hair of his arm.

"She likes you," the Pastor says. "By God's grace are you protected, and by His light within you have you won her over."

Tears sting a path across the old man's cheeks. He raises his arm so that he and the snake look at each other, eye to alien eye.

"Praise be," he whispers. "Praise be to God."

As the last word falls into the still air the snake leaps forward and plunges its fangs deep into the flesh of Abraham's mouth.

He opens his eyes upon darkness. His last memory returns, and with a cry his hands fly to his face. No snake hangs there, nothing save a small path of moisture where sleep has drawn spit from his lips. He turns his head from side to side, recognising details through the dark: pillows beneath his head, the edge of a blanket rubbing against his neck; the square of dimmed light where a window opens onto the night. He is in his room. He is safe.

"You should be dead."

The voice comes from across the room, where a chair has been provided for his reading.

"Who is that?"

"You should be dead."

A form reveals itself through the gloom: larger than a man; graceful and sleek. A human form, elongated and serpentine. It shifts in the seat, and Abraham hears the shiver of scale upon scale.

"You poisoned me," it says. "We should both be dead." It rises from the chair and towers over the bed. "What have you done to me?"

Abraham screams. The creature pauses its progress toward him, then in one fluid movement turns and flies for the window, pushing the panes open and sliding through before he can draw a second breath. By the time the door bursts open, and Pastor Hitchens falls into the room, only the open window stands as testament to the old man's fear.

"Abraham! Are you all right?" The Pastor rushes to his side and pushes him back into the bed's warm embrace. The older man struggles to get out and over to the window. Hitchens' weight is too much. He subsides underneath it.

"The serpent!" Abraham points toward the night. "Please God, the serpent!"

"Margaret, close them will you?" The priest nods at the gaping panes. From behind his bulk a small, pretty woman emerges. She closes them, then stands beside Abraham and places a cool hand on his forehead.

"You're hot, sir," she says, then, "Shall I get a glass of water for him, darling?"

"Yes dear, please." Hitchens looks with worry at his raggedly breathing charge. "You've given us quite a scare, old fellow. To be quite honest, you should be dead."

Abraham winces to hear the words spoken a second time in such quick succession.

"Father, the window. I saw him. I saw the serpent!" He moans into his pillow, face screwed up with old miseries. "I shall never be free of him."

"Abraham, Abraham." The Pastor strokes his hair, calming him, until the tension leaves his muscles and he lies with eyes closed against the soft fabric. "You're not well. A dream, that's all it was, a result of your illness. A bite like that, with such limited medical resources as we have here . . . "

Something in the preacher's tone causes Abraham to unlock his eyes and peer sidewise at him.

"What?"

The younger man shrugs. "I'd have expected death within half a day under normal circumstances. You've lain here without the slightest symptom, and woken as if you've just had a nap. Half my congregation thinks you're the devil. The rest think you're the vessel for miracles."

"What do you mean?" Abraham struggles out from under the Pastor's grip and sits up.

Hitchens eyes him at length. "We teach the signs here. 'They will speak in tongues, they will pick up serpents, and if they drink any deadly thing it will not hurt them'. We remain unbitten when we handle the serpents because the Lord provides us mastery over the beast. You *were* bitten, in full view of everyone, and yet it did no harm to you. And nobody who's passed that door in the last seventy-two hours has failed to hear you. You've been shouting, speaking in tongues the whole time. You haven't said a word we've understood since we brought you in here. You test their faith, my friend."

Abraham stares at the door. "I . . . I can speak languages, I think. I remember many languages, maybe a dozen.'

"Yes, at the church. I remember."

"One thing I know, Father. I am no miracle."

"How can you say that?"

"I have been bitten, Father, by one who has forsaken the Lord. His poison. I bear it. He has touched me, inside and out. Twenty years I've wandered, no memory of the evil I have done . . . " Abraham buries his face in his hands. "I am not touched by God."

"Aren't you? Or do you just hope not, so that you can rationalise it to yourself?"

The door creaks, and Margaret enters, bearing a pitcher upon a tray. Hitchens stands and lets her approach the bed.

"Here," she says. "Drink this."

She pours a glass of water and offers it to the old man. Abraham accepts it, choosing to believe his dry mouth the result of thirst rather than the Pastor's words. As he reaches for the drink he catches a glimpse of his nurse's wrist and stops.

"What is that?"

"This?" She shakes her wrist, encouraging a striped bracelet to fall below the cuff of her nightdress and into his view. "It's nothing. Just a gift."

"The colours." Abraham stares at it, hand caught halfway between the glass and the jewellery. Margaret glances at the bands of red, yellow, white, and black encircling her wrist and laughs.

"Oh, yes. Now there's something."

The old man leans forward and grips the bangle between his fingers.

"The snake," he says through clenched teeth. "The same as . . . aah!" He pulls away from the bracelet as if burned. He buries his hand in the other and falls back into the bed.

"What is it?"

"The bracelet. It moved! I felt it, it *slid* under my touch."

"Hush, now." Margaret places the cold tumbler in his grip, then urges him to drink. "You're not well, sir. It's no surprise you'll feel odd things, maybe even see odd things. You're fevered. It's natural. There's nothing to fear from this." She indicates the bracelet. "It's just a gift, something we give to women here when they begin to show."

"Show?"

"Yes." She stands and moves to her husband, taking his arm and stretching up to kiss his cheek. "Goodnight, sir."

She leaves, taking Abraham's question with her. Hitchens also steps to the door, turning back as he reaches the light switch.

"Three months before she's due," he says with a smile. "Our first. I want a boy, but she's convinced . . . well. Rest now. We'll talk again in the morning. Nothing more will disturb your sleep tonight."

Abraham places the glass on the bedside table and sinks into his pillows.

"Father?"

"Yes?"

"The child. Kill it. Kill it before the serpent finds it. Kill it before it learns what terror we bring it into. Kill them both if you have to."

There is a long pause.

"Go to sleep, Abraham," the Pastor says in a tight voice, and returns the room to darkness.

Nobody will meet his eyes. He walks the streets of Colburg unaccosted by man or woman. People stand aside at his approach, watch him pass, then continue their conversations as if the few seconds of his presence were a bad dream to be washed from the memory. Abraham stalks the populace of the town like a predator, prowling through those who consider him cursed or blessed alike, narrowed eyes searching for the one familiar face that eludes him. Every night he falls into his bed sodden with sweat, exhausted from his hunt, and gives himself over to dreams that slither and caress. He wakes before each dawn, shivering at fears and ecstasies he refuses to face during daylight hours. Sometimes he bears new bite marks into the morning light. On other occasions he finds himself waking with thighs and sheets sticky from nocturnal orgasms the like of which he has not suffered since he was a youth. The window is always open when he rises, no matter how securely he locks it before retiring.

He finds what he has been searching for on the third Sunday. The townspeople might avoid him, but they cannot avoid the call to worship. Abraham watches from nearby bushes as they file up the hill to enter the door of the little church. He counts half a dozen pregnant women among the arrivals, leaning on solicitous partners as they puff up the incline, multi-coloured bracelets clear to the old man's stare.

Soon the doors close, and the sounds of the service begin to drift to him, the raucous chanting of the congregation muted by the walls that contain it. He moves closer, skirting the church until he stands on its blind side, with only the back wall before him and the wilderness behind. It is then that he spies the young man climbing up out of the defile toward him. A burlap bag lies heavy over his shoulder, writhing in the early morning heat. Another youth from the town climbs behind him, an identical bag slung over his bent back. In a flash, Abraham has left the shade of the church and crossed the distance between them, intercepting the youths as they clear the scrub. They pull up short at his approach, moving closer together like cattle at the scent of a dog.

"Where have you been, boy?" he asks. "I've been looking for you."

The young man takes a step backward, eyes sliding left and right as if searching out escape routes.

"Where?"

"I . . . in the hills, sir. Bill and I look for the snakes."

"Where did you get it, boy? Where did it come from?"

"I don't know what you mean, sir. Please, sir. The service."

"Where?" Abraham lunges, and tears the bag from his victim's grip. He upends it, and a stream of snakes strikes the earth between them. He kicks at them, scattering them back into the bushes and across the vacant space between him and the church. Bill drops his bag, and both youths run toward the building. Abraham is oblivious to their desertion. He falls to his knees amongst the creatures, pushing them to either side as he searches amongst the hissing piles. The snakes rear back and attack him, sinking fangs into his dry, unresponsive flesh. Abraham doesn't even pause to brush them off, using the motion of his arms to send the sickened reptiles into the nearby undergrowth.

"Where is it?" he cries, "Where?"

Strong hands grip his shoulders and pull him away from the striking serpents. He lands on his back, glaring up at the frightened stares of the townspeople without recognition. He rises and backs away from them until he is several feet down the incline of the defile. Pastor Hitchens steps forward from the group and reaches out a hand.

"Abraham..."

He breaks at the sound of his name, running into the untamed land. The townspeople watch him go, turning one by one to return to the church to collect their bags and purses. In the end only the Pastor remains, standing silent, looking out over the broken land away from the church.

There is no rain on the night he returns, although the sky is low with clouds. The moon has long ago given up the fight to be seen. Abraham crouches in the bushes of the Pastor's garden, panting through his mouth like an animal, eyes bright in his dirt-encrusted face. Through the shuttered window of the master bedroom he can hear low voices. A female moans somewhere between pain and rapture. A male voice accompanies it in a low chant. Abraham sniffs the air: once, twice. He bares his teeth in a snarl. Then he is up and running toward the house, striking the window and crashing through it into the room beyond, unmindful of the slivers of glass and wood that slice through what remains of his clothes and into flesh that no longer bothers to bleed.

Margaret Hitchens lies naked upon the bed, her swollen belly glistening with oil. Blood and saliva run down from her breasts to pool in the folds and valleys of her lower body. Her husband stands before her. The serpent lounges between them, head bent low over the woman's chest, face buried deep into her breast. The muscles of Hitchens' shoulders and back roll tightly as he grinds his body into the beast's coils, erection appearing and disappearing into the shadows of its body.

Abraham cries out in rage. For perhaps half a second there is no reaction, only the sound of sucking and the hoarse ululations of the human voices. Then Hitchens turns his head, and the threesome disintegrates.

The Pastor twists away from his serpentine lover and throws himself at the intruder. Abraham bats him away, a backhanded swat that sends the unclothed preacher crashing against the wall with a wet smack. Hitchens screeches in pain, and the serpent raises its head to look in Abraham's direction. He stares back at the almost human visage, watching recognition dawn in the creature's drugged eyes. It lifts itself from the Pastor's wife. A single strand of saliva connects the fanged mouth to her breast, before wavering and snapping. The serpent draws up to its full height, seven feet of coils shimmering red, yellow, white and black. It tilts its head, folds muscular arms, and waits. Abraham stalks forward, finger extended like a claw toward the beast's eye.

"Demon," he hisses. "I know what you are."

"And what is that?" the monster replies, voice like sand over dry paper.

"Defiler. Child eater. Blood swallower. Jaracara." He spits the name, as if identifying the creature will result in its destruction. With each word he steps closer. The Pastor's wife gibbers on the bed, barely conscious, hands sliding over her fluid-washed body. The beast tilts backward then shoots its upper body forward until it hangs in the air scant inches from Abraham's twisted visage, face a mask of anger.

"And what of you?" it hisses. "What have you become? What poison courses through you? Your blood addicts. You don't taste like other men. You taste like . . . "

"No!" Abraham's hand shoots out and claws the serpent across the face, nails tearing white-edged furrows across its skin. The snake reels, shrieking. Something cannons into Abraham's back and sends him tumbling across the floor. Fists beat at his face, and the Pastor's voice sounds high and fevered in his ear.

"Leave her! Mistress! Leave the Mistress!"

Abraham twists under the assault and slides his body out from beneath the Pastor. He strikes the younger man a vicious blow to the side of his head with his elbow and Hitchens falls, stunned. Abraham kneels above him. He grabs Hitchens' hair and pulls his head backwards until the younger man is stretched taut, unfocussed eyes pointed toward the evil in the corner and the wet bundle that is his wife.

"Look!" he shouts in the priest's ear. "Look at it! It feeds from you, feeds on the life blood of your wife and child. Don't you understand? It is a *snake*. It must poison in order to feed. For every drop of blood it draws it pumps its own juices into them. Do you want them to end up like me? Do you? It's poisoning your wife and child, man, poisoning them with its own vile fluids!"

"No . . . " Hitchens' voice is dull and muddy, as if the blow has dislodged something fundamental within him. "Mistress . . . protects . . . "

"Damn you!" Abraham pushes his head away in frustration, and rises. The serpent begins to laugh, a dry susurration that stops him in mid-motion.

"And what do you think is in the poison that flows into them, little creature? What do you think draws me to your room night after night?"

"No. No!"

The snake advances upon him now, liquid, deadly, a creature of purpose and poison and lightning-quick speed. Abraham retreats until he is pressed against the window, the wind of the night cutting chill across his lacerated back.

"What is it that courses through your veins, little beast? Your blood is addictive, wampyr. What I draw from you I pass to them." It pushes its face into his, lidless eyes staking him to the wall. "Whose poison do *you* infect the children with?"

Abraham howls, a sound devoid of human reason, and throws himself at the serpent's neck. His hands find purchase round her throat. Feet balance upon her coils. He lunges, and bites into the striped beauty of her face. The snake claws at his face and back, adding new gouges to those already criss-crossing his white flesh. She lurches forward, striking the windowsill and toppling through, carrying her feral burden into the night. On the bed, Margaret Hitchens begins to spasm as the effect of the creature's bite begins to wear off. Her husband stirs, raising his head in time to see the last multi-coloured band at the serpent's tail whip past him and out the window. As his wife begins to scream he lifts one despairing hand toward the night.

"Mistress . . . " he croaks, as the clouds break and rain begins to drive into the ruined bedroom.

They find her the next morning, coiled in front of the church, her hand wrapped around the door handle. Her body lies on the single step, as if dying a single moment before reaching sanctuary. Her head lolls upon a snapped neck. Her throat has been torn out, whether by teeth or claw it is impossible to say, such is the extent of the damage. Her body bears the marks of furious warfare: gashes cross her skin, and ribbons of raw flesh are open where scales have been ripped from their hold. Her torso is covered in bites, so many that the few who dare approach her do not even try to count them. There is no blood, nor any sign of the old man. They find neither him nor proof of his passage in the years to come. The mountains are a treacherous journey for a fit traveller, never mind one so deeply out of his mind. To the townspeople he will remain simply out *there* somewhere, a tale to frighten children into obedience.

They dispose of the body as befits a loving and protective mistress, consecrating a small plot behind the church for the purpose. They pray for the old man, but once the children are born healthy, and free of the terrors he prophesied, he passes from their prayers, and eventually their memories. The people of Colburg, faith in their gods intact, live on.

The air above Amersfoort smells as if it will never again be clean. For the soldiers who move among the emaciated survivors of the German occupation, this is as close to an image of Hell as they will ever see. They walk amongst the prisoners, dispensing blankets and comfort, asking questions to ascertain names, nationalities, occupations: anything to help these tormented ghosts remember the humanity of which they have been so horribly stripped.

One of the privates spies an old man by the fence, crouched over with face buried half in his hands and half in the mud. He touches a skeletal shoulder. It is as cold. The captive peers up from a face little more than a mess of white scars, his features ruined by countless gouges and bite marks. The private takes a step backward, then gathers his composure, and leans down.

"Sir? I have a blanket for you."

"Wat is je naam?"

"Sir?"

"Your name."

"Private Johns, sir. Would you like to come with me? We have some soup, and a bed at the local church."

The old man laughs, a wheeze that wracks his body and causes a line of pasty white drool to fall from his mouth and over his chin. When he recovers he looks up at the younger man, and there is a light in his eyes that gives the private a strange urge to cross himself.

"A church," he says. "Yes. Take me to your church."

AFTERWORD

My vampire story. Everyone has to write at least one, don't they? And there I was, reading about snake cults (as you do), and my friend Stephen had just sent me an email telling me of an anthology of stories about Van Helsing that was open for submissions, and I had a book on vampires next to me (as you do), and I flipped over the page to the 'J' section... The more I wrote, the more over the top the story became, until I thought "The hell with it" and went straight out for the kind of creeping-tentacles-of-doom gothic melodrama I normally hate in other people. What the hell: it was fun.

THE HOBBYIST

I was spreading marmalade on the last of the breakfast toast when Edward brought me the morning mail. Putting aside the usual assortment of worthy charities and distraught Yorkshire mothers begging me to find their daughters (who had, in all probability, run off to far better lives), I unfolded *The Times* and settled down to search for my current favourite hobby. This proved no difficult task. It screamed at me from the front page: Chelsea Strangler Strikes Again! I chuckled as I read the frenzied hyperbole. Without doubt, this writer was training for a first-class career in the penny dreadfuls.

"Listen to this," I read aloud. "The torrent of fear runs rampant through the bustling streets of this embattled suburb. Must citizens now travel only in groups, like miners, or soldiers off to perform their manual labours? The fiend that stalks these streets cares for neither office nor station in life. The merest chambermaid cowers beside the lady-in-waiting at the prospect of coming next into the sight of this frenzied madman." I gave Edward a grin. "Dear, oh dear. What they won't write in order to sell a copy."

"Yes, sir." He busied himself in clearing the table. I continued to scan the front page.

"Look at this. Nothing at all of worth. No details to be had for the wishing. This 'Chelsea Strangler' seems to beggar a description." I folded the paper again and laid it on the now-empty table. "What do you think, old bean? Time I offered my services?"

"If you wish, sir." Edward is a good man, but I've never really been able to get through that stoic air of his, never got him to truly express his views about my little hobby. He was the same with my father. Still, he's given us over fifty years of loyalty. You simply can't buy that nowadays. I stood up.

"Yes, time to see what they really know. Point them in the necessary direction, what?" I smiled at my man's wooden face.

"I'll get your day suit, sir," was his only response.

I jumped from the hansom and made my way up the steps of Scotland Yard. The sergeant at the front desk was insolent enough, eyeing me up and down like some street dip checking his mark, but my name and position soon sent him waddling away to find the man I sought. Presently he returned, his puffy face reddened by his exertions, and waved me through to his superior's office. There I found the man in charge of searching for the Strangler, Inspector William Abbington. He glowered at me from a pile of paper rubble, obscuring what I assumed would be a desk, should anyone care to dig hard enough. I extended my hand, and he flicked ash at it from a cigar perched like a rude sixth finger in his brawny hand. Looking at him, I had the impression of a belligerent farmer's dog, all teeth and anger. His first words did not bode well for our continued association.

"Psychic to Princess Alexandra, are you? Well, I've no idea what you think you're here for, Mr. Douglas."

I settled myself into his visitor's chair and looked around the chaos that was his office. Presumably the room contained some furniture beyond the chair in which I sat, but an archaeological team from the British Museum would have taken one look at the piles of files, obscure bits of machinery, and general debris, and run for Egypt. Drawing out my snuffbox, I took a pinch and offered him some. He declined with a shake of his head.

"You haven't, Inspector?" I replaced the snuffbox in my pocket and leaned back in the chair. "I rather thought it would be obvious. I've come to offer my assistance in clearing up this terrible Chelsea Strangler bother."

"Bother? Seven women dead and you call it 'bother', sir?"

"Seven? The newspapers mention only five."

"Yes. Well, the newspapers, detectives though they feel they are, haven't connected them all yet." He waved a beefy hand towards a map on one wall of the office. I looked at it but could make neither head nor tail of the coloured pins littering its surface. "Frankly, Mr. Douglas, I don't see what you can offer us."

"I'm a psychic, Inspector. Our friends in Fleet Street seem to think you possess no clues, no leads, and apart from that unfortunate business with the wrestler, no suspects. I thought you might like some *professional* help."

Abbington coloured at the mention of the farcical arrest of 'Hercules' Magee, a former circus performer who had presented an alibi for each night the murders had taken place. "Sergeant Dyke's zealousness aside," he rumbled, "we are in the midst of an ongoing investigation, and are not yet so desperate we need to call on the spirit world, witch doctors, or anything other than our own resources." He stood, and moved towards the door. "I'll tell you the same as I told Mr. Conan Doyle and his friend. We *will* catch the Strangler, and it'll be by virtue of police work that we'll do it."

"I understand, Inspector." I left my seat and moved to the doorway. "If you do need me at any time, please feel free." I proffered my card.

"I doubt it." And without ceremony, he slammed the door behind me.

Two nights later The Strangler struck again. Abbington's call came the following afternoon.

This time somebody had alerted the press, and a school of them were circling when I arrived at the station. I pushed through their ranks, ignoring all questions, before pausing on the top step and turning to them with a flourish.

"Gentlemen, gentlemen, please. I am merely here to assist the good Inspector with some questions he believes may fall into my particular sphere of expertise. Beyond that I really know as little as you." I gave them my most engaging smile before moving past the doors and into the scowling presence of the Inspector. If anything the state of his office was even worse than before. A child would have drowned trying to reach safety. Spying an exposed corner of desk, I drew my handkerchief from my pocket and gave it an experimental dab. When the desk didn't immediately collapse under the threat of cleaning I perched upon it and smiled down at the stony face of the policeman.

"You called?"

He jerked a stump-like thumb toward the window behind him.

"What the bloody Hell was that little circus all about?"

"I really can't say. They were there when I arrived. You wouldn't have preferred me to ignore them, would you? Then they could have made up anything they wished."

Abbington said nothing for long moments, merely stroked his moustache and looked at me with an expression of frustrated rage. Finally he managed to hiss, "How do you do whatever the blazes it is you do?"

I grew serious. "It depends on the circumstances, really. I've had some small success with divination and automatic drawing..."

"What?"

"You take a map and a pendulum, hold something related to the person, and wait for the pendulum to point out an area of the map." I demonstrated with empty hands. "Automatic drawing is much the same, except you end up with a picture of a house or something near the object of your search. Anyway, as I was saying, I have some small skill with those approaches, but they're not my preferred method of divination. Generally, I have my best success with sympathetic resonance."

"And what exactly is *that* supposed to be?"

I sighed. "I take it you have something for me to use?"

He grunted, reached into a desk drawer, and pulled out a small piece of paper. He placed it on the desk between us.

"This. A note."

"Are you sure it's from the killer? It's not just something she had on her at the time?"

"Oh, we're fairly sure." He smiled sardonically, and unfolded the note, turning it so I could read it clearly. Once I'd finished, I asked for a glass of water.

"Yes, yes, I see what you mean." I dipped the edge of my handkerchief into the water and dabbed it on my forehead. "Yes."

"So what can you do?"

I poked at the corner of the note. "Well I can use this, certainly. The emanations are . . . strong enough. But why would the Strangler choose to start leaving clues? Nothing for seven times and now something so obvious? It seems so . . . convenient, what?"

"He's taunting us. He's so secure in his superiority he wants us to know he's going to do it again, and again . . . " The Inspector bunched his fists in frustration.

"But he wouldn't have known you'd be calling on me. So let's hope that's his mistake, shall we?" I clapped him on the shoulder. "Never fear, dear fellow, this will lead to something. I'm certain of it."

"It had better." Abbington motioned towards the window, where we could see the waiting pressmen. "It's both our reputations on the line now."

Half an hour later, our preparations were complete. I sat at Abbington's desk, the note before me on its empty surface. Some small, necessary items lay to one side: a glass of water, pen and paper, a small towel. The Inspector sat at the other end of the room, his chin resting on clenched fists, dark eyes boring holes into mine. I returned his stare and raised my eyebrows.

"You understand what you need to do?" He nodded solemnly. "Okay."

I reached out and grasped the note, my face a mask of concentration. Suddenly, my eyes rolled back in my head. A shiver ran the length of my body. Sweat broke out across my face. My body became rigid, my fingers splaying out, my arms rising straight up from the desk. My jaw dropped. A low groan rose in my throat and escaped. After thirty seconds or so of this display, I slid from the chair and slumped to the floor. The note fell from my grasp. At this, Abbington sprang into action. Leaping from his seat, he grabbed the glass of water from the desk and dashed it in my face. As I sputtered in shock, he hauled me back onto my chair, wiped my face with the conveniently placed towel, and pushed pen and paper at me.

"Write!" he hissed.

And I did. With eyes closed, and shaking hand, I wrote the description of the man who within days would be arrested as the Chelsea Strangler. I reported his appearance, his house, the street on which he lived, his profession. I told of his habits, his beliefs, the way in which he spent the hours of his days, the marks upon his body. Madly ripping page after page from the pad, I wrote until I fell exhausted across the desk, ink-stained fingers lying prone before me. For long minutes I lay, eyes unfocussed, no sound breaking the stillness except the gentle ticking of my pocket-watch and the rasping of my depleted breath. Finally, Abbington spoke.

"Are . . . are you alright?"

I raised my head to look at him. "What does it say?" I croaked.

He gathered up the pages and held them in front of me. "Enough."

The morning of the trial found the city in a state of feverish excitement. London never truly pauses, but today even those who would normally still be tucked into their beds seemed to be up and out especially early, as if the whole world found itself drawn without will towards a witnessing of important events. People choked the streets, wandering without purpose, pausing at each paper boy as if the countdown to the trial could be reported anew within each short journey from street corner to street corner, each traveler slowly but inexorably floating on the human tide towards the courts at the Old Bailey. Even the sun had risen bright and full, as if it too wanted to see as much of the forthcoming affair as possible.

As for myself, I was decked out in my finest Saville Row, as befits a gentleman who intends himself to be the star turn at such an important social occasion. Turning backwards and forwards in front of my mirror, I busied myself in making sure I projected the perfect image. Nothing but perfection would suffice. If today were an important day for London, it was doubly so for me. Today was the culmination of many plans, and I meant to take full advantage. Satisfied, I spread my arms and smiled toward Edward.

"How do I look, old chap?"

"Entirely satisfactory, sir." His doleful voice seemed determined to strip the day of any possible enjoyment. I tut-tutted him.

"Really, dear fellow. I do wish you'd allow me to enjoy just this one little hobby."

"Your business is of no interest to me, sir. My sole interest lies in ensuring you are fed, dressed, and otherwise served to the best of my abilities. As you well know. Sir." His reproach hung black in the air.

"Of course, of course," I replied. "Still, the occasional smile might make the day more pleasant for you, no?"

"Smile, sir?" He arched an eyebrow. "My loyalty is not sufficient enough for your purposes?"

I sighed. "Edward, you are a perfect gentleman, and the perfect gentleman's gentleman. I'd be entirely lost without you."

"Yes, sir, you would indeed." He withdrew from the room, taking his mournfulness with him. By the time I descended the stairs he had a hansom at the door and a suitable hat in his hand. I smiled and winked at him as I donned it, and used the hall mirror to check its coordination with the suit.

"Perfect. Absolutely splendid. Well, wish me luck."

"I wouldn't dare to be so presumptuous," was all he would grant me.

The hansom pulled up in front of the Old Bailey. I smiled at the sight of the gathered crowds. This was what London had needed for months, a grand spectacle to add some life to the ever passing days. I could see Abbington at the top of the courthouse steps, in his element, regaling the milling press with yet another account of his valiant pursuit and capture of the monster who awaited trial in the cells below the building. I made my way towards him, pushing through the crowd that gasped and pointed, and even broke out into spontaneous applause as they recognised me. Not so Abbington. His expression clouded as I approached, as if I had dashed some set of hopes by turning up. I doffed my hat in a small bow, and smiled at the journalists.

"How perfectly dramatic, Inspector, but don't give away all your secrets. You'll have nothing left for the memoirs." He shrugged at me, clearly annoyed.

"Charlatans and publicity seekers write 'memoirs'. Policemen simply do their jobs."

"Of course, they do, my dear Abbington. Even when they have to rely on charlatans and publicity seekers for their solutions, what?" I gave a wave to the crowd, and moved on into the building.

Things were in no less of a hubbub inside the courtroom. The public gallery was crammed with onlookers, the press gallery the same, each eager to catch a glimpse of the dreaded Strangler. I nodded to a few familiar faces as I moved to my seat. One by one the principal players in the drama came through the doors and found their places, each one invoking a rise in volume until, looking small and frightened inside his phalanx of burly constables, the man I had identified as the Chelsea Strangler was led into the room.

As I would later see it described in the *Times*, the courtroom 'erupted in a frenzy of hatred'. It took nearly twenty minutes, and several constables armed with truncheons, to quell the near-riot that accompanied the Strangler's entrance. One man even went so far as to brandish a revolver, but he was quickly overpowered and dragged away. Through it all I made a point of reading my paper, ensuring myself a mention in the following morning's news.

Eventually order was restored. The Strangler was deposited in the dock and the judge was able to enter and begin proceedings. I folded my paper and looked serious as a constant stream of his acquaintances proclaimed Jeremy Mathew Dorset to be a loner; a man of intemperate habits; a frequenter of late night public houses and street prostitutes, whose failed marriage and dismissal from his teaching post (for 'unsavoury personal interest in his charges', as the *Times* phrased it) had made him a bitter, vengeful man. I sat, paying little attention. My mind was focussed upon my own upcoming performance.

Eventually it came my turn to rise and approach the witness box. As I passed Abbington, our eyes met, and locked. We both knew that while the preceding testimonies had set up our man, it fell upon we two to place the noose over the Strangler's head. The Inspector was a proud man. He would never have begged me to make a good showing. With his reputation, and indeed his entire career, in the balance, I didn't need him to. I spared him a sly wink as I stepped up and recited the oath. The barrister approached. I did my best to assume a professional air.

It all began innocuously enough. At Counsel's prompting I issued my standard explanations regarding who I was, the extent of my psychic abilities and how I conducted my business. The dear crowd duly oohed and ahhed as I read a personal submission from darling Alix, proclaiming my trustworthiness and general service to the Crown. All rather elementary really. I wasn't forced to deviate too far from the speech I give to entice all those lovely middle class ladies to engage my services. Only once we reached the subject of the unfortunate Mr. Dorset did things get interesting.

"Mr. Douglas, can you tell the court what service you provided to Scotland Yard?"

"Certainly. I used my psychic abilities to provide Inspector Abbington with a description of the fiend who wrote the note found on poor Ms Parrish's body." I drew out a handkerchief and sniffed at it.

"I see. What was the description you provided?"

I looked up at the public gallery. "I had a vision of a man of average height, with a small moustache, a widow's peak, a slight limp from a recently broken ankle, and mismatched eyes, one blue, one light grey. I also provided a description of this person's home street, and the front entrance of their residence."

My interrogator looked doubtful. "That doesn't seem to me to be enough to have a man hanged. Does it you?"

"No, sir, it doesn't. However, I *did* provide the police with two small details that enabled them to positively identify the person before us." I waved my 'kerchief toward the dock.

"Oh?"

I paused, looked around at the packed courtroom. Even without utilising my special gift, I could feel the electric anticipation trilling through the minds of the assembled mass. This was the moment I had worked towards for many months, the culmination of all the research I had accumulated about the life of poor Mr. Dorset. All the time I had spent making sure he had no alibis for the nights of the murders; all the practice to get his handwriting just right; it all added up to this one moment. This crowded room, the excitement in the air, the intoxication that had gripped the country these past weeks, all because of my work. I drew a breath.

"As part of my vision, I saw the star-shaped birthmark that the accused has to the rear of his left ear, and," I delivered my final blow, "at the last, I saw the face of the accused through the dying eyes of Ms Parrish, the last of his unfortunate victims!"

There was more of course. Abbington had his turn, with all his little pieces of evidence. The doctors came with their autopsy reports. But it was anticlimactic. I've been a friend of Oscar Wilde's for many years. I know how to structure a drama. It really didn't matter what they had to say. The outcome was as inevitable as the dawn.

Jeremy Mathew Dorset was found guilty of the murders of eight women in the Chelsea area, and sentenced to death. Five days later, I watched from my private room at 'The Magpie and Stump' as the Chelsea Strangler was taken from the cells of the Old Bailey and hanged.

I was pouring myself one last cup of tea from the bottom of the breakfast pot when Edward brought in the morning mail. Grabbing the *Times*, I rifled the pages, but there was nothing to catch my eye. With no Strangler, and no murders, life in London had soon settled back into its routines and habits. My fame had ensured me a number of new commissions. I was the centre of society attention for some little while, much to poor Oscar's disgust (We still don't talk.) The Strangler hung on in the more vulgar of the popular magazines and disreputable theatres for a couple of months, but the novelty wore off over time. And now here I sat, less than half a year after I created him, and the Chelsea Strangler had made his sad, slow exit from the popular consciousness. Once more the papers were filled with shipping notices, political mud slinging, cats caught in trees... the whole civilized world seemed sunken into a morass of boredom and mundanity. It simply was not good enough.

I folded the paper and laid it aside. As Edward stood by, I sat, lost in thought, pondering what task I might perform to add a little excitement to the lives of the souls who had to wade through this catalogue of tedium each day. There seemed nothing for it: with a sigh I settled back into my chair, closed my eyes, and focussed.

My mind expanded, spilling out of the room and into the streets of London, hunting, seeking out the star of my next charade. Further and further afield, my consciousness roamed. I gloried in colours unseen by the mere eye, sounds unheard by the crude flesh of the ear. Hither and thither across the breadth of England, long years of practice steering my mental gift so that I absorbed the myriad minds that dotted the land. Until... I found him. There, on the south coast. The perfect marionette.

I drew my mind back in towards my seat, feeling as always an indefinable sadness as my consciousness shrank in the direction of the cage that is my body. Finally, I drew a deep breath and motioned Edward forward.

"Southampton, I think. Some trunk murders this time. Leave them with some torsos to pick at and ponder, what? That hotel porter who was so rude to us last year will do nicely."

Edward made no response, merely sniffed and took his own good time clearing the table and leaving the room.

He is a good man, but he really does disapprove of my little hobby.

AFTERWORD

Oscar Wilde, Jack The Ripper, and a Victorian-era psychic walk into a bar... This was a very deliberate attempt to write in a different style, and to throw a few of my own pet Ripper theories around without starring the old liver-gnawer himself. An object lesson in red herring creation: a review at the time pointed out that in a murder mystery with only two suspects, it's always the narrator. Oops. Still, I think our hero is a likeable enough character, and his voice carries the reader along nicely. He's someone I'd like to bring back for a second outing, if I could find a plot to suit.

MIKAL

Mikal wants to be different. This is a problem.

I've asked Liam and Nigel. As his closest brothers in name, they are accountable for his welfare. That is the rule. We decided when we came to the house. You have to have rules. Without them, nobody can be sure we are all the same. We have to be the same.

We have dinner in the upstairs room, with the window facing onto the garden. It is my turn to be head of the table. Tomorrow it will be Graeme's responsibility, but today I can look over my brothers and see the graves outside. There are more than the last time I sat in this position. Mikal sees my gaze and turns his head. He knows what I am thinking. We all think the same thing. There is no need to discuss it.

"Why?" I ask.

He pauses over his vegetables, places his fork gently upon the edge of the plate, gazes at the wooden surface of the table as if studying the grain. We all lay our forks on the edge of our plates and wait for his response. Nigel leans forward, steepling his fingers and resting his chin against them. The rest of us follow his action, as well as each is able.

"I . . . " Mikal starts, stops, then starts again. "I just want . . . " He waves a hand in the air, signifying thoughts he lacks words to explain. I feel a twinge of sympathy. We all do. Mikal lapses into silence again, staring at his reflection in the polished table. After a time I pick up my fork and begin eating. The others follow suit. We say nothing more. There is nothing more to say.

After dinner, Mikal tells us that he does not wish to join us in the lounge room. There is consternation at this announcement. We always gather in the lounge room after dinner. Liam is very upset. He says some bad things. Others counter, including myself. An argument ensues, and almost a fight. Then we look at each other, lower our fists and voices.

"You see?" I tell Mikal. "This is what comes from wanting to be different. We are the same, all the same. It is what saves us."

Mikal looks past me at my brothers. He raises an eyebrow. When no-one responds he shakes his head. He walks to the staircase and begins to climb, not looking back at us. We stare at his departure in shock. There are no games this night, nothing to occupy us. We sit alone inside our own heads, pondering this new and frightening thing. I stand from my chair more than once, ready to go to Mikal and bring him down to join us, but something stops me. I am not alone: all of us, except Liam of course, get up at some stage. All of us reseat ourselves in silence. I am aware of how few we are, and how many of us lie outside, together in peace.

The next day it is Graeme's turn at the head of the table. I sit at his right hand, aware of how many names lie between mine and his. We surround the wooden expanse; unsure, nervous. Mikal has not come down. He was not in our room. Liam and Nigel spent all night searching for him. They are tired, and distraught. Nigel's good hand twitches from lack of sleep. None of us look at each other, or at Mikal's empty chair. Instead we focus on our untouched plates, watching the vegetables cool and congeal. I am very hungry. We all know what happens if we do not eat our vegetables, the sickness and pain that ensues. I cannot see the graves from where I sit at Graeme's right, but my memory of the view is strong. Still, none of us eat. We must all eat together. We must be the same. We cannot begin until Mikal is with us. He knows this. We all do.

There is a noise. It is the door from the hallway, squeaking on the hinges we do not have oil to silence. Mikal stands in the doorway. My eyes widen. I rise to my feet. Someone stifles a sob. It might be Nigel: he is the most prone among us to crying. It might just as well be me.

"What have you . . . ?'

Mikal says nothing, merely shuffles to his place and sits. He picks up his fork and begins to eat his cold vegetables. We face him, none of us except Liam sitting, our dinner ignored. Mikal talks around his food, mumbles words bitter and quiet in the barren air.

"Please stop staring. It is nothing."

"Nothing." Graeme is scared. Today is his responsibility. He must do something, but he does not wish to be the one to face this. We all understand. It would be the same were it us. I see Nigel from the corner of my eye, leaning toward Simon and explaining what he sees. Simon raises one shrunken hand to his mouth, face twisted with fear, and grief, and memories we are all trying to avoid. Mikal continues to eat, raising and lowering his fork with mechanical precision. I am so hungry. I fall back into my chair. The others follow, Graeme last of all, although he is the first to eat. Our eyes never leave Mikal. We are still staring at him as he finishes his breakfast and waits patiently for us to catch up. He sits with head bowed, hands in his lap, as if spurning the casual touches which give us such constant comfort.

"It's just hair," he says into the silence.

It is my errand to gather and wash the dishes. Once we have all eaten I make my way round the table, spending slightly longer than normal in contact with each brother as I pass. Mikal holds his plate up for me long before I get to him. I reach out to stroke his shoulder, to re-establish the connection I so desperately crave. He will not look at me. As my hand approaches he flinches away from my fingers. I stop, my hand lost in the air between us. I make my way to the kitchen. I cannot concentrate. It is only the long habit of experience that enables me to run the water and place the dishes in without burning myself. I hear voices in the other room, angry and confused. I bend to my task, unwilling to open myself to the pain of the others. The door opens. Mikal runs past me and out to the garden, hands covering his face. A low keening emanates from between them. I want to go after him, to give him what peace I can. I know it will do no good. He does not want us. We can see that. Mikal wants to be different. All we can do is hope it is not permanent, and that he will return to us. We must be the same. I return to my dishes, and once I have finished, to the bosom of my brothers.

Mikal is nowhere to be found. Graeme decides we must search for him. Nobody wants a repeat of what happened at breakfast. We set off to separate parts of the grounds to bring him back to us. For no reason I can explain, I choose the upper floors of the house. I have no success. I am at a loss, wandering the lonely upper corridors without thought. We never come here. It is too quiet, too isolated, too far from the warmth and coziness provided by the bright lower rooms and our brothers. Besides, Simon and Liam's infirmities mean they cannot climb this high, and we do not leave each other behind.

I climb to the corridor bisecting the uppermost floor, the one I have never been to. A trapdoor has been set into the ceiling, a blemish against the smoothness of plaster. It disturbs me. I do not like such perfection to be broken. I approach and look closer. The trapdoor has been left open. I jump. I am able to reach it with my fingertips. Ever so slowly I lower it so the ladder on its upper side slides out. I look up into the square of darkness. I do not want to go into that black uncertainty. I am already too far from my brothers. Their fear is palpable, their knowledge that we are spread out across the grounds, so distant from each other. I need touch, comfort. But I have promised Graeme: I will search the upper floors. And this is a new upper floor, a new responsibility. Graeme will be proud of me. And Mikal might be here, hurt and needing the touch of a brother. My touch. I put a hesitant foot onto the lowest step. With Mikal's image fixed in my mind, I climb into the darkness.

I find a switch as I reach around the frame to haul myself up the last step. I turn it on. The light flickers, finds life. I cannot help it: I cry out at the sight laid out before my frightened eyes.

How can he have done this? Where can he have found the time, the resources? I scan walls papered with pictures, drawn in a beautiful hand. Strange places confront me, vistas I have never seen. My brothers and I look out at the world, striking poses filled with drama and action. And looking back at me with a thousand different expressions: Mikal. Mikal in clothes he has never owned; Mikal in conversations with people we have never met; Mikal skiing, surfing, walking through public parks with a variety of pretty women . . . I never even knew he could draw. We spend so little time apart. Even sleeping, we confine ourselves to one room of the house. We are the same. We need to be together. It is what we wanted, what we needed. It is a rare event indeed, such as the one we find ourselves in now, where we ever spend time truly alone. But this, this is evidence that Mikal has turned his back on us, has spurned us more than we thought. I see myself sleeping, and Mikal sneaking out of our room past me. He hauls furniture up stairwells, gathers papers and pens and chalks, clears space in the corner for that bed, sets up and practices with that easel, hangs those curtains across the window. And all the while I sleep on.

The curtains are parted. I cannot contain my curiosity. I shiver with fear at the thought of walking so deeply into the interior of Mikal's mind, laid bare by this hole-in-the-wall. I fix my eyes upon the gap and walk over. I raise one trembling hand and grasp the edge of the thin material. In one swift movement I pull it back far enough to push my face against the glass.

I want to cry. The window is set into the same side of the house as the big one in the dining room, but the view is different, oh so different. I never knew, never realised. So much distance. So much world.

I can see the garden. All of the garden. All at once. Nigel and Graeme stand together by the willow in the darkest corner where the sun rarely reaches. For a moment I am surprised. Graeme does not like the dark. He has said so often, and avoids that part of the plot. My brothers talk, hand in hand. They push aside the fronds of the willow and step into the bell-jar space beneath. The branches fall behind them, and they are concealed from me. That is not what brings tears to my eyes. It is what lies beyond the willow, beyond the dark corner, beyond the hedge which has formed the outer boundary of my world for as long as I choose to remember.

There are houses out there, countless roofs staining the landscape like a forgotten pack of cards strewn across carpet. And people, so many people I could spend my day counting them and still not reach their end. They walk in the open air, ride bicycles, drive cars and talk to each other and go in and out of the houses and shops and buildings and . . . and . . . I am crying freely now. The faint thumping sounds I hear come from my fist banging against the window, ever so lightly, again and again in time to my voice whispering "No, no, no" .

"Beautiful, isn't it?" says a voice behind me. I turn with guilty speed. My movement causes the curtain to close, blocking out that wonderful, terrible, alien world. Mikal has climbed the steps. He leans on the floor, half in his world and half in mine. His chin balances upon his pale fist. Large brown eyes fix me with a gaze in which I recognize amusement and love and . . . is that pity?

I want to scream with rage. I want to banish my sudden despair by grabbing his obscene haircut and using it to batter his head against the wooden planks. I want to shriek "How could you? How could you do these things, see these things?" at him until he lies still, and broken, and I never have to know the answer. All I can do is cling to the curtain. All I can whisper is "How?"

He levers himself out of the hole and steps into his room with confident grace. I shrink away, and that frightens me more than anything I have seen. I retreat from my own brother as if he were some foreign, dangerous creature. And yet . . . He is. He moves to me, raises a hand and runs it down my wet cheek in a gesture that used to signify love but now heralds some emotion I cannot recognize.

"How?" he replies in a soft voice. "Oh, Darius, don't you know?"

I recoil from his touch, staggering back until I tangle myself in the curtain and fall to the floor with a thump. He kneels in front of me, head tilted in amused enquiry.

"You really don't know, do you?" He reaches past me and opens the curtains with a quick tug. The awful light of the world floods the room. I balk from it and raise my hand to cover my eyes. Mikal takes my wrist and lowers my arm. He hauls me to my feet and spins around, forcing me to confront the view beyond our safe border again.

"Look," he says in a tight little voice, "down there. Look!"

I close my eyes, but he grabs my shoulders and shakes me until I open them. He presses against my back and grasps my chin, twists my head. I see the willow. The fronds part. Nigel and Graeme emerge, hand in hand. They kiss, and part, heading for opposite ends of the garden.

"Shall we go?" Mikal asks, dragging me away from the window and across to the trapdoor. I am too sick with grief and fear to offer anything real in the way of resistance. Mikal bundles me down the steps. We are passing through the kitchen when Liam confronts us, blocking our path with his wheelchair.

"Help me," I whisper. "Madness. Help me."

Liam looks at me, then Mikal.

"He doesn't know," Mikal says, as if that explains everything. "It's gone on long enough."

"Please." I hold out an imploring hand. My brother will save me from this mad creature dressed in Mikal's flesh. My brother. He looks at me again, then wheels out of the way. I scream and flail, but Mikal drags me toward the open door. Liam does not glance at us as we pass. He sits perfectly still, one hand smoothing his trouser creases as if my pain is the most normal thing in the world.

We are halfway across the garden before Mikal looses his grip. I drop, retching, onto the hard-packed grass. Tears scald me on their way to the unforgiving ground. My fingers clench and unclench in sad attempts to drag my dead weight away from the torturer who stands above me. He is silent. When at last I gather the strength to raise my head, he is not alone. They surround me. My brothers, looking at me with the same mix of amusement and pity across their white faces.

"What?" I scream. "Why?"

It is Simon who answers, Simon who never speaks, and who must be carried everywhere lest his brittle and twisted bones break beyond our ability to repair.

"It has to end," he says. "We have to live."

They move forward as one, and lift me to my feet. They carry my limp, howling form to the willow tree and part the fronds so I can see the horror within.

Pillows, I see, and sheets spread across the dry, sheltered earth. There is the smell of love in the air, mixed with the memory of candle flame and oils. What little strength I had deserts me. Creatures stand around me, aliens, mocking me with their flesh and their declarations of love.

"Simon has a room in the basement, where you've always feared to go," Mikal says in a soft voice, "Liam's is at the end of the upper hallway. We told you it was sealed because of fumes."

"Why?" I ask again. A part of me hears how small and whining I sound, like a child who has had his favourite dream exposed.

"We need to live," he replies. "We need to be alive. We can't just sit in this house and wait to die."

"We *are* dying!" I scream. The forbidden words cause birds to fly from the house's eaves. "They are killing us!" I point to the hedge, toward the poisonous world outside, and the evil we fled so very long ago. I lunge at Mikal, throw my weight against him and drive him to the ground. I press him into the dirt. He does not fight back, does not attempt to free himself from my grip. He wraps his arms around me and hugs me against his chest.

"Darius," he says into my ear. "Darius!" again as I scream at him. "Stop it."

I fold in on myself. My sudden rage abandons me. I draw comfort from his warmth, despite my fear and loathing. He rests his cheek against the top of my head.

"We *are* dying, Darius. We are. But it's not them. It's never been them." He strokes my hair, like a mother calming a hysterical child. "Oh, Darius, we all come to this, sooner or later."

I pull away, wipe my wet face with the back of my hand.

"Come to what?"

He stands, pulling me to my feet. He walks me to the graves sitting peaceful and quiet in their open patch of lawn.

"This is the truth," he says. "Just this. We'll all come here, one after the other. It's how we fill the time until then that counts, not how we cower in fright and denial." He looks at me, reaches out a hand to caress my cheek. "We have to live, Darius. Even you."

I look past him, at the headstones of my dear brothers. Those who are still alive stand beyond them, their white faces tilted toward me in love and hope. I turn away from them, and walk back toward the house. It will be dinner soon. I have to prepare the vegetables. That is the rule. We must have rules. Otherwise, how can I tell we are all the same?

We have to be the same. And I am the only one left who is.

AFTERWORD

What to do when you're blocked? Write one sentence. Any sentence. Don't think about it. Then add the next. If you can add a third, go for it. If you can get to ten, don't stop. If you can get a whole story out, *without thinking about it*, you're unblocked. Which is where this one came from. Everybody who has read it has a different idea about who Mikal and his brethren are, where they came from, how they got to the house, and why they don't just leave. So, dear reader, I can give you the answer to all of those questions: Buggered if I know. This is a story straight from the lizard mind. No internal editor was harmed in the making.

LETTERS TO JOSIE

Warlympic Village
Game Day 001
My darling Josie,

    Here I am, safe and sound. I got off the plane (Disembarked at the Rear LZ. I must get used to speaking in the proper manner!) with the other fellows about an hour ago, and already I've taken to one of the local customs: I've removed my shirt, and I don't think it'll come back out of my kit-bag again unless it has to. It is so *hot* here! And humid, too. Even the flies don't buzz above your chest, as if they can't muster the energy to fly higher.
    Right now, I'm lying on a cot in a marquis, with three lads I was grouped with on the plane over. We've been told we won't be heading out for a couple of days while our papers are processed, so for the moment, this is home. We might be companions for some time. I'd best describe them to you so that you get an image when I mention them again. I'm sure I will.
    Dinger is a tall chap, frighteningly thin. How he passed the medical I have no idea. He's almost skeletal. He has a cigarette permanently attached to his lip. I've not seen him without one yet, although he never seems to light or replace it. Perhaps it's the same one, and he'll spend the entire year with it hanging there!
    Farley is the complete opposite, a red-faced, roly-poly little man with a

voice that carries on like a dozen stenographers all working their typewriters at once. He's very nervous, and jumps at every shadow. I don't think he's gone away to a Warlympics before. Like me, he's probably wondering what possessed him to volunteer for this one. His nerves are contagious. I doubt I'll spend much time around him, not if I want to get through this injury-free.

Finally, there's Thompson. He's a big man, burly. He says he comes from out back, but volunteers little more about himself or indeed much of anything, other than the occasional monosyllable, or snort. He seems to be waiting for something to reveal itself. I find myself drawn to him. We all do. He's confident and capable. I get the impression he's experienced this kind of thing a few times before. I hope so. I'll need to stick close to someone who knows how to get through, at least until I find my feet.

As for myself, I still can't believe I'm here, and that we'll be apart for a whole year! It must be difficult for you, moving into the estate when I haven't really let you get used to the family. Don't let mother boss you around! She can be domineering if you let her, but her heart is in the right place. Just stand up to her if you need to and she'll be okay. Father is a real softie (you'll love him), so look to him if you need any support. I know you'll all get on famously and that I'll be back before you know it. You probably won't want to leave them by then!

Anyway, I must go now, darling. It's nearly 'chow time', and around here the saying is "if you snooze, you lose!"

All My Love,
Geoffrey

1st Round: Location AX2
Game Day 017
Dearest Josie,

Thank you for the mail, and the much-needed socks and cake. You don't know how much it means to have some real food, and dry clothes, after so many weeks of tack, camp stew and damp fatigues, and also to hear your sweet voice. I'm sorry this letter is so late to come back to you. We've been in-country for a fortnight and this is my first night back at HQ. We're still in a state of shock. All except Thompson, anyway. I knew we were here for a reason, but I don't think any of us really had reconciled ourselves to just what we were expected to do. Not until we were out there, at night, with no contact and nothing around us but our teammates, and somewhere, the opposition.

I was so frightened I don't think I slept at all during my first week. Even though the recruiting officer tells you all about how the Warlympics is for real, and how you'll be facing real enemies with real weapons, it's hard to get away from the carnival aspect of what we're used to seeing on the telecasts. That is until you're out here, in a tent with only your fellow recruits and the darkness around you. Every creak or groan became an enemy patrol sneaking in to kill me. I know the Sarge keeps telling us that we're a medal fancy, and that we're up against an unseeded opposition, but it doesn't make the nights any easier. Especially not since . . . but I'd better tell you the whole story.

It happened five nights ago. Thompson, myself, and a little guy called Newsome were at an OP (that's Observation Post, Josie) on our perimeter. I saw movement just outside the camp and pointed it out to the others. I thought it might have been an animal that had strayed too close to camp. The designers have done a marvellous job here. Unless you'd watched them building it on the telecasts, you'd swear you'd travelled back to the 20th Century. This place looks like a jungle from those old films your father used to watch. Anyway, to me it looked like a bush pig or some other aimless animal, but Thompson simply smiled, drew out his knife, and disappeared out of the OP. Newsome and I didn't know what to do. We stayed glued to the viewport and tried to make out what has happening out there in the dark. Fat chance. We didn't even see Thompson returning, we were so strung out. The first clue we had was when he burst back through the flap, dropped a dead body onto the floor and raised the general alarm. I'm afraid I let out a bit of a cry of shock when I saw what he'd done to the poor fellow. Better than Newsome though, who lost his cookies in the corner.

I'm not supposed to tell you who our opponents are, although if you've been watching the telecasts you probably know anyway. (I'm sorry Mother is being so unreasonable. She's only like that with Father's nurses. I really can't understand what's got into her.) I recognised the uniform from my pre-reading. I must say, I'm glad they're as unused to a jungle setting as we are. Sergeant Brown keeps telling us that we'll become more like "real soldiers" (he's an old-school type, and refuses to use 'pitty-patty TV words" like Troopathlete) Still, it's not been easy to get the poor devil's face out of my mind. Even though it was our first confirmed kill, and Thompson shared credit with me for spotting him, I keep wondering what he was before he came here and got on the wrong end of a knife. An accountant? A teacher? A banker, like me?

Anyway, I'd best stop now. I've been promoted to Lance Corporal, what with the kill and the heavy rate at which we're losing men. Thompson too. I've got a couple of men under my command. We're going out again tomorrow, so I'd better be up nice and early to make sure they're ready. I don't know what happens if we win this engagement. I know each round is based in a different time period and that we'll have to organise ourselves like armies did in whatever time the Games Organisers recreate, but they don't tell you how that works in regards to anything other than fighting. Write me again soon anyway, my dear wife, and I'll hope to be around to read it.

With Love,
Geoff

2nd Round: Location BFG
Game Day 026
Dearest Josephine,

Thank you for your letter dated Game Day 21. I'm pleased to hear you and Father have taken to each other so well. I'm sure he is enjoying the long walks you've been taking. The beach is one of his favourite places. In fact, to hear him tell it, it's where he first met Mother. No, I don't know why she continues to behave in such a combative manner. Her letter mentions no possible reason for her anger. She barely mentions you or Father at all, in fact. Her continuing illness is a worry, although I'm sure your cooking has nothing to do with it! (A joke, Josephine, my darling)

You've probably seen from the telecasts that we made the second round quite comfortably. In the end, the Ragheads weren't up to much. After our initial confusion we all managed to get on the scoreboard before they surrendered. Thompson and I have formed quite a team, and I scored a further brace after my last letter, second only to Farley. Hard to believe, but the little fella's taken to it like a pig to shit. When the old man caught one, he was an automatic to make Sergeant. Even Newsome can look through a sight without puking now.

The only bad news in the last couple of weeks was poor old Dinger copping one. Turns out he *does* smoke those fags of his. A sniper caught him lighting one, and took his jaw off for him. Still, it means getting shipped home, and the International Warlympics Committee will pay for a prosthetic, so I'm sure we'll see him at the first reunion as good as new. His replacement's been slated for my squad, so I'll have to assign a Lance to babysit him until he's dug in.

We've changed times and locations, of course, and have to get used to more archaic equipment and command structures. We're out in the sand this round, looks like something from the Second Big One, all diesel tanks around us and prop jobs flying overhead. Damn sand gets into everything The underwear you sent'll be shredded inside a fortnight Thanks anyway for the thought. Situation looks a bit tougher than last round. I think this lot are Ities, and they've got a history of desert fighting.

I'll write you again if I get the chance, but maybe not soon. Thommo and me and some of the other lads are about to conduct a combined op with elements of 3Div, in an attempt to interdict the enemy's MSR. It'll be covert throughout, and fairly long-term, so I'll have to contact you when I'm back.

Love
Corporal G Winter

Quarter Final Round: Location Classified
Game Day 038
Dear Wife,

Sorry to hear about the confrontation with your mother-in-law. I don't know what basis she has for her accusations. I trust you shall endeavour to work towards an appropriate solution. I have not, as yet, discussed the situation with Father. I am confident that her accusations are baseless. I am sure you will be able to continue your accommodation arrangements with them, especially now Mother is reliant upon your care.

The sitrep here is improving after the heavy losses suffered in the last round. I have taken up my new command. With 2nd Lieutenant Thompson, I have formed two companies under Major Farley, who for the last three weeks has been acting Battalion Commander. We are starting to see the arrival of large numbers of newly-trained troops from the rear, and hope to be able to disperse them amongst the veterans left over from the initial stages of our campaign. I send to you for safekeeping the 'Distinguished Games Performance' medal I was awarded during the final battle with the Italians, as well as my letter of commission. Please keep them for my return.

I am afraid this communication must remain brief. Standing orders for all participants in Medal Round engagements prohibit release of sensitive or classified information. I am therefore unable to divulge to you details of our enemy or location, other than to tell you that we continue to regress through Historical Military campaigns. Due to reconstruction of command structure upon entering the third round, any letters should now address me as 'Ensign', even though I am nominally ranked within current nomenclature. You should be aware of this already; as the civilian telecasts you are able to access have more information than we receive.

The drummers have begun to beat the formation tattoo, so I must leave you. May God grant us victory on this day, and allow me to correspond with you further.

G.W. Winter
2nd Lieutenant.

Semi-Final Round: Location Classified
Game Day 044
Mrs Josephine Winter
PS 346821LX

Terrible news about Mother stop. Please contribute wreath on behalf stop. Legion currently hard-pressed stop. Campaign under threat stop. Am now 2IC to Brigadier Farley stop. Thompson killed during recent enemy interdiction stop. Only two originals left stop. Currently recuperating from losing hand to enemy gladius stop. Expect to rejoin forces before conclusion of battle stop. Trying to remain hopeful stop. One last push coming stop. May have to resign self to bronze medal stop. By time this delivered will know either way stop. Ends

Tribune Winter

Warlympic Village
Game Day 051
Dear Mrs Winter,

It is with the deepest regret that I find myself writing this letter. In truth, this is perhaps the saddest duty I have been asked to perform during these Games. It is my duty to tell you that your husband, Colonel Geoffrey William Winter, was killed in the line of Troopathletic duty on the night of the 18th September.

On that night, Colonel Winter was overseeing the construction of a Britannic style hillfort as part of our semi-final round. His detachment, numbering no more than two companies of engineers, was struck by the total remaining strength of the enemy forces. Unbeknownst to our intelligence, the enemy had chosen this night to make their final assault upon our positions. Their attack was aimed squarely at the point in our lines occupied by your husband's command.

Although their forces numbered approximately a battalion, Colonel Winter was able to marshal his forces and provide significant defence.

Survivor accounts have indicated that, although the battle became a fierce close quarters melee within the area of the partly completed fortifications, your husband was able to organise his outnumbered troops. They provided fierce resistance until message runners were dispatched to summon reinforcements. These accounts, which I have overseen personally, state that Colonel Winter was responsible for numerous enemy casualties. His actions held up significant numbers of the attacking force, until being overwhelmed through sheer weight of numbers.

It was your husband's deeds in both personal combat and excellence of command that helped ensure our final victory on this night, and thus our passage into the Gold Medal round. As Commanding Officer of our forces I have recommended to the International Warlympics Committee that Colonel Winter be awarded the highest individual honour available to a participant of the Games.

On a more personal note, I have served with your husband since the day of our arrival, and have been proud to have considered him my friend. He set an example of bravery, strength and commitment that has been the model for all that have competed with him at these Fifteenth Warlympiad.

I must also tell you, that as your letter arrived after his death, I took the liberty as his Commanding Officer of opening and reading it, in order that you may receive a personal reply to any matters raised. As his friend, I am glad that Geoffrey never had the chance to read of the plans that you and his Father have decided upon. It would have dealt him a major blow, coming as it does in the midst of a battle to preserve the way of life you enjoy, a contest to which he was committed both body and soul. I know from our conversations that he looked forward to the day in which you and he were to be reunited.

As he will not be able to sign the enclosed papers, I return them to you with this advice: Your husband is a national hero. He will be accorded a parade and state funeral should we be victorious in the final round and our Governmental authority be confirmed for the next four years. Once you have received the flag from his coffin, and his Games Medal, you may do as you wish. Until then, do not shame his sacrifice. I ask you to keep the union between yourself and his Father secret until afterwards.

> Until then, I remain your obedient servant,
> Brigadier Charles Farley,
> AusJap Warlympic Team Management

AFTERWORD

For a long time I attended a group on a Thursday morning at my local writing centre. Like many such groups there was a real feeling of "By nannas, for nannas" about it. But still, I went because they were lovely ladies and I enjoyed being exposed to some poetry, and biography, and reminiscences, and you know, you're never sure what's coming down your own story pipe next and it's good to keep your options open. Each week, we would run an exercise, and read the results. This came out of an exercise in letter writing, which I'd not seen done in a science fiction workshop before. Naturally, I've pinched the idea and run it in all my workshops now. Groucho's first rule of comedy: Only steal from the best.

A STONE TO MARK MY PASSING

I was somewhere between Bridgetown and Pemberton when the car died. Not that location mattered very much to me at that point. For the last fifty kilometers my head had barely left the steering wheel. I'd been fighting sleep for hours; afraid to close my eyes and see the end of my happiness replayed. It was still too soon, still too painful, to look at the events that had precipitated my headlong flight.

When the engine stopped ticking and creaking, I found the strength to raise my head and peer through the windscreen. I had left the road, and appeared to be in a cemetery. In front of me were rank after rank of upright headstones, standing to attention at an even spacing: shoulders back; stomachs in; like so many terracotta warriors awaiting the next life. The rows receded twenty or thirty feet, before fetching up against a chain-link fence.

Dimly, I recognised that something about them seemed wrong. It took a few minutes to realise what that was. The stones bore no inscriptions. They were as blank and smooth as painted doors. What was more, they were separated by no more than one or two feet. If this was a graveyard, it was one for nameless dwarves, or newborns.

The door opened at the second attempt. I fumbled out and fell to my knees on the hard pavement, then used the door to pull myself up and look around. The car had rolled through an open gate, bowling a path over four or five rows of headstones before bumping to a stop against one in the shape of a large Celtic cross. A sign swung on poles above the gate. It read 'Purge's Masons: When You Need Us'.

I shook my head. I wasn't in a cemetery. Fair enough. I'd started to realise that anyway. But the second half of the sentence didn't make sense. Or if it did, it was the worst sales pitch I'd ever seen. At the other side of what I now knew to be the display yard stood an open-sided workshop. I would need to talk to whoever ran the place, I supposed, to explain my entrance and pay for any damage. The strength returning to my legs, I walked towards the building.

As I got closer I saw someone hunched over a table, running their hands across an indistinct object that lay in front of them. I managed to avoid knocking over any more stones, by good luck rather than good aim, and made my way over. The figure glanced up as I approached. He was an old man, with long snow-white hair that dissolved into a spray of stubble across his jaw and lower face. What had appeared to be a patterned shirt from a distance proved to be a crisscrossing of old scars on his bare chest and back, a spider-web of white creases against the dark brown of his skin. He tilted his head in enquiry.

"I, uh . . . " I managed, "I seem to have had a bit of a bingle." I pointed a thumb behind me at the car.

He tilted his head further to follow my thumb, then smiled.

"Looks like it. Pardon the observation, but you look like shit. Want a drink?"

"Love one."

He pointed to a bar fridge underneath a nearby workbench. "Help yourself. The VB's mine, you can have the Nookie Broon."

I opened the fridge and saw the promised cans, handed his across and pulled the tab on mine. A welter of froth overflowed, and I sucked some from my fingers. The old man looked at it with a wry grimace.

"Pommy beer," he smiled. "Your stomach will throttle you in your sleep one night, you just wait."

I grinned back at him, my first smile in well over a week. The muscles in my face felt unfamiliar. He motioned towards a stool and I dropped onto it. "Listen, about the damage . . . "

"Don't worry. Nothing's broken." He turned back to his work, which I now saw was a large headstone upon which he was carving somebody's details. "In fact, I'm glad you're here. I have another stone outside that I have to finish today. I could do with a hand getting it in here."

"Sure."

"Won't be long." While he worked, I watched his back, losing myself in the white scar tissue that wallpapered his skin. His shifting muscles, and the blunt sounds of the hammer striking the chisel, retrieved a memory of similar dimensions.

I stood in a street in Hanoi watching a young man, no more than sixteen or seventeen years old and delicate as a doll, carve a grave for his grandfather's stall.

The letters he carved were perfect: better than I could have written even had I a template to guide me. I fell into the pattern his hands made through the air: tiny olive butterflies darting here and there, chewing away the stone and leaving behind the memory of a man's life.

Then my companion had touched my shoulder and caused me to jump in shock. I remember the boy's smile, shy and amused, offered without so much as a glimpse up from his art.

The companion hadn't lasted the holiday. Later I returned to the street to find the boy with the butterfly hands, but he was gone as well.

A cough interrupted my reverie. The mason had stopped his carving, and was talking to me once again.

"I'm sorry?" I said. "I was miles away."

"I asked you if you were looking at something in particular." He sat facing me, exposing his chest fully to my view.

"I . . . uh . . . um . . . " I avoided his even gaze, feeling a blush begin.

"It's okay," he said. "I'm so used to them that I forget how they must look the first time." He ran a finger along a path of scars. I followed its progress.

"How . . . how did they . . . ?" I shadowed his finger with my own.

"One of the outcomes of my profession. You'll see a bit later, I think. Each scar here represents a work completed, and a gift given. Now, are you ready to give me a hand?"

"Huh?" Hypnotised by his voice and slowly moving hand, it took a moment to refocus myself.

"I asked if you were ready." He stood, and waited patiently for me to come to my senses and do the same. We walked into the yard; he pushing a trolley from the workshop, me with head bowed, shuffling in his wake. He led me over to the corner furthest from the building, stopping before a simple, round-cornered stone.

"This one."

The marker was nothing special. Simple, even elegant perhaps, the kind of restrained style of which I personally approved. I've never been one for ostentation. Then I saw the name that ran across the top, the date of birth below, the all-too-familiar details underneath, the quote from Byron I can recite in my sleep. The space where the date of death would be chiseled in: final, immutable.

"I still have to put that bit in." His voice came from very far away.

"I . . . what . . . what is this?" I choked from a throat suddenly empty of air. I couldn't tear my eyes away to show him my sudden terror.

"Something I've been working on for a couple of days." His hand fell on my shoulder, hard and heavy and stone cold. "I wasn't sure if you'd make it here or not. The way you've been driving you might have run off the road at any time, and the path here isn't always that easy to find. You really have to be looking for it, in one way or another."

I twisted aside from his touch, stumbled away from him. The back of my legs collided with a headstone and I thumped to the ground. "You didn't . . . who are you? Where is this place?"

He shrugged, and squatted down across from me, leaning his back against my carved name. "This place? An end to a journey, for some. For others, it's a departure point. Depends on the person, and why they came here."

"What are you, Tom Bloody Bombadil?" Now the initial shock had passed, my fear began to bubble up as anger. "Can't you give a straight question a straight answer?"

He laughed. "No fantasy stories here, I'm afraid. It's far more mundane than that."

"Mundane? How can you even know my name? How can you know all this stuff about me? How can you have been working on this thing for ... since ... ?"

"Since you ran out on Aaron?" His voice was soft, but the words hit me like a stoning. I stared, dumbstruck. He continued as if he were simply talking about the weather.

"Sometimes people run, David. Not all that often, but sometimes. If a person is in enough despair, or the pain finally closes over their heads and they begin to drown, they run. They don't look where they're running. They just obey the urge to get away, anywhere, as long as it's as quickly and as far as possible."

"No. It wasn't like that. I just had to move out, that's all."

"Pack all your furniture in the car then, or is the truck coming later?"

"What would you know?"

"I've seen it before."

His eyes stared just over my shoulder, as if he was not speaking so much to me as to a group of people who sat with me at their head. He looked very sad, as if he recognised each one of us, and knew why we were all there. His hand traced the white paths on his chest, jumping from one quadrant of skin to another as if searching out individual scars.

"People don't realise that the pain is within them. It's not tied to place or time. They don't leave it behind. Sometimes, when they run, they find a path between somewhere and somewhere else. That's when they come to a place like this." He waved a hand at our surroundings. I followed it, half expecting to see the audience behind me doing the same. There was nobody there. We were alone.

"It's not always a mason's yard. For some it might be a bar in a back alley that nobody else seems to notice. For others a school oval with an old gardener painting running tracks in the grass." He looked straight at me. "For you, it's here."

"I don't understand."

He stood up, rubbing his hands against his thighs. "Oof. I'm not so young I can crouch like that for very long. I don't know any better way to explain it, really. It's just that there's this place, you came here because you needed to, and this is what you'll take away. Now come on. I still have to finish it, and you're leaving soon." He leant down and held out his hand.

"But why? What is this all about?"

"You'll understand when you get the first new opportunity, but you won't find it sitting on your arse here, will you? Come on." He pulled me to my feet.

"Everyone understands in the end, David. Everyone takes something away. Everyone leaves something behind in return."

"What do I leave?"

His fingers hovered over the scars on his chest. "We'll work that out later. Help me lift this up, now."

We lifted my marker onto his trolley. I ran my hands across its surface, feeling the warmth where he had leant against it. In silence we trooped back to the workshop, setting the stone onto the workbench and then stepping back. He clapped his hands in satisfaction.

"Right then. I'll need a number four chisel for this, I think." He pointed to a rack on the workbench next to me. I picked out the right tool and handed it across to him.

He pulled a pair of glasses from the pocket of his shorts, sat down, and bent over the marker. He rubbed his hand over the blank area, then picked up a mallet and put his chisel on the spot. He raised his arm for the first strike. I made a small, uncertain noise in my throat. He looked up at me over the rim of his glasses.

"Should I . . . I mean, do you think I should watch? You know, see what you . . . ?"

He shrugged. "Some do. Some don't. I'm not sure it makes all that much of a difference in the end, really." He bent back over his work. "Just a few small knocks, that's all it takes. Then you'll give me what you need to give me, and you'll be on your way. A few," his mallet descended and the chisel took its first bite, "small knocks. That's all it ever takes."

I watched him carve the date of my death into the rock. With every arc of the mallet, every flake of discarded granite that spun off and fell to the floor, a small sliver of pain split away from the heavy weight inside me. A chunk of stone leapt into the air and whirled away, an image bright on its glassy surface. Time slowed. It was Aaron I could see, trapped on the madly twisting fragment. Standing in isolation, neither the superman he had appeared at the start of our relationship, nor the monster at the end. A man, just a man. With that knowledge came a little understanding of my own part in our story. The ache shifted within me.

Then Bang! Time sped up as hammer met chisel once more. Aaron's fragment fell to the floor unheeded, and another shard of my life spun into the air. My father's face, alone on a chip of stone . . .

It went on that way until I lost measure of time. Chip. I understood just how long ago the schoolyard bullying was. Chip. Another number was revealed. Chip. A month began to appear, and it wasn't so important that my job lay in tatters. Chip. A year emerged. The mason began to talk, his voice as even and measured as his careful mallet blows.

"When you were twenty-five your world ended, and you were faced with a horrible decision, a terrible decision. Nothing was as you thought it was. You could either run from that truth, or you could face the fact that no matter what had happened you still had to live through the future. No matter what happened you would be thirty in five years, fifty in twenty five, and dead sometime between now and the heat death of the Universe. So you made your decision, whatever it was . . . there, it's done "

I looked down at the stone before him. There lay my death, coldly displayed. Final, immutable, unchangeable. The mason ran a gentle hand over it.

"Does that seem like a long time to you, or short?"

I touched the cold lettering. "It doesn't matter, does it? It's not what's already happened. It's how I fill in the time left that's important."

"Puts it into perspective, doesn't it?"

And just like that it let me go. All the pent-up hurt, and confusion, and fear. The anger at Aaron for not being the perfect answer to my needs; the terror I felt at being alone and not being able to see what came next; the wishing that it would all just end and I wouldn't have to lift my head and try all over again. They faded into the past. It still hurt. Maybe it always would, when I stopped to think of them. But I understood that those things were not all there was to my life. Pain is only *part* of living. I smiled, and it wasn't such an unfamiliar sensation this time. The old man had said I made a decision. It was no decision at all, really.

Then he gasped, snapping me out of my newfound peace. His chest was covered with blood, bright and viscous in the mote-filled light.

"Above the shelf. Medicine cabinet."

I ran to it and dumped its contents on the bench, finding bandages and gauze and returning to clean and dress the wound.

"What happened?"

"It's not deep. It'll leave a scar, though."

"Did you slip? I didn't see . . . "

He stopped my hands with his. "This is what you give. We're both better for it."

"But . . . "

"Gifts work both ways. Just accept it, okay?" He brushed his dressings. "Nice job. Now, I still have to polish this stone and get started on a new one. Fetch us a drink would you?" He winced as he pointed at the little bar fridge. "Mine's the VB . . . "

When it was over, we took the canvas-wrapped headstone and laid it in the boot of my car. The old mason looked down at it.

"When you need to remember."

I closed the boot. He held the driver's door open.

"Okay, then."

I climbed into my seat, put the key in the ignition, and turned it once. The engine that had given up and died only hours earlier now roared into life. The fuel gauge needle climbed towards the 'F'. The rev counter rose to eight hundred and sat there, steady as a rock.

"It's not dead anymore."

"It has no reason to be."

He closed the door, then reached through the open window and touched my shoulder, once. I put the car into reverse and moved backward out of the yard.

Through the windscreen I saw him unwind the bandage and show me the red scar that ran from the top of his left shoulder to just above his nipple. He waved once, then walked back amongst the headstones. By the time I reached the road, he was already re-arranging those that had fallen. The road stretched away in two directions. I picked one, and drove away.

AFTERWORD

A nod of the head to Michael Barry, here. Michael was editing an anthology called *Elsewhere* for the Canberra Speculative Fiction Guild, and when I submitted this story, took it in hand and worked with me over many months to get it to the version you've just read. In particular, he didn't gripe when I stole one of his holiday reminiscences wholesale, and dumped it right in the middle of the tale. The story made Datlow & Windling's Recommended Reading List, so we did all right, in the end. I thought writing outside my own sexuality would be a challenge, but in the end, it proved to be easy. Love is love, after all.

VORTLE

Deep in the middle of the Poolshug Swampland, where even Giant Grells tiptoe for fear of drawing attention to themselves, lives Vortle alone in his little hut.

Small is Vortle, and smelly. His ears are hairy, and his toes have fungus, and not even Kerrits stop to ask him for directions. In all the years since I was assigned my post at the Snakeborder entrance, I have known of only a single entity who has wanted a thing to do with him. And about *that* I would not have spoken, if you had not offered me so many fermented Rebfruit.

It happened, (if indeed it did happen, and I am not saying it did, mind) twenty Turns ago, quite some time in anyone's language, and I am long-lived for one of our people. The Snakeborder was still new. Any number of people were employed to keep track of the Grells, and Beis, and Snezzles, still able to cross through and wreak havoc amongst the outer barrows of the Epicity. I had only been at my post for two or three cycles, barely half a Turn. I was busy, watching a team of underhandlers trying to persuade a newly second-hatched Snezzle to turn away from its path and return to the Swampland. I was cheerfully dispensing advice to the panicky underhandlers, when my attention was drawn to a sudden brightness in the sky, a point of harsh light on the horizon that fizzled and sang like a heat-source meant only for me. It grew as I watched, turning into a shining sphere that resembled a crackseed pod. Only this was a crackseed pod that farted white smoke, and gleamed in the sunlight, and *flew*. It roared over my head and disappeared towards the centre of the Swamp. I heard a crashing, and a cracking, and a big thud like a thousand Grells lying down all at once. I looked towards the underhandlers, but not one had raised their heads; they being too busy negotiating with the recalcitrant Snezzle. Anyway, underhandlers are not noted for their interest outside their appointed tasks.

I, however, was still young, and had not even reached my Cutting Age. I gave no thought to the desertion of my lucky post, only to this strange new arrival. I shouted in the general direction of the Snezzle that I would return as soon as I could, and strode into the Swampland.

What you need to understand is that in those days, the Poolshug Swampland was not as it is now, with the Snakes big, and fat, and teaching each other the laws, and nice, neat paths, and even Beis too afraid to have more than a nibble of your toes if you happen to find a comfy moss pad and decide to have a nap. No, in those days it crept right up to the borders of the Epicity. It was dark and scary, and certainly no place to be unless you had lost your love of heat and wanted to become a Cold One before your time.

Only Vortle has ever made a home there. Vortle can have it as far as decent, civilized, Barrow-loving people are concerned. But I was full of heat, so in I walked like I had business to attend to, and little time in which to do it.

Within seconds I was hacking my way through the stitchcutters and hackbracken, and trying to avoid the Snezzle eggs that littered the muddy ground, all the while keeping one set of eyes skyward to follow the direction the shining mystery had taken. This was early in the Turn. I was able to open my chloroglands nice and wide and feed off the solar energy, so that all the slashing and chopping made little demands on my heat store. I found myself deep inside the Swamp, so deep that the trees bore no notch-branches, and I was soon turned about and lost.

With my chloroglands open, my attention was not all it could have been. I am, by descent, a Southerner and my ears are low in my neck. I failed to hear the clicking that should have warned me of a troop of approaching Beis. I was unprepared when they burst through the bushes and attacked me.

Luckily for me the Beis were immature, not even having grown their primary pincers, or I should have ended my adventure right there and then. However, being youthful and strong, and with a heat-store so large that a fight was something to be enjoyed so long as the odds were favourable, I was able to hold my own for quite a period. In next to no time, I was stepping to avoid tripping over the corpses of those who had ventured too close. Even so, it was not long before I found myself retreating. I would have become food and shelter for their symbiosouls, were it not for an astonishing piece of luck, although in truth, it did not seem it at the time.

Put simply, I fell. I tumbled down an incline I had not noticed, and which now slid my feet from beneath me. My fall left me lying on my back. Beis crowded the incline's edge many feet above me. They turned away, and the air was filled with the sound of survivors eating their dead. I lay on the new soil, catching my breath, and feeling the pain throbbing in the chloroglands I had not thought to close.

Before long the ground began to grow cold, and I felt the desire to continue my journey. I stood and looked around. During the fight I had lost track of which route the flying pod was following. This meant the direction from which I had entered the Swampland was also unknown to me. I felt sore and sorry, and the cold made me regret my exertions. In truth, all I wanted was to return to my post and crawl inside my barrow for a good long sleep. One direction was as good as another under the circumstances. I picked a path that led away from the feeding Beis, and began to walk.

I had no idea of time this deep into the Swamp. I did not know when eating and fasting periods should be observed, but here the untamed Swamplands came to my aid. Many young Snakes travelled the paths. I was not the quiet, dignified being you see today. I was possessed of quite the liquid tongues, at least according to the overfemales of the Epicity's spawning quarters. I was able to persuade the younger Snakes to vent their heat so I could feed.

I managed to keep my strength up as I wandered along, marvelling at the wild beauty that differed so greatly from the ordered civility of my home. It was in this mood of quiet contemplation that I pushed through a row of lickleaf bushes and saw the pod.

It lay in a pool of water, bright white in colour where mud and weeds had not risen up and covered its smooth surface. This close it was larger than I had assumed, so tall and round that even Councillor Plackmacket could not have stretched his arms around it. One end was flat and grey, and from that surface three stalks protruded, radiating smoke and a delicious glowing heat. I must confess: I opened myself wide and soaked in the energizing warmth until I thought I must shed a half-year early or risk bursting my skin apart. However my curiosity soon began to prick at me, and I wandered around to the pod's far side.

And what a wonder I found! For here the pod had cracked open from the impact. A circular section had come away, and now hung by an edge. I sloshed my way through the water and peered into its hollow interior. To this day I have never truly believed what I saw inside, even though I tell you now with the truth colour in my eyes, and my gland-horn long burnt to appease the all-powerful Shlebbershlurmen. For I saw none of the sweetmeat one would expect to see in an open crackseed, even a giant one such as this.

A seat was inside. A *seat*, although one for a single-hatched or a malform. I saw straight away that it could hold no more than one buttock, maybe two, as if the others were expected to hang in the air to either side. More wonders greeted my turning eyes: lights hung everywhere, tiny square ones that blinked and flashed like lightbugs. I bruised three fingers trying to catch them, before I realised they were part of the walls. The last one I reached for made a strange clicking sound. A voice boomed across the Swampland.

"Greetings!" it cried in an accent I had never before heard, but which I have since learnt was much like that of our barbarian cousins from the Bigdryland to the East, "I come in something something." (I did not understand some of the words and would not care to try and repeat them.) "I offer friendship and something from the something something something of Earth."

"Who are you? *Where* are you?" I yelled, stumbling backward out of the pod and cracking my head against the edge of the hole, an edge I will swear by my barrow was not wood. I fell into the water. The voice continued to thunder out around the clearing.

"Greetings! I come in something something . . . "

I heard the snap of a breaking branch and turned over, expecting to see the giant who spoke in such an ear-rippling voice. Instead, I caught my first glimpse of Vortle, moments before his club descended and knocked the heat right out of me.

I woke face down in the mud. When I raised my head and looked about I found myself in a small clearing, surrounded by trees so crowded upon each other I could not see the smallest gap between their twisted boles. A filthy hut of bones, and branches, and things I chose not to identify stood bandy-legged behind me. Vortle squeezed out of its only entrance and smiled in my direction.

"Sorry I knocked you out like that," he wheezed. I closed my orifices to avoid unconsciousness once more, this time from his breath. "I took you for another Pink Pod Thingy."

"I beg your pardon?"

"You have it." He smiled again, exposing a mass of pulpy, half-chewed mush. The occasional grey tooth poked through, like a first-hatched peering round his warmth-nurse's skirts.

"A Pink what?" I asked, trying to shake the fog from my head.

"Pod Thingy. Like the one came out of the pod you were talking to."

"I wasn't talking to it. It was talking to me."

"Whatever," he shrugged, disturbing the air between us. Most of my orifices were already closed, so the smell from his clothes only caused my eyes to sting and water. "Anyway, I still have some left. Want to share?"

"Want to share what?" I shook my head again, wondering whether he always made such little sense, or whether the blow to my head had caused some sort of permanent damage.

"Pink Pod Thingy." He reached down into a foodpit next to the entrance door, pulled something out, and handed it to me. I looked at it dubiously. It was an arm. Well, it was sort of an arm, except it was small like a new-hatched, and only had five stiff stubby podules on the end, and was quite, quite pink.

"Eat," Vortle commanded. I nibbled at one of the podules. To my lasting surprise it was the most delicious thing I have ever tasted. I held out my hand for more. Vortle gave me another piece, smiling as if this settled some matter between us.

Anyway, it all went rather well from that point. Friendly did Vortle prove to be, and lonely, and quite the conversationalist, as long as I took care to sit downwind and only talk when I was absolutely sure he wasn't breathing in my direction.

While we finished the rest of the Pink Pod Thingy he told me how he had come across the pod in the water and killed the strange beast within. It hadn't had the sense to lower its heat image at his approach but had held out its two arms (Two!) as if *begging* to give up its life. Vortle shrugged. There is never enough to eat when you are Vortle, and if a beast wants to save you the trouble of hunting, no matter how strange it may look, well . . .

Luckily for us, the Pink Pod Thingy provided plenty of sustenance, so Vortle was happy to share. He even packed some meat to take with me. When night began to fall, I told him I needed to return home, and he guided me to a spot near my Snakeborder post. As we parted he looked at me askance.

"What will you tell the Epicity Council?"

I considered him. The Snakeborder plans were well under way. Soon the Swamplands would be isolated, and the fringes would be developed to accept those who no longer felt the song of heat. If I told the Epicity Council of the wondrous pod and the delicious creature it contained, they would call a halt to their developments. The whole Swamp would be explored, catalogued, turned into a place to be visited by hatchlings and students from the Underschool.

Vortle would be forced to join civilisation, or run from the lands he considered his home. Pathways would criss-cross the Swamp, and I saw him being forced to cavort and perform for the amusement of the crowds who wandered past his little hut; saw how his loneliness would be all the greater for the mass of gawking tourists who would surround him. That was no way to repay his kindness. I shook my head.

"A grand adventure," I said, "but I didn't see a thing. It's a mystery."

Vortle said nothing, just gave me one last, stomach-churning smile and ran back into the clinging arms of the Swamplands.

Small is Vortle, and smelly. His ears are hairy, and his toes have fungus, and not even Kerrits have the strength to stop and ask him directions. And I have never again seen a crackseed pod that flies and farts white smoke across the sky.

But I have heard stories from those who travel from the Bigdryland to the East; stories of two-armed pink creatures who come down from the sky in round white pods and visit the Barrow Councils and the Underschools of that faraway land.

They tell tales of pods that set out to journey North and South and West, to visit all the Epicities of the world and spread wisdom and gifts amongst all. I look in dismay at these travellers, how they turn their backs on the natural ways, and ride vehicles that fart white smoke and clog the orifices of those who sit on them. I think that perhaps it would be a good thing if no such pods ever came this far.

And sometimes, not very often at all, but every now and then, I come out of my barrow to begin my duties and find a little parcel of delicious pink meat in my foodpit. Then I know that Vortle is well and hunting, and that the pods of the strange creatures will not reach our beautiful Epicity just yet, and that I am still the only person who calls him friend.

AFTERWORD

The first time I sent this story to a magazine, it was rejected with the comment "I don't know why anybody bothers writing 1st person POV alien stories anymore." Because it's *fun*, goldurnit! That's all there was to this one, a feeling of fun and a chance to play Poul Anderson and name things. And yet, by the end, I kind of liked the ugly little bugger at the heart of his swamp. Not that I'd ever accept a dinner invitation, mind.

ECDYSIS

The body was naked, and black. Not African-American black, or Aborigine black. Black. Like somebody had soaked him in dye. Like one of those white guys pretending to be 'Nigrahs' in the old racist Griffith movies you sometimes get on the Classics channel. He was lying behind a mound of trash bags three times my height. It looked as if a space had been cleared for the task: bags surrounded him at a respectful distance. I knelt and wiped a gloved finger across his skin. It wasn't make-up.

"What else is there?" I snapped at the Uniform standing over the body. I'd been taken away from an old 'Brady Bunch' episode for this. I was not prepared to be pleased. Spending my evenings at rubbish tips does that to me.

"There's no hair, sir."

"He's bald."

"No, sir. Well, yeah, sir, but there's no hair at all, anywhere. He's bald everywhere."

"Worst case of alopecia I've ever seen." Frank Ramirez wandered between hills of refuse and blew cigarette smoke at the body. Frank's the owner of The Cop Cabana, the policing company I work for, so I'm nice to him. First thing you learn in this business: be nice to everybody. They might be trying to find your killer one day. I gave him a nod.

"Hairless and funny colored. Good so far." Uniforms do the normals.

I'm Special Squad. We do the loons. This is LA. I've always got plenty of work.

"Check out the eyes."

I kneeled down and looked again. Dead skin doesn't bounce back into shape the way live skin does. The lids held a faint impression, as if something had been pressed into them. I gave Frank a quizzical glance.

"Coins?"

"Nice guess. Two more on the palms as well."

"Ritual?" I peeked to see how far the Uniform had moved away from us. Uniforms don't get paid very well, and newspages know it.

"Could be," Frank said. "Look here." He reached into his pocket and drew out a plastic baggie. Four coins, gold ones by the look of them, jingled inside, along with a slip of folded paper. I opened the bag and picked out the sheet. Someone had shown enough sense to note which coin had been where, and what side had been facing upwards. Frank scuffed his shoe across the mud.

"I'm off, then."

"Off? Why?"

"This is your show now Marcus. Besides, Brady's a two-parter tonight."

I watched his back recede all the way towards his nice dry, car. The bastard knows I love that show.

I didn't get much done in the next couple of hours. Frank was Johnny-On-The-Spot, so the forensics guys had already been over every square inch of the surrounding area, and a Bag Squad was on its way to pick up the body. Nevertheless, I made them wait while I conducted my own search. My name would be on the reports. I found zip. The scene was clean, the body was clean, everything was clean. There were no clues my poor, underpaid, eyes could find. By the time I was finished my alarm bells were ringing loud and clear. Accidental deaths aren't clean. Cleanliness only happens when someone cleans up.

I had teams of Uniforms tote digipics of the dead guy from door to door, interviewing everyone in the neighborhood. Usually, this achieves nothing—"Nobody never sees nuttin' "—other than keeping the Uniforms away from my investigations, which is usually a good thing.

I spent the time pacing my office, waiting for the forensics report. I read for less than ten minutes before I threw it across the room and had a good curse. According to forensics there was nothing wrong with the dead guy. No cause of death could be established, not by any test they ran over him. He was just . . . 'inert' was the word they used. That was an odd choice of word.

"It's an accurate word." Doctor Friedel sounded confused, something I've rarely heard from him. "Normally there would be cellular degradation, blood-settle, any number of things we could use to determine a cause of death. But I've got nothing. He's heavier than I would expect a man of his size to be, but that's it. I'm dry on this one, Marcus."

"But what about his skin? How did it get that color?"

"That," he said, after a long pause, "would appear to be natural. There's no chemical or physical reason we can find for the coloration. It just . . . is. He's a perfectly normal, strangely coloured, inert body without a single reason not to be alive."

I thanked him, and hung up. Now I was really worried. I've known Friedel for twenty-four years. He's never failed to give me an answer. Someone out there had just committed murder, and left no trace of how. Without at least one lead there wasn't a damn thing I could do to find him.

As expected, the door to door turned up nothing. A Uniform dumped the pile of sheets on my desk and shook his head.

"Sorry, sir."

I waved him out. I sighed, and pushed the reports onto the floor, making sure they landed on the side of my desk I don't walk around to get to the door. I pulled the baggie from my pocket and looked at the coins. According to the slip of paper, I had four identical specimens. They bore no distinguishing features, no clues as to who had used them or where they might have come from. Unless this guy had a serious allergy to gold, my only clue was that the death resembled a ritual killing. These coins had to be part of the ceremony; there was no other reason to leave good money lying on a dead guy in such a way. I turned to my DeskPilot and netted on. I searched every Sourcepage I could find dealing with rituals involving coins, and objects associated with the eyes and hands. Apart from the old myth about paying the ferryman, I found nothing that seemed useful. And that one didn't explain why he would have coins on his palms, so I dismissed it too. Rituals are generic wholes. Every aspect of them has to be accounted for. They're not a mix and match job. I was just about to give up and call Ramirez to admit failure when a link at the bottom of the search listings caught my attention. It was for someone calling herself Madame Zelda, Dream Analyst. I wasn't sure how it had ended up within my search parameters, but as the alternative was calling the boss and virtually guaranteeing the result of my next Performance Appraisal, I clicked the link. Ten minutes later I had Ramirez out of bed and on his way to the office.

"Dreams?" Frank Ramirez scratched fingers through unbrushed hair and stared at me as if I was asking to be fired on grounds of insanity.

"Couldn't be anything else. Look." I dimmed the lights, projected the Deskpilot's screen onto my office wall, and began clicking links as I talked. "No other explanation fits all the pieces together. The eyes are a dream symbol. So are the hands. I couldn't find anything specifically about coins, but money's in there and so is an interpretation for the color black. Hell, even the number four means something." I pointed to the evidence, still sitting in the middle of the desk.

"So?"

"So try this: Money is a symbol for energy, okay? You place it on the eyes . . . " I clicked to the appropriate definition, " . . . which are how you receive insight, and the hands . . . " another click, " . . . which symbolize the way you grasp and take hold of things, how you make things happen."

"And the black skin?"

"The color of death, which I guess is obvious, but it also means gestation, absorption, receptivity . . . "

"So?"

"So you kill the guy for his energy, which you draw out with the money. Where do you put this energy? Right where you can use it to increase your insight, and right where you can increase your power to make things happen. The eyes and hands, Frank. And you want to receive it all quickly, absorb it quickly, so you make the guy black somehow . . . "

"Marcus." Frank's voice was flat and tired, and it stopped me short. "Is this the answer you said you had for me?"

"Well, yeah. I mean it's . . . "

"I'm going back to bed now, Marcus. When I come back to work at our actual opening time tomorrow . . . " He glanced at the clock on the projected screen's lower corner " . . . later today, you're going to give me the results of some *police* work. Otherwise I'll give *you* a nightmare, you understand?"

"But . . . "

"How was he killed, huh? What caused the coloration? Where does a complete lack of any body hair fit into your theory, even?" He moved to the door and opened it. "Don't let this be all you have when I get back, Marcus. I really mean that."

Live in LA longer than a week and you find yourself wondering if there's anybody pushing a shopping trolley who isn't homeless. Live here as long as I have and you learn that there's homeless, and then there's *homeless*. Some people manage quite well with what they can fit into a shopping trolley. It just helps to know where to find them when you need them. I had no other options, so I was heading over to the Beverly Centre to speak to one of those special kind of homeless people.

The Beverly Centre was a mall once, five floors of carpark topped by another three of shops. It even had a cinema. After The Bust, some enterprising soul bought the whole complex for a song. He started renting out the parking spaces to the new ranks of homeless clogging up the streets, and the Bum-Bay was born. As long as you had something to barter, you could secure one of the numbered bays for your very own. Sleep in it, run a business, even park a car if you wanted. It was all yours, border inviolate, security guaranteed. Hand over something nice enough, and you'd be allowed access to the mall above, to wander with your escort down to the cinema and use the still-functioning bathrooms to wash yourself or your clothes, or just save yourself from having to empty a bucket into the streets each morning. And what the hell but it worked. Honour might not exist amongst thieves, but it seems the homeless know how to respect another's castle, even if it only consists of a painted number and a few lines on the tarmac.

The man I was meeting was known to most people as Vincent. He'd been a jeweller, an antiques dealer, a coin merchant, and a spectacularly unsuccessful fence, which is how we'd first met. I'd helped turn ten years away into three, so we got on just fine. Now he ran a trade in jewellery barter from the trolleys crowding his bay on the third floor. I waited patiently while he dealt with a couple of customers, swapping various bits of crap for various other bits of crap. Finally they departed and he turned to me with a grimace.

"You frighten customers away just by being here, man."

I held up the bag so he could see the coins. He didn't even pause.

"I give you fifty bucks."

"Money? They're rare, then."

He shrugged. "I seen them before."

"That rare?"

He grinned. "Shit. You getting too good at this." He held out his hand. I dropped the bag into it. "What's the deal?"

"I need your critical eye, Vincent. Tell me what you can."

"And?"

I sighed. "And same as always. Once everything's wrapped up and all the evidence is bagged and tagged, if no-one claims them you can have one of these nice shiny coins for your very own."

"Hmm." He looked at them through the plastic then raised an eyebrow at me. "May I?"

"Be my guest. We've exhausted them and found nothing."

"Of course. You cops."

He opened the bag and spilled the coins onto his palm. I tried to wait patiently while he examined each one in turn, occasionally delving into one trolley or another to retrieve a watchmaker's eyepiece or calipers to aid in his examination. He put down an instrument I couldn't even begin to understand, and looked at me in exasperation.

"Haven't you got any cop things you could be doing? I can't concentrate with you fidgeting like that."

"I really need to know about them. It's important."

"Well go away and let me work, man. I got your number. I ring when I'm done. Go be a cop. Buy yourself a doughnut or something. Shit," he looked me up and down, "Buy two. You getting skinnier every time I see you."

He waved me away and bent back to his work. Lacking any better ideas, I left him to it.

The end and the beginning are often the same place. I forget who said that, but in police work it means this: when you've got nothing else to do, go back to the beginning and start again. I read the forensic reports. I scanned at my scene-of-death notes. I even hauled myself downstairs to our morgue and gave the body another once-over, trying to find the one little clue I might have missed the first time. I didn't find a thing.

In desperation, I scooped up the door-to-door reports from the floor. I needed something to take my mind off signing my official Letgo papers when Ramirez arrived. I viewed them glumly, denial after denial passing my eyes. There was a knock on the door.

"Yes?"

A Uniform popped his head round.

"Call for you, sir."

"Well?"

"It's coming from a public box."

"Ah." We'd been rerouting public calls through the switchboard since a nasty episode a couple of years ago involving some clever electrical apparatus and a lot of scorched ears. "Where from?"

"La Cieniga, just outside the Beverley."

I smiled. That was quick. "Put it through."

Vincent was not impressed when I picked up the line.

"What the hell you playing at man? You think I got a trolley full of dimes?"

"Don't you?"

"That's not the point. You want to know what I've found out or not?"

"Not really."

"What?"

"Kidding."

"You funny as crib death, you know that? I see you soon."

Within ten minutes I was back at his Bum-Bay. He had the coins laid out on top of a felt-covered box, where he could play with them while we talked.

"What you got here is a Quarter Eagle."

"Can I have a drumstick?"

"You don't get any better, you know that, don't you? It a two buck fifty piece, quarter of ten dollars. You let me know if I going too fast for you, okay? Now, they rare enough these days, but check this."

He turned one of the coins over so the reverse side was uppermost.

"See that little mark there?"

"There?"

"No. There. Where it say Cal. Mean it was made right here in California, man. I betting these things never even left the state."

"How the hell did we miss this stuff? Our experts spent hours looking these over."

"You should know better than that. You want it worked out, you go to a real expert. Police expert like Santa Claus, man. He don't exist. You do know Santa don't exist, don't you?"

"You're so much funnier than I am. Anything else?"

"Yeah, that mark means one more thing. Dates it. Only coins made in 1848 had this mark, show it was made from Californian gold."

"Gold. These things are pure gold?"

"Close as, ninety percent or more."

"That'd be good enough, I guess."

"Good enough? What are you, a gold merchant? Good enough for a couple hundred years. Good enough this guy kept them to himself once he got them."

"So these haven't been in circulation for some time?"

"Hell, by the looks of them I say they never left this guy's collection. These ain't spending coins, they keeping coins. Last time any of this type recorded they were sold for ten grand, man. Ten *grand*."

"When was that? I checked coin auctions. I didn't see that."

He snorted. "Oh, you mean legal auctions? I wouldn't know nothing about them. Now, you said I could keep these, right?"

He made to sweep up the coins. I got there before him, and scooped them into my own hand.

"Nice try, pal. One only, and only when everything's finished and dead."

"Just don't forget, okay? Ten grand, man."

I was about to move off when on a whim I pulled the picture of the dead guy out of my pocket.

"Hey, while I'm wasting my time with you, does this guy look familiar?"

Vincent took the picture. "Hey, that look like Mister Exis."

"Exis?"

"Yeah. Had a bay a couple of rows over for a while. Real weird guy, you know? Left because he said everyone was poisoning his aura or something like that. These coins were his?"

"That's what we're trying to find out. How long ago was this?"

"Man, would have been five, six months ago? Hey, Harvey!" he yelled out to a man in a bay just across from us. "When did The new guy move in?"

"Round about Christmas, wasn't it?"

"There you go." Vincent said to me.

"So where did this Mister Exis say he was going?"

"Said something about there being better air in the hills, but it was a while ago, man. I really don't know."

The Hills. I took the photo from Vincent and put it in my pocket. As I walked away he called out.

"Hey! Hey! That was important, wasn't it? That mean I can have another coin? Hey!"

Now I had a location for our mysterious friend, and even better, it looked like I had a name. I went back to the office, for another look at the reports.

I was halfway through the pile before I found him. Uniform reports are largely tick-and-flick affairs, designed to help the Uniform note such details as the interviewee's apparent age, height, weight and so on. I'd waded through hundreds with nothing more significant than a few misspellings. Just about the time my attention would normally start to wander I came across the one I was looking for. Under the 'Skin Color' heading the Uniform had ticked 'Other' and written, "White. Really, really white." According to Madame Zelda, white is the color of purity, enlightenment, and joy. The color of rebirth. And in the field marked surname was written something close enough to 'Exis' to make me cry out. I tore the sheet from the pile and headed for the door.

"Yes?"

As soon as he opened the door I knew it was him. He was white: really, really white. White like someone had soaked him in dye bleach?. And if I could hold him down long enough to shave his hair and pluck his eyelashes then his face would be snow-white Yang to the black Yin in our morgue.

"Mister Ecdysis?"

"Yes, can I help you?"

"I think you can." I pulled the dead man's picture from my pocket, and held it up so he could see. "You can come quietly."

They never do, of course. He paused for maybe half a second before turning back into his apartment. In that half-second I was already dropping the digipic and reaching for my pocket. I tasered him before he took three steps. As he fell, I stepped into the room and closed the door behind me. I locked it, picked up his twitching body, and carried him to the couch in the middle of the room. He was light.

It takes ten minutes or so to recover from a taser shot. I spent the time making myself a cup of coffee, and checking the apartment. Apart from the couch, a vidset in the corner, and a few bits and pieces, the place was empty. There wasn't even a picture on the wall. A quick search of the drawers and shelves failed to locate anything I would call a personal effect. As Ecdysis began to stir, I stood before him and did a quick mental inventory. It seemed to me that if you really tried, you could fit everything in this man's apartment into three, maybe four shopping trolleys. I looked into my empty cup. It was almost dawn, I'd been up all night, and I wasn't going to get any sleep in the immediate future. I could afford a second shot of caffeine. I made another cup, then pulled a chair over so I sat facing Ecdysis. I sipped the black brew and watched him slowly recover. When he sat up I made sure he could see the taser pointing toward him. I smiled.

"So. Shall we start again?"

He said nothing, just stared at me with a look halfway between fear and anger. I sighed.

"Shall I read your Ailsa rights to you, Mister Ecdysis? The ones that say how I can detain you for forty-eight hours without counsel, so long as I guarantee your basic rights to food, water, and ablutions? But you have a Three-Vee." I nodded towards the projector in the far corner of the room. "I'm sure you watch the news, so you know all about how our powers have changed when it comes to murder. That's what it is, isn't it? Murder."

He should have been worried about that. Shit, he should have been downright terrified. Two days alone in a cell without some jackal in a suit telling him what answers would have him back on the street and out of our reach? He should have peed his pants. Instead, he leant back in his seat and smirked.

"And how do you know it's murder?" he asked, in an accent I'd never heard before. "I thought you needed means and motives to prove a murder."

"I can arrest you on suspicion. And then of course, you ran away from me. That's avoiding arrest, refusing to help police with their enquiries... I'm sure I could think up plenty more non-specific charges like that given, say, forty-eight hours."

His smile slipped a little. "It wasn't murder."

That was it. That was the admission I needed. He had been there when the black man died.

"What was it then?"

He looked down at the floor for a long time. I waited, sipping my coffee. Silence is a powerful tool when interviewing. It's human nature to want to fill the vacuum. A confession in a minor key can become a symphony when you give them a patient silence to fill. I let this one fill the room.

"What was it, Mister Ecdysis?"

"A dream." He looked up at me. "Nothing more than a dream."

"Ober WHAT?" Frank Ramirez was not pleased. We were in the interview room at The Cop Cobana. Ecdysis sat on a chair across the table from us, his too-white skin in stark contrast to the black t-shirt and jeans he had changed into before I brought him in.

"Oberhautchen," he replied. "The body is an oberhautchen."

"And what the fuck is that supposed to be?" Ramirez was not happy to find me bringing in a man who wouldn't confess to a killing, but wanted to tell us about his dreams. Ecdysis' single word explanations were not helping.

"It means an epidermal sheath, Frank." I said. "Like a snake shedding its skin. I looked it up."

He turned a baleful glare upon me. "And what does that have to do with whitey here and our boy in the morgue?"

"It is my skin," Ecdysis said in a small voice, "my dead skin."

"We agree on that at least." Ramirez leant over the table and jabbed an angry finger. "He's dead all right. And you did it. Now tell me before I shake the answer from your skinny pencil neck!" He banged the table so hard with his fist that even I jumped a little. Ecdysis sat back, ramrod stiff in his chair, his eyes wide with sudden fear.

"It's my rebirth, my change. I have to leave it behind, you see; I have to discard it so I can become something new. I cannot carry it with me, can I? Can I?" He turned pleading eyes toward me. I stood.

"Boss, can we take a break for a couple of minutes? Leave Mister Ecdysis to think over his statement, eh?"

I tilted my head towards the door. Ramirez gave me a look that told me exactly what he'd like to do with Ecdysis' statement, but he nodded and followed. Once we were outside, I spoke quickly, hoping to avert any explosion coming my way now we had left the easier target behind us.

"I know he's crazy, Frank, but listen for a second. In the absence of any proof, why don't you let me try another angle?"

Ramirez stared at me for a few seconds. Then he sucked in his top lip, always a sign his mind is beginning to run over-time.

"What angle?"

"Let's believe him. Give him the chance to keep explaining this rebirth and this shedding and what-not. Let him trip himself up. If he insists that our man downstairs is just an old skin, then let him show us. When he's got incontrovertible proof in front of him then bang, we've got him dead to rights."

"What have you got in mind?"

I grinned at him and headed back towards the interview room. "Watch and see."

I opened the door. Ecdysis started in surprise, then looked up at my friendly smile.

'Right then," I said to him, "we've got some things to do."

Doc Friedel looked through the one-way glass into the interview room, then at me, then back towards the silent figure seated on the other side.

"Are you sure?"

"Yep. Give him the works. Skin samples, hair analysis, mucus, make him piss in a jar, whatever. As many tests as you can think of. Then take him down to the morgue and let him watch while you do the same to the body. I want you to explain yourself every step of the way. Let him understand what you're going to do with the tests. He needs to know that you're going to compare him with this guy down to a cellular level."

"But I am!"

"Good, then it should be easy."

"Then what?"

"Take him back to his cell, run the comparisons, and come wake me."

I left him to make his own way into the interview room. I went back to my office, lay down behind my desk, and fell asleep.

Two hours later the door crashed open and Friedel came charging in.

"Marcus!"

I looked up at him blearily.

"What is it? Found our loophole?"

"You need to come see."

I stood in the middle of Friedel's office and viewed the printouts covering his walls. Each sheet bore a table or graph, and each sheet had a twin next to it.

"All the same?"

"Every last one." Friedel stood beside me, his confusion echoing my own. "I ran every test we have, from retinal scans to mitochondrial DNA cross-analysis. These two guys are the same to a degree power high enough to max out a Pocket Pilot."

"Twins?"

"Beyond that. Even with twins you'd get some difference, particularly post-puberty. Fingerprints will differ, iris configuration, any one out of a hundred tiny little things. These two are the same, Marcus, exactly the same. Except . . ."

"Yes?"

"Well, there's one thing." He took two sheets from the wall and handed them to me. "These readings measure mean cellular age. The one on the left is the body in the morgue. It's off the chart, right over the upper edge.

These tests aren't always accurate of course, so a reading of two hundred and fifty years or so . . . " he waved his hand, " . . . he ain't in bad shape for a guy born in the eighteen twenties."

He dropped it on the desk and picked up another. "It would have been easy to dismiss as a wild reading. I mean, they happen, right? Now look at the one for our albino friend."

I did.

"It's less."

"Miles less. Like a baby. The thing is, I've never known the test to go bad twice in a row. But this one's got to be a wild reading, too. No way this guy is a baby, right? I did some wide-range checks on the net. Nothing matches up. The only type of statistical variation that's even in the same zip code as the ballpark comes from . . . "

"Don't tell me," I said, my skin grown cold, "From a snake that's just shed its skin."

Ecdysis sat on the bunk in his cell. Ramirez, Friedel, and I filled the rest of the space, each one of us trying not to get too close to our prisoner. We were all nervous, uncertain of where to start. Ecdysis' eyes scanned across our faces, receiving nothing but mute questions and a little fear. He finally settled his gaze upon me. I cleared my throat.

"Explain this to us, please."

"I . . . I told you. It's my skin. I . . . I have to discard it when I grow too heavy, too . . . too full of the life I have been leading."

"But the coins? The color of his . . . of your skin?"

"It is my dream. I told you." His accent grew thicker as he talked. "I must enter the dream to change. I live for a long time in a life. I absorb things."

"What things?"

"Just things. Poisons, metals, things in the air. You, you would process them, excrete them. Smog, chemicals in the water, you don't even think about them. I cannot rid myself of them. They change me, my colour, my . . . " he swallowed, " . . . my dreams. When I grow so dark I must . . . shed." He swallowed another nervous gulp and looked up at me.

"But why the coins?" Ramirez spoke up. "Why go to all that trouble? Why not just move to the fucking country if this, poison, bothers you so much?"

Ecdysis snorted. "Have you lived amongst country folk, Mister Ramirez? Do they still call you 'spick' out there?" Ramirez fell silent and looked at the floor. "There are psychic poisons too, Mister Ramirez. In my building there are four homosexual couples and their children, three *something-elses*, and a total of seventeen nationalities, not including the man on the roof who calls himself a citizen of the sky. I do not stand out so much. I am accepted."

"But what's with all this ritual stuff? Who is that downstairs, huh?" Ramirez was gone. There was no way he was accepting this stuff. I could barely understand it myself, but I'd seen the evidence and I knew, somehow just knew, that the little man in front of us was telling the truth.

"I think I know." I said, glancing sideways at my boss. "It's what I said before, the transfer of energy, isn't it?" I raised my eyebrows toward Ecdysis. "Money for energy, eyes for perception, hands for the power to make things happen, right? You enter your, uh, dream state, and you can influence what happens in your next life?"

Ecdysis nodded. "Yes, yes, crude but you understand."

"But that hair. What about the hair?"

He shrugged. "It does not fall out. I don't know why. Maybe it is already dead, yes?"

"Can you show us?"

"I..." He shook his head. "It is too soon to change. But maybe... if I have the symbols, I can perhaps explain."

I dug in my pocket and pulled the coins out. "Good enough?"

Ecdysis smiled a small thank you. He took them from me and laid them on the bunk. He removed his t-shirt and laid down. I nudged Friedel.

"Is there something...?"

"Too many ribs. No navel," the doctor answered in a whisper, eyes anchored to Ecdysis.

Ecdysis gathered up the coins and placed them at the same points as they'd been discovered on the corpse. He spoke in a chant, his accent thickening and distorting.

"Money to pass values, to enfold energy. Four for tradition, for loyalty to yourself and for karma. I am reborn but with new energy, focused energy, the power to choose a new path."

I felt the air congeal in front of me. Things writhed there, things without form or substance. I gasped, feeling my muscles loosen from my bones, feeling the invisible core of me begin to move toward the front of my chest, seeking escape.

"Stop! For God's sake stop!" Friedel was on his knees, retching, the words coming between gasps for breath. Ecdysis sat up and placed the coins on the bunk beside him. Ramirez knelt beside the doctor and helped him to his feet. I stared at Ecdysis, feeling the pain in my chest where something had tried to separate itself from me. Ecdysis looked back, his eyes calm and knowing. I thought I saw the irises change color, darken slightly.

"I am sorry," he said. "I did not wish to cause alarm."

"What did you do? I felt . . . It's not possible!" Ramirez sounded lost, stranded outside his frames of reference.

"I don't think so." I said slowly. "There have been others, haven't there?"

"Yes, yes." More eager nods from the seated figure. "Not many, but there have been others, yes."

"Jesus Christ died and then rose from the dead."

"Osiris." Friedel blurted, his cheeks red from his exertions. "Egyptian myth, killed and cut into pieces, yeah? His wife put him together and he came back to life."

"This is crazy!" Ramirez shouted us down. "You're talking about fairy stories!"

"Maybe. But where do things like that begin? They have to start with something. If you saw him," I nodded at Ecdysis, "and you were living in ancient Judea, what would you think?"

We fell silent. Ecdysis returned our stares, his eyes large in his too-white face. Finally, he turned to me once more.

"So what will you do to me?" he asked in a small voice.

In the end we let him go. What else could we do, charge him with littering? There had been no murder, so there was no crime. Friedel wanted to study him, of course, but Ramirez said no and Ramirez was still his boss, like it or not. A man has a right to personal freedom, or at least whatever it was that Ecdysis really was has a right.

So we shredded the print-outs, wiped our reports, and recorded the dead thing in the morgue as 'John Doe, death by natural causes'. I drove Ecdysis back to his apartment while Ramirez was busy reading the good doctor the Riot Act, the Secrecy Act, and any other Acts he thought might help. As Ecdysis opened his door to get out, I laid a hand on his arm.

"We won't be able to keep it a secret for long, you know, even if we gag Friedel."

He didn't look at me.

"I know."

"Is there somewhere you can go?"

"I will find somewhere. It gets harder each time, but I can always find somewhere."

I took my hand from his arm.

"I'm sorry it came to this."

"Yes." He stood out of the car, closed the door, and leant back to the open window. "Goodbye, Mister Marcus."

"Ecdysis, wait."

"Yes?"

"How many of you are there?"

"Of me? Just one."

"That's not what I meant."

He reached into his pocket, pulled something out and flipped it toward me. I caught it and looked at it. It was a Quarter Eagle. I turned it over, saw the 'Cal' inscribed on the back.

"Gold. For wisdom, and an enlightened mind."

"I..."

"Goodbye, Mister Marcus."

He turned and walked into the building. I let him go. Then I drove home, unplugged the phone, and went to bed. If I had any dreams, I don't remember them.

AFTERWORD

Blame Tim Powers for this one. Tim was tutor for my week in LA at the Writers of The Future workshop. On Tuesday he gave each of us a small object, and said "Don't think about it, give it back to me tomorrow." On Wednesday morning he drove us out to a library and said "Remember that object? That's your starting point. You have three hours research time, and you'll turn the story in to me by this time tomorrow morning." Huh? There was my comfort zone thrown away! My object? Four quarter bits. And there's another reason for me to love this story: my future wife Lyn bought it when she was editing for *Andromeda Spaceways In-flight Magazine*, which is how we first began our relationship. Always a non-traditionalist, me: sleep with the editor **after** you sell her the story . . .

A VERY GOOD LAWYER

Charles Montilliard III is a very good lawyer. He remains cool and unruffled, despite the heat in the cramped courtroom. He strides around his performance space with the step of a dancer, soft-soled shoes making no noise against the floor. He pauses, draws one deep breath, and tilts his head to an angle calculated to show his handsome face to his audience from the best possible viewpoint.

"Ladies and gentlemen of the jury," he begins, his voice as handsome as his features, "my client is not the criminal here. He is the victim." He sweeps his hand toward where his client, dressed in suit and discreet au de cologne, sits with downcast eyes. "It is not his nature that has led to the crimes for which he sits trial today. It is the culmination of factors that have combined to destroy his reputation"

Montilliard studied drama before he took to law. It shows. As he views the jury before him he sees how they hang upon his words, the way they follow his gestures. He already has them hooked. He allows himself a small pause, tries to ignore the trickle of sweat tickling his ribs.

"My client is the product of a single parent family. If you have read anything in the media, if you have any understanding of our society, you will know that crime rates are highest in such families. He never knew his mother. His father was distant to him, and demanding, and when he dared question his iron rule do you know what happened?"

Montilliard draws himself up to his full height. His eyes fill with rage at the injustice. "He threw him out! Threw him out from the only home he had ever known, into the cold and dark with no belongings, none of the things you and I take for granted, not even a single word of comfort to take with him. Simply discarded him as if he'd never existed. I ask you, ladies and gentlemen, what hope could my client have had, when his only role model treated him in such a way?"

Montilliard's voice echoes round the stone chamber. He waits until silence once more descends, then resumes in a softer tone, noting with satisfaction that the jury leans forward as one to catch his words.

"I ask you to look at the faces in the public gallery. Even on this most important day, my client's only parent chooses not to be here."

He watches as the jurors turn and scan the assembled audience, seeing with gratification their shaking heads and mutterings. He takes the opportunity to wipe a hand across his moist brow before they turn back towards him. Pointing once more to the respectable figure seated at the defence table, he presses forward with his arguments.

"Is it any wonder, with no guidance or love to support him, that my client fell in with an unsuitable crowd? Is it any surprise that he was drawn into the flashy embrace of the robbers and prostitutes and murderers of the underworld? Confused, looking for acceptance, can you blame him for being attracted to people who greeted him with open arms? Can you condemn him for being blind to the ulterior motives of those who used him for their own twisted agendas?"

Montilliard pauses, and uses a perfectly manicured finger to point to the jury.

"Can you honestly say that you would not have done the same had *you* shared his fragile emotional state?"

He knows he has them, by the looks of sorrow and pity on their faces. Despite the heat of his surroundings, Montilliard feels just a little bit cooler. His chiselled features soften, and a well-practiced look of sadness settles upon it. He places one hand on the obsidian table, draws pleasure from the smoothness under his touch.

"Let us not ignore, ladies and gentlemen, that my client is no ordinary person. Look up please," he instructs his charge. Slowly, with great dignity, the defendant raises his head and gazes toward the jury. Montilliard hears their collective gasp, and measures his success by the distance they shrink from his client's gaze. His heart fills with triumph. He enunciates each word separately, and with great clarity. The chamber's acoustics add Shakespearean timbre to his speech.

"Multiple Neurofibromatosis. Colloquially called Von Rickenhausen's Disease. It's the same affliction that cursed Joseph Merrick, who you might know as the Elephant Man. Not a pretty sight, is it?" He scans the horrified jurors. "Can you, can any of us, understand what it must be like to go through life looking the way my client does?"

He moves over to place a hand upon the defendant's shoulder, radiating friendship and support.

"How can we begin to comprehend the pain of being cursed by all who meet you? Of being the object of hatred and superstition, just because you are different?"

He stands in front of his audience again, noting their reluctance to tear their gazes from the spectacle behind him. He talks to them while they stare at the defendant's deformities. Three of the jurors draw hands down pale and sweating faces.

"They throw salt at him. They bar him from their churches. They warn their children against him. His very name is used as a curse. This poor being before you has been the victim of vicious lies and discrimination his whole life. His entire existence has been little more than a procession of misfortunes and rejection."

Montilliard raises his voice once more, and it rings out with the power of a trained actor. "This is why I say to you, ladies and gentlemen: If you have any pity in your hearts, you must absolve my client of any wrongdoing. You must find him without guilt, without sin, if only for the sake of your own souls."

Passion shakes his voice, and he takes long moments to draw breath and gather himself. Then, with a quiet and dignified "Thank you", he sits beside his client.

It is a long time before the jury return from their deliberations. Montilliard sits with bowed head, watching the tabletop flicker beneath his drumming fingertips. He fancies he can hear the ticking of a clock, although no timepiece hangs from the walls of this special room. Eventually, the jury members shuffle in and regain their seats. Lawyer and defendant rise. The judge speaks.

"Foreman of the jury, have you reached a verdict?"

The man nearest the judge stands and nods.

"We have, your honour."

"And what say you?"

The foreman clears his throat, unfolds a piece of paper, and reads from it.

"Your honour, despite the eloquence of counsel, we find the defendant's guilt to be proven."

"So be it." The judge bangs his gavel, and disappears. The jury box dissolves, taking the jury with it. Montilliard's starts as his client clears his throat. His voice, when he speaks, is warm as blood.

"Well?" he says.

"I really thought . . . I really thought it would work."

"Well, you were a good lawyer."

"I am. I had the jury right there, right *there* . . . " Montilliard clenches a sweaty fist, and isn't the least bit surprised when dots of blood appear where his nails bite into the flesh. "Where did they come from anyway?"

His client smiles, an unpleasant, knowing smile.

"Where else?"

"But . . . but it's supposed to be a jury of your peers!"

"And where do I find twelve peers, hmm?"

"But . . . it shouldn't be . . . they didn't even care, they didn't even care that they were going back."

"Don't blame them. In time you'll be as used to it as they are."

Montilliard slumps in his chair, presses his head against the tabletop. Despite the heat, the stone is cool. Montilliard tries not to consider why.

He is reminded of the sacrificial benches used by High priests of cabalistic sects. His client coughs.

"You had a good shot. I liked the Elephant Man bit."

Montilliard smiles a small, sad smile to himself.

"Yeah. That was good, wasn't it?" He raises his head. "Listen, I don't suppose . . ."

"Sorry. A deal's a deal."

"But I could do so much for you. I could . . . I could get people off, I could let them do more, well, more of what you like people to do . . ."

"Charles, don't. I gave you a chance, just like we'd bargained. And there are always more lawyers."

The client snaps clawed fingers. The walls and floor of the chamber disappear, revealing the flaming pits behind. Heat licks them, followed by a tongue of flame that leaps up and caresses the rock island upon which they stand. The beginning of Montilliard's scream is cut off as he is engulfed in a burst of flame and yellow smoke. His voice echoes away, falling and falling and falling for a long time. All that remains is a small pile of sulphurous ash, and the smell of brimstone.

Charles Montilliard III was a very good lawyer. But not *that* good.

AFTERWORD

A whimsy, but one born from yet another fascination—in this case, Joseph Merrick, the Elephant Man. Take a story that makes you cry like a baby every time, then make a joke of it. Sure. But it's an object lesson in how doing what you love can lead to other things: because I wrote this story, Zoran Zivkovic read it. Because he read it, and liked it, he invited me to contribute to his anthology *The Devil in Brisbane*. Because he did that, I made friends with a man of extraordinary talent. Not a bad return, all things considered.

GOODFELLOW

It was Monday, and it started perfectly. Right outside my window, so close I could smell their need, two young lovers sat on a bench, kissing each other with such sweet abandon it made me giggle like a squirrel. I watched their hands move across each other for a few moments, then reached out and slipped a pair of woman's panties into the boy's jacket pocket. Before I had time to remember how to breathe, the panties were clutched in her hands and the day's fun had started.

The streets were full of frivolous people. It's always a carnival somewhere in the world, and my window looks out at them all. I picked a destination at random, put on my best fooling smile, and leaped. Where I landed I could not have cared: it was sunny, and happy, and the herds that swallowed up the streets looked oblivious and ripe for the tricking.

I began in lazy fashion, plucking wallets from the pockets of tourists and pressing them into the outstretched hands of beggars and children, chortling with early morning glee at the pursuit of unwilling Artful Dodgers. I poked balls of ice-cream off their cones, slid hotdogs from their buns and onto shirts, pricked balloons, caught sneezes in mid-air and deposited them on the necks of fat fools and pretty young things alike. By mid-morning, I had warmed myself up for some real mischief. I snacked upon a toffee apple, and a bag-trapped goldfish carried by a strutting child. Then I began to look around in earnest.

There. Over by the fountain in the town square, ignoring the festivities as she worked her way through a thermos of coffee and a sandwich she'd doubtless brought from home. I am a creature of spirit. Bodies hold little fascination for me. If I was to guess I would have put her at no younger than seventy, and no older than seven hundred. Her air of contentment was palpable. I skipped a dance and kissed the cheek of a passing policewoman just for the heck of it. Old people are such tumblesome fun.

The coffee was an obvious place to start. Such a nice big thermos, such beautiful steam making patterns in the air above its open mouth. I imagined the screams, the attempts to scoop water from the pool behind her to damp the scald across skirt and stockinged legs. Perhaps that police horse over there would panic, those young men standing so close might be angry at having their new trousers splashed with hot, staining liquid. Either way, confusion. Chaos. Fun and laughter and entertainment galore. I snuck my way over, pausing in my creep to wipe my nose on the sleeve of a young man in a snow-white business shirt. I reached out, giggling through my ears to stifle the sound of my laughter. My nail brushed the surface of the thermos. At that very moment the old lady reached down without looking and swept it up to pour herself another cup. I toppled forward and fell splat-splash into the fountain water. My head bounced off the bottom, and I rose, spluttering and shaking, fingers arched into claws, ready to scratch the smile of anyone who laughed at my misfortune. No-one had noticed, of course. My victim had replaced the thermos and now sat with cup to lip, smiling at her surroundings.

I stalked off to a nearby laundrette to dry, consoling myself by plucking every red handkerchief I own out of the air and dropping one into each of the washers. By the time I climbed out of the dryer and returned to the street, the old woman had finished her lunch and disappeared. I leapt to the top of a nut vendor's stall to look. I spied her near a puppet show on the other side of the square and smiled. It was a small matter to push the cart over and spread the vendor's wares under the feet of nearby pedestrians. Then I bounded to where her blue-rinsed head bobbed in time to the puppeteer's songs. Removing him from behind his curtains with a well-timed foot, I grabbed two puppets and flung them over the stage and into the woman's lap. By dint of my nimble fingers, I had them copulating like starving animals before she disentangled them with a tug that sent their wires fizzing across my fingertips. She returned them to their stage and joined the other audience members in helping the stunned puppeteer to his feet. I contented myself with drawing out a small paint set and painting such leering countenances on the dolls tiny faces that the school group who waited their turn by their nearby bus would receive an unexpected education when the next performance started. Happy with my work I looked up, only to see her home-curled hair vanishing into the nearby museum.

I love museums. I love the way they get so much wrong, and I should know. I caused half the accidents that stock their coffers, and it's amazing what people will do with just a whisper in their ear, be they king or commoner as the saying used to go. I skipped to the entrance and dropped a dead rat in the donations box. Just my happy luck! A display of commedia dell'arte masks was her destination. If anyone knows anything about the commedia it is I. After all, who else are they about? I reached back into my cupboard at home and drew out a staff into the here and now. With a wave, I turned it into the slap stick from which it was descended. One must go to the theatre properly attired, after all.

Inside the hall, I found my prey amongst a group of wrinkled dilettantes surrounding a fat docent. He stood in front of a mask, droning on and on concerning things of which he knew nothing. I, who have lived them, listened and laughed. Why, I recognised this creature! I knew his sweaty face, the supercilious look he wore across his skin as he showed his ignorance to the world. I have jousted with this lovely fool too many times to resist another opportunity.

"Doctor!" I cried and leaped upon his shoulders, gripping his ears and shoving my ever-erect dibble into his face. He remained oblivious to my presence, but the flapping of his lips upon my member made me whoop and holler in lusty joy. I beat out a tattoo upon his oily head, made monkey noises in his ears, slid my hands down into his trouser pockets and drew out the handful of breath mints stashed within. I scattered them high into the air, somersaulting off the docent's flabby shoulders and kicking one into the mouth of a child laughing nearby. While the crowd scurried to collect the fallen sweets, I grabbed the mask from the wall and ran to the next room, using the display cases for a private game of Pirates, feet free of the shark-infested floor until I reached the safe ground beyond the doorway.

Once inside, I ran my fingers across the soot-black mask with fond remembrance. So much more comfortable than my little domino, so snug, so easy to hide behind. I slipped it over my face, felt the plaster flow and conform to my features like a lover's welcome. I smiled, and the mask smiled with me. I glanced back into the hallway. The group had moved on, mints back in the keeping of their gaoler. Only the old woman remained, head tilted toward a display case I had leaped across on my exit. I followed her gaze, ready for my next bit of fun.

When I saw what she was looking at, I laughed like a drunk. A Phallophorus! Beautiful black beauty, standing rude and proud, as jovial and delicious as it stood when held to the body of a beautiful dancing Roman boy. I smiled at the memory of bottoms pinched, of firm young boys fighting and wrestling in the fun of hot Latin afternoons. There were glorious days back then, tumbling and rolling with boy and girl and beast until not one was distinguishable from the other, and the love and laughter filled both the air and my soul. I clicked my fingers in a long-dead tune and snuck back into the room. Soot-faced and oil-bodied, I slid between the air like smoke from a pagan hearth house. If my lady wanted a giant pintle, well, she would have all she wanted and more.

Unseen by rheumy old-woman eyes, I flipped through the glass case, snatched up my long-discarded friend and thrust my hips into its embrace. Like the mask it welcomed me home, hugging itself to me. With joy, I felt myself stiffen even further, and the phallophorus rose in response, jutting out like the prow of a randy trireme.

I jumped toward my pretty septuagenarian, prodding my member at her Cock Inn, skipping a jig and waggling my hips to make it dance and wave in front of her. To my surprise she didn't fall back, didn't cover her mouth with a hand and cry out in dust-voiced shock at the sight of a museum display taking flight with no visible means of support. Instead, she reached into her bag and pulled out her thermos. Gripping it in one hand as if it were a club, she bought its metal down upon the head of my bouncing bell-end. There was a loud 'boing', like the sound of a young Roman boy striking an amphora with a wadded stick. I fancied I heard the sound of barbarian laughter.

"Stop that," she said, and whacked it once again for emphasis. I looked down at her in astonishment, and recoiled at the anger in her gaze.

"You can see me."

"Of course, I can, you silly man." She brandished the flask again and I took a step back.

"But how?"

She reached into her bag and I flinched. She smiled when she saw that, before drawing out a bag of boiled sweets and popping one into her mouth.

"None of your business. I don't expect you to know what it's like to die on an operating table and I don't intend to tell you. Now take that stupid thing off and put it back." She waved a disdainful hand at the phallophorus.

"But . . . "

She raised the thermos once more and I complied.

"And the mask."

I slid it off with regret, plodding over to the wall and hanging it back onto its hook.

"And the other one."

"But . . . "

"Do as you're told."

I heard the slosh of coffee and she raised her weapon. I unhooked my domino and hung it over the first one.

"Now turn around and let me see you."

"No."

"Why not?"

"I . . . I'm embarrassed," I admitted.

"Don't be silly. Hasn't anybody ever seen your face before?"

Nobody had, I realised with a start. In all these years, all these incarnations, I had never been without my mask.

"No."

"Well, it's about time then. Come on."

A gentle hand took my shoulder and turned me to face her. She grabbed my chin with her other hand and raised my head so that we looked into each other's eyes again.

"My, aren't you handsome?" she said. "Why on Earth would you want to hide away behind a mask?"

I made to answer, then paused with mouth half open. Truth, I didn't really know. Because it has always been what I have done. Because it is what has to be done. Because . . . I don't know why. I am Merry Andrew. I simply do.

She saw my confusion and smiled.

"I expect you have a lot to learn." She patted my shoulder and walked toward the exit. "Come on."

I made to grab my domino.

"Leave that. You won't need any of this anymore."

I stilled my fingers, dropped my hand to my side. With slow, reluctant steps I followed her out into the light of the afternoon sun.

"What's your name?" I asked as we stood on the museum steps and looked around the chaos of the festival.

"Isabella," she replied. "Isabella Puncino."

I may have cried then. Certainly, I forgot how to breathe. After all this time, after all the Columbines and Flaminias and Silvias I had chased . . .

"Isabella." I tasted the name, and it was as sweet as it had always been. "I have something for you."

She raised an eyebrow.

"It has always been yours."

I reached up to my chest and drew open the little drawer I keep there. I took out my heart, laid it in a velvet-lined box from my pocket, and gave it to her. She put it in her handbag.

"You know that's not enough."

"I know," I said, and flourished my staff, changed back from its ludicrous slap stick beginnings. Behind me the world quivered, and I saw the location of all the little and big wrongs I had ever wronged. To right them all would be a mighty task, a task fit for a lover. I took a hop, skip and jump away from her, then looked back. "This may take some time."

"I know."

Smiling, I stepped into history for the final time. Just before I disappeared, I heard her whisper, "I'll be waiting."

AFTERWORD

It's not often I'm directly inspired by another piece of fiction, but this is one case. After reading a Neil Gaiman graphic novel, in which Puncinello finds a type of cathartic love, I turned to my darling wife Lyn and said "That was great, but in *my* story . . . " The only natural response, of course, is "Well get off your arse and write it then." So I did. I sold the story to European magazine *Znak Sagite*, but to date I've never seen a copy of the magazine so don't know if it ever saw print. And Neil, if you're reading this, feel free to say "That was great, but in *my* story . . . oh, wait . . . "

STALAG HOLLYWOOD

Our first day in captivity started with the 'zhang zhang' of the big 16-bank klieg lights firing up, sodium glare blasting away the artificial night. Then we were up and out, into the exercise yard, hidden from the studio tours by backdrops and flats and painted signs.

They'd lined us up and marched us into the back lots, made up an old World War Two camp from their memories and the sets they'd found out there. They'd locked us in, manned the gun towers, walked up and down outside with Rin Tin Tin and a bunch of Lassies on their tight, tight leashes: muzzles on; snarling. And we just stood there, we who could cause audiences to scream, or cry, with nothing but a light on our faces. We shivered in the drizzle from the rain machines, and waited for them to tell us what was going on. The main street from a hundred thousand westerns was our only gathering place, a few feet before it ended in a flat pained with the view of a castle from Olivier's Henry V. We could see the path to Xanadu but would never get there.

Then the gate opened, just a sliver. We shuffled forward, but it was only Thalberg, leather hat covering his greasy hair, and an armband round his bicep. He sauntered along our massed frontage, Bogey and Mitchum to either side, staring at us like they'd love it if we tried something, anything. When they reached the middle of the street Thalberg paused, let the shuffling die down, and in that prissy, precise voice of his, he began to speak.

"Right, chaps." He actually called us chaps, as if we were sitting in his office with a three picture deal on the desk between us. "We know the way the studios want this to run, so let's all of us just knuckle down and work together and see to it that things proceed as they should, shall we?"

"Why?" a voice behind me shouted, all pain, and confusion, and belligerent need, "Why we gotta? Why you do this?"

"Oh God," I heard Rondo mutter, "it's Max."

I felt him move through the crowd, felt bodies adjust to allow him passage. I could have stopped him. I could have. We come from the same part of the world. He would have listened to me, maybe. I never even moved. I saw the look in Bogey's eyes, saw him shake his head 'no' just a little bit, knew he wanted this to play out. I'd worked with Bogey before it all changed. I stood still.

Max came blundering out of the crowd, blinking in the light, bald head and rat face covered with a sheen of sweat. I could see his long, long, fingernails arch like claws as he held them up towards our captors.

"You can no do this. You no have right. We is stars too. We is..."

A single shot rang out. Max fell. From a window to our right a Stetson-clad head appeared.

"We do this," it drawled, "because we have an image to maintain."

"Thank you, Mister McQueen," Thalberg called out, and I realised that this had been expected. They knew someone would break. They knew they would make an example. They wanted to show us the power of the system, so there would be no mistaking where we stood. I looked at Bogey. A quarter of an inch at the corner of his lip smiled at me. It said, "See?"

After that we were at their mercy. We no longer had the will to try to break free, if we ever had. Every day, work parties were taken out along that street and through the gates to where the film sets waited. Every week, Thalberg and his cronies would post attendance figures, next to the big picture of Marilyn looking down at us and blowing a kiss. A special Thalberg cruelty that: a kiss she would never blow at the likes of us. He knew we would look at it every week, just to see if we were still bringing the audiences in. From time to time, a name was underlined, and that person would be taken away, marched through the gate with Thalberg sauntering along behind, smiling because he knew he couldn't be touched. Those who left never came back.

"We have to do something."

A group of us were gathered at one end of the yard. As always, the subject was our incarceration. As always, Charlie Laughton was raving. As always, we knew there could be no answer, no plan.

"Do what?" Schnoz replied. "Tunnel our way out? Build a glider and fly? You know nobody makes them the way we do."

"Europe. We could go to Europe. Italy, Germany, Spain. They still make them. I heard Douglas did one in Greece. We could go there, start something of our own. England. Come on Boris, you're English too. We'd be appreciated there, wouldn't we?"

His appeal was in vain. Boris said nothing. Boris never says anything. I watched his heavy-lidded eyes blink once, twice, one hand scratch at the stitches across his other wrist. One or two of the others began to drift away.

"Please. Somewhere, surely?" Charlie began to plead. I was about go when I saw Gabby waddling towards us at speed.

"They're taking Rondo," he gasped. I took off for the gate at a flat run. It was true. Rondo was being marched away.

"No!" I don't know why, but I raced through the standing crowd and jumped out in front of the little procession. "No, not Rondo. Please."

Bogey and Mitchum had him strung out between them. Mithcum was a dead-eyed bastard. You knew he enjoyed it when they dragged us away. But Bogey . . . I turned to him, ignoring Thalberg as he stepped forward and ordered me away.

"Humph, please, for pity's sake, don't do this. Not after what he's been through. Damn it, he was one of you. You've seen the photos, you know what he was like before . . . before . . . "

Rondo hung between them, too gone to even fight for his own life. We all knew the work he'd been put in, the way they'd exploited his deformities. Who knows? Maybe this was what he'd wanted. Maybe this was preferable to the humiliation he endured every time he stepped onto the set of another "Creeper" movie. Seeing him slumped there, with the light gone from his eyes, killed the boldness in me. My voice ran down, and I could only manage another weak "Please?"

Bogey let go of his prey and stepped toward me. I stared up at him, expecting violence, perhaps even welcoming the thought of physical pain to match that inside me. Instead, he placed his hand on my shoulder. His knowing, dangerous eyes gazed down into mine. He pushed me aside. They took Rondo away.

That night Bela killed himself. I don't know how he got his hands on it. It must have been agony to hold it for so long, or to have it hidden so close. But I heard him stop his ceaseless pacing (Bela was always more active after they powered down the lights) and whisper something that sounded like "No more". Then he moved out of the room. I roused Boris and the others and raced out of the barrack in his wake.

We found him sitting against the gate, his face contorted in agony. Half a clove of garlic lay next to him where it had dropped from his dying hand. Boris picked it up without a word, and placed it in the chest pocket of Bela's dinner jacket. Boris had always been thankful to Bela.

"Charlie's right," I heard myself say, "something has to be done."

"What do we do? What do we do?" asked Dwight, his voice falling from Igor to Renfield and climbing back again. "What do we do?" He broke into tears and hid his face against Boris' chest. Boris said nothing. Boris always says nothing.

Bela crumbled as we watched. A breeze sprang out of nowhere, and the dust started to fly away. I shaded my eyes and looked through the gates towards where the wind machines were. I saw Mitchum standing there, his face impassive. I knew if I were closer I would see the smile in the bastard's lizard eyes.

Soon after, my performances began to suffer, then my roles. Gradually, over the course of a few weeks, I went from A list releases to B list, until I found myself in two-reelers. One day I walked onto the set and found myself doing a walk-on in a serial that had the 'Educational Films' logo all over it. I'd seen Buster go this way. After this, there was the only the underlined name on a sheet of paper, and a walk through the gates from which you didn't return. When I got back to the room that night I told everyone.

"It'll be tomorrow."

They nodded, eager now that the time was near. They moved to their bunks and began to get ready for bed. I glanced at Boris. He stared back.

"Have I done the right thing?" I asked him. "Have I condemned us all?"

Boris took in our surroundings: the discarded flats that formed the walls; the bundles of rags from Costuming that we had made into our blankets and our clothes, the Commissary left-overs that lay half-eaten on the table at the far end of the room. He leaned down and glared at me with an intensity I had never seen in him before.

"You stay, we better off dead," he said in a halting voice.

I watched him walk away and lie on his bunk. I found my way to my own bed, and tried to draw what little warmth I could from the threadbare sheets they had provided. Dwight turned off the lights. I caught one last glimpse of the Lons, curled up like dogs on a thin mattress on the floor. That night I did not sleep at all.

They came for me the next day. Thalberg, flanked by his two cronies, Bogart and Mitchum. They strode up the street and over to the picture of Marilyn, their feet refusing to stir the dust of our studio-made dirt. Nobody moved. Only our eyes followed their passage. Thalberg nailed the notice upon the wall then stood back, awaiting the rush that always accompanied the weekly ritual. This time there was no charge. There was no movement at all. Except me. Exuding a calm I didn't feel, I walked to the board. I read the notice. I turned to face the three studio men. Thalberg looked nervous. This was not normal. I saw his eyes look beyond me, to the windows above the street, and knew my guess had been correct. There was nobody there: they had become so secure in their superiority that the McQueens and Bronsons and Garners had left their stations long ago, confident that we had been so cowed that their authority would no longer need reinforcement. These three men were alone, amongst hundreds of us. I looked at Bogey, and at Mitchum. They realised it too. Their eyes were slitted, their bodies tense.

"Come on then," I said, and began to walk towards the gate. I held my breath as I walked. My entire plan hinged on their reaction. If they paused at my audacity, the power they had over us would be broken.

Power is not a physical thing. It exists only in the mind. Thalberg was not a big man. He was short, and thin. But he held sway over us because we *believed* he did. The studios did not keep us penned in because they had authority over us. We had allowed ourselves to be caged because they had made us *believe* they had the right. But I had taken control over my own decisions. If Thalberg and his cronies acted as if nothing had happened, and simply marched me out of the gates, then I would die, and things wouldn't have changed at all. But if they paused, and then followed me *because I had told them to do so*, then I would also have taken their power. And every one of the hundreds of inmates would realise it.

They paused.

Perhaps they realised what they had done, or at least realised that something intangible had suddenly shifted, because they tried to stop me. Someone gripped my shoulder, hard. I was spun around, and there stood Bogey, hand raised to slap me as he had done so many times in the past. I looked down at his hold on me, and smiled.

"Look what you did to my shirt."

"What?"

"This is the second time you have laid hands on me."

Now he knew something was wrong. We'd spoken these words before. He knew the script to which I referred. I should have been wild, crazy, screaming and tearing at my hair. And he could have reacted to that, could have wrested control in the same way he had done on set, by physical violence. But I was calm, sincere. And because I had control, he lost his. His eyes snapped left-right-left. Hundreds of gazes focussed upon us. He backed away from me, head turning in all directions. Thalberg and Mitchum joined him, ranks of monsters and villains surrounding them. They saw the eyes staring back. They saw the knowledge of what had happened. They tried to run for the gates.

Thalberg was not a big man. Neither was Bogart, not really. Mitchum was a big man, but not next to Boris or Lon Junior.

It was ugly, but then, we have been in horror movies, we have been in westerns, we have been in Noir and crime and mysteries. We have always been the ones to murder, and torture, and kill, while the hero gets to deliver us with one clean shot and win the girl. We know all about ugly endings. They do not bother us.

The inmates engulfed their captors. Thalberg tried to run. Mitchum tried to fight them off. Only Bogey stood still, looking at me as if this was what he had expected all along. As the first hands reached for him he gave me one of his quarter-inch smiles and shrugged as if to say, "I see."

It didn't take long.

The crowds moved through the park as if life was ordinary, and nobody ever had to find a way to escape just so they could survive. The sun was warm, and real, and I couldn't find a way to stand comfortably.

Boris was with me, still as ever, his eyes fixed on a little girl playing by the edge of the lake. His fingers clenched and unclenched in rhythm to the pulse in her neck. I glanced up at his calm, blank face.

"What now?" I asked. "What do we do now?"

Boris smiled, a thin stretching of the lips that did nothing to create a light in his eyes. He stepped away from me, and began to walk down toward the lake. Halfway there, he turned and favoured me with a small wave.

He didn't say anything. He never does.

AFTERWORD

Another fascination taken out of context and played with: the grand old Hollywood Uglies, particularly the tragic Rondo Hatton. I'm also a huge fan of Buster Keaton. Like a lot of writers of my acquaintance, I tend to have a bunch of books on the go at once, so I was reading a biography of Keaton, and a history of Hollywood Horror movies during the same period, and it struck me how the studio system that derailed Keaton was like a chain gang of sorts, and how right Karloff was about not wanting the Monster to speak, and one thing led to another... Under the title "In The Dream Factory" this story won the 2003 Katharine Susannah Prichard Writer's Centre SF & Fantasy Competition, over 108 other entries, so I'm fond of it.

BRILLIG

Life, like a dome of many coloured glass,
Stains the white radiance of Eternity,
Until Death tramples it to fragments.

—Percy Bysse Shelley
ADONAIS

During the operation, Brillig opened his eyes. For a moment he was blinded by the light hanging over him. The Man leaned over, the bottom half of his face obscured by a mask. He held a scalpel and, when he spoke, Brillig was surprised to find he understood the words.

"Don't worry," The Man said. "The pain will be over soon."

Soothed by his voice, Brillig closed his eyes.

Repeat after me: Those who don't learn their history are bound to repeat it.

There is a room beneath The City. Machines line the walls. They crackle and pulse with hidden energies. Water drips from the ceiling, forming grey puddles. Brillig sits strapped to a chair in the centre of the room, blinded by the light hanging over him. A metal cap covers his head, pinning his ears back against his scalp. Wires lead from the cap to a box at the chair's feet. More wires exit the box to a machine that stands clean and uncaring against the wall behind him. A shadow falls across his closed eyes. He opens them, and sees his torturer standing above him.

Often The Man would gather them round and explain things.

"I gave myself this name because it is a name that other men do not have." He once told them. "Once a person reaches a certain status, a particular level of usefulness, a unique name is appropriate. Most people are called 'J Soldier 463' and 'R Clerk 601' or somesuch."

"But why is my name Brillig?"

"It's from a poem, written by a man long ago. All your names are taken from poems. Poems are unknown these days, or nearly so. I may be the only person in the world who has any, and even I didn't know about them until I found this mixed in amongst the datanet."

The Man reached up to a shelf and took down a crudely bound sheaf of paper. One of the others had smiled.

"It's a textbook."

"No," said The Man. "Listen." And he began to read.

FILE VISION 001   BLACK AND WHITE

Frankenstein, 1931 (Dir. James Whale). The Monster (Boris Karloff) lies inert on the operating table. By means of chains attached to each corner, the table is winched upwards through a hole in the roof. Below him, Doctor Frankenstein (Colin Clive) shouts.

Pink has a name. All members of Information Retrieval have names. Brillig screams. Pink raises a massive arm to its full extension and brings it sweeping down across Brillig's face, following through until his fingers brush the floor. Across the room, Brown sits in front of a large machine crooning senselessly to himself, fingering the electrodes that lead from his temples to a socket in the machine's midsection. At the sound of the slap he lurches to his feet and moves across to the mother-machine, pushing buttons, turning knobs, suckling at the electric nipples that feed him. Pink slaps Brillig again, screeching from his seven feet of height at the bleeding prisoner.

"Where?"

Brillig makes a soft choking sound and faints. Brown pulls down a lever, halting the flow of electrons to the chair. Pink turns away.

"He's lost consciousness again. Get him out of here."

FILE VISION 002   BLACK AND WHITE

A young human female, her curly blonde hair tied with a ribbon. She is singing.

GIRL

How much is that doggy in the window?

Brillig wakes. He stands slowly, shaking his head to try and relieve the electric-sharp pain nestling behind his brow. He is in the cell in which he was first incarcerated, after his capture. The metal door behind him bangs open, and he turns to face it. A man shuffles in, carrying a tray piled high with bones. Brillig looks at him in disgust. He is a parody of humanity, even worse than those who have been torturing him. One leg must be shorter than the other under his rough robe, for he leans to one side as he walks. What Brillig can see of his face is covered in hard, leathery nodules, ranging in size from no bigger than acne to one the size of a concussion grenade. Seeing his look, the stranger snorts.

"You no picture youself muttsey. You want something eat? This look good?"

He grunts and puts the tray down on the floor. As he does so his robe draws back from his arms, revealing hands that are no more than duo-digital claws.

"You no thank me? Up to him," he tilts a head towards the door, "not even this."

"Why am I here?" Brillig asks, pressing one hand against the pain in his forehead. "What have I done to you? What happened to your hands?"

"These? These legacy muttsey. Daddy give these, and Daddy before and before. Foot-soldier hands these, no pretty scientists hands."

"But what about me? Why am I here?"

The ragged man smiles up at him. Brillig sees only gums behind the scarred lips.

"You monster, muttsey. You unnatural. You not live not natural. We find you scientist man, he no make no more mutsseys, eh?"

Brillig finds his reasonable tone frightening, more so than if he was ranting. He edges towards the door, but the torturer's assistant looks up sharply.

"No try leave, no, no. Me shout little shout, they come get you."

Brillig stops. "I could kill you." He bares his teeth in what he hopes is a fearsome manner.

"Then what?" the little man laughs. "Go back in city? City dead." He stops laughing, and his voice turns harsh. "No. Stay here, tell us he where. Much better."

Brillig forces his face to become still. "I don't know anything about him."

"Pity. Only pain then." The awful little man backs out of the room, swinging the door shut behind him.

It was easy, in the before-time, in the days before capture. He and The Man had played together in the public park outside The City, a last vestige of green that The Man had called 'Our Little Sherwood'. All the others had gone back, returned to the grey steel buildings and concrete paths within, determined to live like their former masters had lived. But The Man had chosen to stay. He had hidden as the others had left. Brillig had stayed. They played together beneath the shadows of the walls.

He told them once.

"I was a surgeon. Well, molecular engineer was the correct term. Did most of my work with a computer and a DNA string, but I still got into the surgery when I could. You were my best friends, but you couldn't share my life fully. So I worked upon you in secret. I used my knowledge to accelerate your potential, pushed forward your evolution a few hundred millennia or so. The clues were all there in your genes. You would have reached this point anyway, eventually, maybe, at least your race would. But you and I would have been long dead, and I just didn't want to wait."

Like so much of what he told them, they did not understand.

In the chair once more. Pink looms over him.

"Tell us, or we'll give your bones to the crows."

FILE VISION 003   COLOUR

A music video. The Mad Hatter and his friends sit around a giant table. Alice lies spread-eagled on top. As the Mad Hatter sings, he cuts a slice from Alice's body. It looks like cake.

> MAD HATTER
> Don't come around here no more,
> Whatever you're looking for, hey!
> Don't come around here no more.

They had stood together and watched as the rest of his people had readied themselves to move down into The City. The Man was talking to one of the Canan.

"I wish you'd reconsider."

The Canan smiled.

"I was about to say the same thing." He tilted his head at Brillig. "And you?"

Brillig tried to think of something to say, some reason he could give for his decision to stay. He recalled a line from one of the movies they had watched together on the nights when they had punched into the Tainmentnet, and offered it.

"If you build it, they will come."

They leave him in the chair while they take a break from their endeavours. He feigns unconsciousness, and catches snippets of their conversation.

"I don't understand. How could such a noble creature become such a twisted and hateful object?"

"They pervert nature to their own ends. Beasts that offer such an affront to nature should not be allowed to live, don't you think?"

"I was talking of the Doctor."

"As was I."

Pink raises a blackstick and brings it crashing down on Brillig's shoulder. Brillig screams as the bones snap. Brown sits with his eyes luminous, one hand moving under his robe, masturbating. The ruined man who had bought him the bones lurches about in the shadows, laughing.

"Kill him! Kill him!"

Repeat after me: In the land of the blind, the one-eyed man is King.

FILE VISION 004   BLACK AND WHITE

Culloden. A young Scots warrior, dead, stares blindly past the camera.

Lying in his cell, turned so that his shoulder avoids the floor, Brillig finds solace in his earliest memory. The Man, much younger than he had been when Brillig left him, was sitting on the back steps of his house. In the distance, just in front of the flitter pad, two gardenbots tended the flowerbeds. He watched them depositing twigs and weeds into the top of their waist-high, barrel-shaped bodies, and saw the mulched remains emerge from between their legs. Reaching down between his feet The Man grabbed a small rubber ball and threw it to where Brillig and a friend fought and played. A servitor robot, taller and thinner than the gardenbots, came out of the house and gently cleared its throat.

"Will there be anything else, sir?"

"No, take the . . . wait a minute, yes." He looked up at the robot. "Could you fetch me the book on nano-surgery please?"

"Sir?" The robot's face was impassive. Only its voice betrayed its uncertainty.

"The Singer book. Effects of N. Masipulaoria on . . . ." He got to his feet. Brillig stopped playing and watched him, hoping he was coming down the steps to join in the game. Instead The Man pushed past the servitor.

"I'll get it myself," he said, and entered the house. Brillig's friend jumped on him, and Brillig rolled over, momentarily blinded by the light hanging over him.

Pink raises the blackstick and brings it down again, but instead of the impact of carbonite on flesh there is a strangled scream. Pink pulls his hand away, letting go of the blackstick so that it flies off and lands dangerously close to the mother-machine.

"He bit me!" he shouts, clutching his wrist. Between his fingertips Brillig can see the beginnings of blood, dark and thick. "A full load. Give him a full load."

Brown pulls down on a lever and the electricity courses up through the chair and into Brillig. The light and the flames flow through him. Raped by electrons, he screams, and the scream seems to last forever.

They stood on the Hill and looked out over the highway where once their people had walked down to The City. Now it was a twisted concrete ruin, lacking all purpose and definition. Smoke rose like funeral pyres from the few buildings still burning. Many of the structures had fallen. As they watched, another slid glacier-like into the rubble.

"Dead," Brillig said.

"Yes," agreed The Man. "They've got hold of the city now. They'll chew it up and spit out the bones before they're through. At least we're still free, eh boy?"

He tried to smile, but the wetness of his eyes betrayed him.

Brillig opens burning eyes. Pink towers over him. Through ears still humming with electric agony he hears his tormentor speak.

"If you do that again you won't have time to make whatever prayers it is you creatures have."

Brown pulls the lever the final distance to its resting position. Brillig slumps. The last trickle of electricity is banished. Pink straightens.

"Now. Tell us once and for all. You know where he is. We want to be told. Tell us, or there will only be more pain."

Brillig lies in his cell, trying to ignore the pain blanketing his body. Come what may it will only last for a short while longer. In his mind, The Man sits once more on the back steps of his house, a book in his lap. A puppy lies next to him, head resting on the open pages.

"How about this then?" The Man says, and reads, "Neural activity in the frontal lobes can be traced to the direct reception of aural and oral stimuli. Thus, neural activity can, to an extent, be stimulated both by increasing the intensity of the stimuli received and improving the receptors."

He reaches down and scratches the puppy on the top of his head.

"How does that sound, boy? Fancy getting fed more sights and sounds, do you?"

The puppy wags his tail and barks.

A tank, leading a platoon of foot soldiers, rumbled along the highway towards the dying City. Explosions sounded from distant quadrants. Gouts of flame erupted from between buildings. Above them, a stick of paratroopers descended from an aircraft, dropping like rain before slowing as their HALO chutes opened mere hundreds of feet from the ground. From within the walls came the echo of fierce fighting: gunfire; shouting; and screaming. Brillig and The Man turned away and walked back towards their cottage.

"One of the other Cities. People like me, they don't understand the Canan. You're too new, too different. They're afraid of you, of the rapid progress you've made. They're scared that the Canan will replace them, and that our two races will never be able to co-exist. They want you all dead."

As they went inside Brillig took a final look over his shoulder.

"They're getting their wish."

"He going be dead."

Pink turns and backhands the knob-faced assistant in one movement, sending him lengthways onto the floor.

"Shutup! If you want to question my methods you can be the next to test them." His lackey grovels on the floor, trying to scoop up the blood that flows from his nose and push it back in.

"No questioning, no questioning. Thought it was planned plan, is all."

Pink stoops and hauls him upward by the front of his robe. He dangles from the giant's outstretched arm, nose level with his master's but his feet a good metre above the floor. Pink shakes him.

"You do not have the rank to assume anything of my plans. You are useful, not expendable. Do you understand?"

His underling nods feebly, choking. Pink opens his fist, and once more he falls to the floor in a filthy heap. Pink kicks him.

"Put him in his cell. And get out of my sight."

While the little man scurries to do his bidding Pink turns his massive head towards where Brown crouches grinning at the mother-machine.

"And you! Find me something special in those infernal wires of yours. If I can't break him next time, I'll break you instead."

Brown smiles a smile of sharp teeth. From somewhere beneath his robe a voice hisses.

"What will you do? If I'm dead, you cannot hope to operate the machines. If I'm alive, I don't think you can afford to threaten me every time your little plan goes astray, do you?" The voice dissolves into a sibilant giggle.

"Just do it." Pink storms from the room, Brown's laughter at his back.

Repeat after me: Power corrupts. Electric power corrupts electrically.

One night, a week after it had happened, he found The Man talking into a small device. When The Man went to bed he stole it and took it back into the woods. He found buttons marked 'rewind' and 'play', and learnt their functions. Holding it up to his ear, he heard The Man speak.

"The Canan progressed quickly in technological matters once they left us, but that proved their undoing as I had tried to warn them it would. They thought that to live like the Hierarchy was the only way to live, but the Hierarchy monitored their outputs and saw them as a travesty. The Canan thought all people were like me, and would love them and treasure their uniqueness. They were destroyed for this innocence. The prime subject and myself have remained hidden, or we would also have been killed. Once the Hierarchy has satisfied themself that they have removed the threat, and recall their Extermination squad, I should be able to continue the work. This time I shall be sure to modify my approaches to teaching."

Brillig sat a long time, in the dark, mulling over the words he found on the recorder. In the darkness before dawn, he began to understand.

In the garden, the man reads to the pup.

"Artificial Intelligence: the simulation of intelligent behaviour so that it is indistinguishable from that displayed by a human being."

He puts the book down and picks the pup up.

"We don't want simulations, do we, boy? We want the real thing, don't we?"

FILE VISION 005   BLACK AND WHITE

An Australian soldier, with bandages over his eyes and left arm in a splint, is helped across a Papua New Guinean stream by another soldier. In the background, two more wounded have also begun to cross.

"See?" The Man had asked, pointing out various parts of The City. "The Canan are fighting back."

"Who is winning?"

The Man took a long time to answer.

"Only you and I."

They bring him back to his cell and dump him in a corner. The nameless one, who has carried him here, turns to leave, but then changes his mind.

"Not found him yet, no no, soon will," he says softly, and not without some feeling. "Save you both pain you tell us. He remain hid not much longer. What your pain to him? Nothing. Nothing or he have come for you." He reaches out a claw and runs it across the back of Brillig's unmoving head. For all his agony Brillig manages to sketch something like a smile.

"I don't remember anything about him."

"You die then." There is pity in his voice. He leaves, and the door clangs shut behind him.

Listen: you might think it surprising that they have not thought to look outside The City's walls for their prey. But it is not so really odd, for these people have been locked away in their separate bolt-holes since the Gene Wars all those generations ago, societies curled up in fetal positions, sucking their thumbs and afraid of the dark, only venturing forth to fight or trade or when the radclouds gather and fear sends whole cities out to the old shelters for a time. To live under open skies, to surround oneself with trees and grass and the uncontrollable whims of nature, this is as unthinkable to them as poetry. Like all monsters, cleanliness and freshness offends them and fills them with fear.

"I don't understand," The Man had said/ "After all you've seen and heard, after all I've told you, you're still going? What if there are people down there?"

"Yours or mine?" he had replied, and for once there seemed no answer.

"It will be dangerous."

He remembered the voice recorder, and the words he had listened to that night.

"So is staying here," he said, "if your people think to come and look."

So he had gone down into The City, many months after the last bomb had fallen and the tanks had rumbled away. He padded through rusting jaws that were once buildings, eyes and ears opened in the hope of hearing a voice he recognised, seeing a face he once knew.

And they captured him, overlooking a pit where they had thrown many of the bodies. A military flitter lay half in and half out of a nearby building, a human body hanging head first from the shattered cockpit. A nearby water main had burst and transformed it into a surreal waterfall, water spraying high over the craft before running into the street below and down the drains. He had raised his crying eyes from his dead friends and seen it, had stopped to look at it for a moment, and they had stepped out of a building right in front of him.

"Well, well, well," the ugly giant had said, "I don't believe we've met."

Repeat after me: you don't miss what you've never had.

So they found him amongst his dead, trapped him and took him to the deep dark down-under halls and dungeons of The City where they felt most safe, and raped him with their machines and their tortures. When he would not tell, their play grew more vicious. The knives and truncheons; the deprivation of light, food and water; the constant repetition of sound; all the methods of Information Retrieval they knew so well would not break him. In the end, pain and reality and memory fused into one liquid whole and all that was left was the mother-machine and her electric love-making, and even then he still would not tell.

"Well?"

"Yes." Brown nods, and turns back to his machine. Pink stands once more above his captive.

"Where is he?" he says in a soft voice. "This is the last time. Where is he?"

Brillig says nothing, but a triumphant smile plays across his features. Pink throws up his hands.

"All right, all right. Do it."

Brown glides to a large, gleaming box newly attached to the bank of machines. Tendrils of wire emanate from the front, coiling into one thick, multi-hued cable that wraps itself round his throat and disappears into the socket at the base of his neck. He presses the button that is the box's only feature.

The room hums. Brillig and Brown arch in obscene choreography as the cable that joins them leaps into the air and becomes taut. From inside Brillig a brightness emerges as whatever arcane power the electric-suckling Brown has harnessed pours through his body. The brightness grows until Pink can no longer look in his direction for fear of being blinded. Still it grows; pulsing with a life that threatens to drain every fibre of vitality from those present. Pink hears someone screaming, "Turn it off, turn it off", and is surprised to recognise his own voice. But Brown can no longer respond. His drained, lifeless husk hangs, suspended feet above the ground, turning on lines of force that whip through the air. Pink covers his eyes and runs for the door, blinded by the light that hangs above them all.

Brillig and his friend play together on the grass, rolling and fighting in the waning sunlight. The Man sits watching, smiling. The sun begins to settle into its bed, and he calls out to them.

"Watch the sunset. Have you ever seen anything so beautiful?" and Brillig understands him, even though he is still just a pup and the surgery is many years in his future.

"I'm dreaming," he thinks, but the dream is good. The sun goes down, taking the light with it.

Rain mists the air as two men, perhaps Pink and his misshapen assistant, but looking many years older as if part of their lives have been sucked from them, emerge from a doorway. They carry a man between them. At least, it looks like one in the dim and uncertain light. They take the crushed and battered body into the street and drop it in a nearby shell crater, half-filled by rain. The body lies, partway in the water, face turned away from them as if in disgust. They look down at it. It is a long time before the smaller man speaks.

"Brave," he says.

"Shutup. He was an animal." The giant turns away and hobbles back inside.

"Maybe," the other agrees. "Beat you though. Like a dog."

AFTERWORD

It's a long story: way back in the days before computers, I read Algys Budrys' "Michaelmas" in the same week as a Writers of The Future anthology. The WOTF book had address details so you could write away and get the guidelines, and Algis was the name at the top. So I wrote a half-query, half-fan letter, in which I jokingly referred to myself as "the world's greatest unpublished 18 year old". I received the guidelines, wrapped around a copy of the 1st WOTF anthology, signed by Algis " To Lee Battersby, the world's greatest unpublished 18 year old". I had written "Brillig" for a University assignment, turned it into a film script for another Uni assignment, and had turned back into a story and sent to the competition within a week of Algis' letter. It got nowhere, but thirteen years later I found it in a drawer, rewrote it, and sold it to *EOTU* ezine, just in time to fly to LA and tell everyone at WOTF what had happened. My one regret is that Algis was too sick to attend, and to this day I've never met him. I would have liked to have told him what he'd inspired in me.

HIS CALLIOPE

It was during the winter of 1940 that I found myself mounting the stairs to the house of Michael McKee. Though we roomed at Oxford, and remained close after, my work with the Ministry had ensured an absence of well over a year. Besides, his success had me convinced that such a famous composer would no longer wish to continue a friendship with a mere clerk, no matter how secret that clerk's work might be. So when a message was left at my lodgings, saying he wished me to dinner had I the time, I made the journey to his Chelsea residence. One thing Michael was good for was a party: I didn't expect to get home before morning, and not without a devilish hangover.

The man who opened the door, however, clearly had no such intentions. Michael was a mess. His hair fell lank and unwashed around his face, framing the stubble and sour breath that spoke of long days without care. His clothes hung stained and crumpled, pressed against him where sweat and neglect had soaked through to the outside air. His gaze wandered across my face to hover some inches above my shoulder, as if too tired to maintain any pretence of interest at my arrival. Without acknowledging my gasp of shock he croaked a weary "Come in" and retreated into the hallway, leaving me to navigate the fetid air of the passageway alone. I found him in the living room, slumped into an armchair amidst a ring-fort of empty bottles and half-eaten food. I negotiated my way to a nearby chair and settled into it, taking care to avoid the detritus balanced upon its arms. I had the overwhelming impression that should I cause one item to fall I would start a general collapse, forever burying us in crockery.

I waited, uneasy in the gloom and unsure how to approach the subject of his apparent breakdown. Michael stared at the blackout curtains, looking past them at a sight I had no hope of sharing. After his first words he had paid me no attention. Just as I was wondering whether I should make some noise, or better yet, get up and check to see if the motionless form before me still bore life, he spoke.

"She's gone."

"Who's gone, Michael?"

"I went up to her room. She hadn't touched her food. She'd gone."

"Gone where?"

I studied him with worry. Michael had never been the type for a single woman. Now it seemed as if he had found one to love, and her departure had sent him into a depression unheard of by those of us with a more monogamous temperament.

"I went up this morning," he repeated. "She was *gone*."

The inflection he put on the word made me frown. Was he trying to suggest something greater than just a departure, something he couldn't say outright?

"Michael, what do you mean?"

For the first time since my entrance he turned to look at me. He stared at me for several seconds, and even through the gloom I could feel the light lurking behind his dulled and strangled eyes.

"Gone."

There didn't seem much to say after that. We lapsed into silence, and let the room darken into night around us. I was considering making my exit, in order to prepare for the morning's work, when he spoke again, as if we'd merely paused instead of sitting mute for over half an hour.

"I did everything right. I read all the books, studied the spells and incantations. I bound her with cold iron. I fed her only honey and ambrosia, and water from a stream."

"You . . . *bound* her?"

"It was fine for a while. She blessed me with inspiration. But then she stopped talking, and then she stopped moving, and then . . ." He laid his head upon one hand. "I went up and she was gone." He choked, and I realised he was crying. "I haven't written a note in six months."

"You bound her, Michael? You tied someone up?" I had leaned forward in my chair. Now I rose to my feet. "Who was it, Michael? Where did she go?"

"The guest bedroom," he gestured toward the stairwell. "I captured her correctly. She was mine by right."

I ran for the stairs, his voice following me in childish insistence. "I followed the lore, Edward. She was mine. Calliope, Edward. She was mine. I had the right."

I took the steps three at a time, ran along the hall, and hit the door to the guest bedroom without pausing to make sure it was unlocked. All I achieved was to disturb the host of flies within the room. Whoever the girl on the bed had been, she was nothing more than decay and stench now. What little remained writhed with insect life, maggots providing food for things that scuttled and crawled over the architecture of her bones.

My urge to vomit sent me staggering outside, banging the door shut behind me and grasping for the hall banister as I fell. I spent long minutes retching, trying to clear my senses of the sight and smell I had just witnessed. When at last I was able to drag myself down the stairs and into the living room, I found Michael still staring at the curtains.

"How long?" I managed to croak. "How long has she been like that?"

"Six months since I've written a note," he replied. "I'm finished, Edward."

"Finished? Michael, you're a murderer! They'll hang you for this! Who the hell *is* she, anyway?"

"I told you. Calliope. She's my Muse."

"Oh God. Oh God." I backed away from him. "Look, don't move, don't . . . " I looked around at the pigsty surrounding us. "For God's sake, don't touch anything. I've got to . . . I've got to think about this."

I left him then, and stumbled gagging and weeping, into the street. Michael was mad, of that there was no doubt. And the girl . . . I had been away too long. I couldn't connect her with anything I'd read or heard. What had happened seemed obvious: Michael had seen her somewhere, perhaps a party, and in his madness had abducted her and kept her chained in his house until she'd starved, or he'd killed her in a fit of lunacy or . . . or what else I didn't wish to believe.

Now I was involved. I *knew*. I lurched toward my lodgings, building scenarios in my mind, groping for the right course of action. I should call the police, that was the right thing to do, call the police and have them arrest Michael. Arrest my friend, the foremost composer of the day; the man Churchill called "the voice that gives song to our hopes and prayers."

And the girl, what of her? Had she suffered? Did her parents suffer even now, wondering at her fate? Or did they grieve as so many wartime families grieved, at the loss of a loved one amidst the nightly bombings, and the bodies that would never be found in a city more rubble than structure? I wandered for hours, past homes living on despite the destruction that threatened them each day. Everywhere I looked, London survived in the face of loss, grim dignity coloured by flashes of joy which did nothing to ease my torment. It was long past 3:00 a.m. when I reached my bed, and fell down upon it an exhausted and heart-broken man.

And God help me: as I fell asleep I made my decision.

The next day, I found myself in Michael's front hallway by noon. He still sat in his chair, heavy eyes fixed upon the closed blackout curtain. The same clothes as yesterday hung on his frame. It was obvious he had not stirred since I left him. He didn't acknowledge my entrance, not even when I took the burlap bags I had brought with me and filled them with the stinking remains of the creature from the bedroom. One by one, I left them in the coal cellar, returning with bleach and scrubbing brush once the task was completed. By evening, I was dizzy from fumes and hard labour, sick to my core at the work I had set myself, and the sensations of guilt and revulsion they stirred within me. Michael made no move, neither to assist nor prevent me. Now as I stood before him in the murky living room, skin red and stinging from disinfectant, tears streaming down my face from all manner of things, he raised his dull and lifeless face to me.

"I had the right," he said calmly, as if our conversation had not suffered a lapse of nearly twenty four hours.

I snapped. Throwing down my bucket of dirty water, I lunged across the room and planted my hands around his throat. The force of my dive broke the chair beneath us, sending us tumbling to the floor. I didn't notice. I pummelled his face and neck with my fists, months of combat experience forgotten as I bludgeoned him again and again, my voice an inarticulate scream. He lay still, neither fighting back nor attempting to avoid the beating he was receiving. He merely absorbed my fury, until he lay a bloodied mess of skin and bruises and I collapsed half on and half off him, my breathing no more than a series of ragged sobs that fractured the evening air. Eventually, I forced myself to stand and grabbed his unresisting body by the shoulders.

"Get up."

Somehow he found his feet. I half-pushed, half-pulled him down the hallway to the coal cellar. I opened the door and drew out two of the heavy bags, thrusting them at him without a word. He took them, and I removed the other three before forcing him toward the back door and the yard beyond.

"Move."

London was battening down for the night, huddling together in the dark to wait for the inevitable bombs. The air around us reeked of fear. During sunlight hours people lived each day as if it were their last. When night fell, they succumbed to the fear that it might have been. We shuffled unheeded through the darkened avenues, making for a nearby area where the bombs had wrought three square streets of destruction. It soon loomed out at us: a wasteland, where the only things moving against the barrows of rubble were rats, dogs, and ghosts. I shoved Michael between the piles of concrete and twisted metal, uncaring as to whether he went over or into each obstacle. Within minutes, we came to a small clearing, barely big enough for us both to stand. Several beams, and lumps of masonry, had landed in such a way as to form a small tunnel. I shined my torch into it, watching as light fell toward the hidden earth.

"Down there," I said. "Start digging." I grabbed his shoulder and pushed him toward the opening. He looked back at me from its mouth.

"I don't have a spade."

"Use your hands, you bastard." I gave him a final thrust. He toppled over the nearby outcropping and into the hole. He sorted his limbs out spastically, gave me a look bordering on surprise, and slid head first into the pit.

It took a little over five hours. I spurred Michael on as much as I could, without giving vent to noise that would bring wardens running from all directions. As it was I stopped at every little sound from the street, returning to my threats once I had identified it as animal, creaking building, or ambulance. Only when the sirens began their inescapable wailing did I call on him to dig regardless of the racket we made, scooping great handfuls of dirt and flinging them back out of the tunnel until we had a hole deep enough to bury the five lumps of horror under tons of brickwork and a few empty feet of earth. When we returned to the front room of Michael's house we were dirty, exhausted, and numbed by our efforts. Michael stood in the doorway and looked around.

"My chair's broken," he said, with such a note of despair to his voice that I could not help but laugh. I laughed until I gave way to hysteria, and I sank down onto my haunches, wrapping my hands around my head to hide myself away from my poor, mad friend and his unknowing evil.

Then I felt his hand on my shoulder, and he spoke, his voice calm and quiet.

"It's all right, Edward. I can get another one."

Whether he referred to his chair or the other of our evening's tasks I was too afraid to ask.

AFTERWORD

An attempt to write a non-genre piece, just for something different to do, and it still turned into one (if you squint and turn your head). Maybe it's my English background, but I seem to write an awful lot of stories about the two World Wars (I also write a lot of stories about Hollywood monsters. Hmmm. Now there's a thought.) A story with a deliberate non-ending: it's a personal philosophy that each time I sit down to write a new story, I twist it in as different a direction from the last as possible. This followed "Mikal" in my writing order, so it was plotted out, researched, had that open ending, and was 'built' rather than the result of unleashing my subconscious.

FATHER RENOIR'S HANDS

Father Renoir has the largest hands in the village. There are only three hundred or so souls in Santa Rosaria. Many of them are women and children. Even so, the burly priest's hands would be the object of discussion in the larger towns inhabiting the more fertile lands north and south. Father Renoir has spent time in these towns. He does not talk about them, preferring instead to discuss the salvation of the flock he has chosen as his own.

He lives by his hands. He has used them to great effect in the three years he has resided in Santa Rosaria: gripping poles that youths take turns to hammer into the ground; spreading them wide and splaying artillery shell-shaped fingers to illustrate some high point of his weekly homily; wrapping them around a boule and propelling it with force toward a shy cochonnet.

Right now, those meaty, massive, hands are clenched round the throat of Maria Trote, and the little slut is paying the price for leading his thoughts into peril.

Maria's hands are tiny and soft. They scrabble against his fingers. Her lips spasm, forming screams of terror she has no breath to fuel. Renoir hunches his beast-like shoulders and tenses. Stress runs in ripples along his arm. His fingers whiten, and burrow further into the velvet skin of the young girl's neck. There is a sharp crack. Maria stops fighting. Her head lolls forward, moisture dripping from her open mouth onto his flesh. Her body hangs broken in the air below his grip.

The priest stares at her for long moments, then shakes his head as if dispelling the last traces of some befuddling fog. He lowers her to the ground, and spends several minutes gathering the shreds of her pretty Sunday dress from the surrounding grass. He drapes them over her still form, then lifts her in his big, strong arms. He gives her one last kiss, filled with all the passion he has ever held for her, then drops her six-year-old body over the cliff and into the protesting sea below. As the body strikes the water he is already turning away from the edge and striding back toward the town.

He is washing his trousers in the big iron tub at the back of the church when a delegation of visitors rounds the corner of the building. He removes his hands from the soapy water and wipes them across the front of his shirt. The men are upon him before he can dry them completely.

"Father, you must help."

"What is it?" He rests his wet arms on the speaker's shoulders. Gabriel Trote is a small man, stooped and balding. The eyes he raises toward the priest have been dulled by years of subsistence survival. It is a look that Father Renoir has yet to grow used to. "What's the matter?"

"Little Maria . . ."

"Yes?" He tightens his grip, wills himself to relax.

"She did not return to the house after . . . playing in the street. We've looked everywhere."

Father Renoir frowns. "What about the beach?"

"Everywhere." Trote shakes his head. "She is nowhere. Please, Father . . ."

"Come inside. We will organise a proper search." He turns, and one arm around the shoulders of Maria's father, leads them into the warm confines of the Church.

It takes several hours to scour the town. No rock remains unmoved, no floorboard unlifted. At the centre of it all stands Renoir, hands in constant motion: pointing villagers towards new areas to investigate, clapping men on the back in encouragement of their efforts, directing the people around him like a puppeteer commanding his toys. Maria Trote is a popular child, pretty, joyful, a friend to all. No effort is spared. Dusk is falling when the exhausted Santa Rosarians gather at the open end of the town.

"Nowhere?"

The crowd murmurs unhappily. The priest hangs his head, hiding his reaction.

"Then there is nothing to do but pray for her safe return."

"Wait!" Gabriel Trote pushes to the front of the crowd. He looks up at the bigger man, his gnarled farmer's hands spread wide in supplication. "What about the cliffs? The forest?"

"It is getting dark. It is too dangerous."

"All the more reason! My daughter . . . out there alone . . . " He waves an arm at the darkening world beyond the clearing. The villagers rumble agreement. Father Renoir scans their faces, then tilts his head toward the forest.

"Very well," he says at last, "But not the cliffs. I don't want anyone to fall, and in this light . . . I don't want anyone else . . . " He does not finish the thought. The villagers' faces tell him he does not need to. Gabriel closes his eyes in pain, and nods once.

"The forest, then," he says, his voice thick with sorrow. "We may still be fortunate."

"God allows fortune to those who love him," the priest replies, a relieved smile creasing the corners of his eyes.

A party of a dozen men is assembled and fitted out with lanterns and warm clothing. Father Renoir leads the way to the forest edge, a lamp held like a toy between thick fingers. Once there, he pairs the men off and sends them in different directions, until only he and the shivering Gabriel Trote are left.

"Are you ready?"

"Yes." The smaller man draws his jacket closer around his wiry shoulders.

"Are you cold?"

"No, no, I . . . " Gabriel looks at the ground. "It is not the cold. I am afraid. Maria, she . . . she's dead, isn't she Father?"

The priest steps back, and hides his reaction from the light.

"I don't know, Gabriel. You should hope God's will is not set on it."

Trote looks as if he wishes to say something more. Instead, he turns his head toward the forest and draws his arms in tight to his body. Renoir pulls back a low-hanging branch. The two men step through, into the embrace of the trees.

The forest is an old place, twisted and tangled upon itself. Renoir and Trote struggle forward by inches, cut off from all thought of their fellow searchers within seconds. It takes them fifteen minutes to push through as many metres. They strain through the heavy branches, Gabriel Trote's breath growing more laboured with each step. Eventually he falls to his knees, and buries his face into his hands.

"Maria," he moans. "Oh, my little darling. Forgive me. Forgive me, Maria."

Renoir stops and slumps against a tree, wiping his forehead with one hand and pointing the lantern at his companion with the other. He frowns.

"Gabriel?"

"Oh, Father. Forgive me, Father. Maria, she . . . she . . . oh God . . ."

"What is it, man? What are you saying?"

"Maria." Trote raises his grief-ravaged face toward the priest. "She was dressed up, so pretty. So pretty, in her Sunday dress" he holds out his hands toward Renoir. "I just . . . she was meant to wear it to Church, but she wanted to show you. I shouted at her to get changed. I was so angry . . ."

Renoir stares in shock, feeling his knees buckle. He reaches out to the tree and steadies himself.

"So pretty . . . She said . . ."

"Where could she have gone, Father? She ran into the street. Where?" Trote looks at the priest as if seeing him for the first time. "You live at the end of our street, Father. She wanted you to see her dress."

"I . . . I saw her . . ."

"All this time, waiting for you to say something. And you've said nothing. Why is that? What did she say, Father? What did she tell you?"

Renoir falls back from the volley of questions, the lantern falling to his side.

"Gabriel, I . . . "

"She did come to you, didn't she?" Trote rises to his feet, hands forming into claws. "You saw her. You talked to her. What did she say, Father?"

"Nothing. She said nothing!"

"What?"

"The whole time, not a word." Renoir looks down at the farmer, his hands clenching involuntarily. "I tried not to. But she wouldn't say anything . . . just lay there . . . lay there, looking at me . . . "

Trote talks a step forward, then another "Lay there? She just lay there?"

"I tried. I tried not to . . . "

"You tried not to what? You tried not to *what*?" Gabriel throws himself at the priest's tortured eyes, screaming, "What have you done with my daughter?"

Renoir's reaction is automatic. His arm swings up, the heavy lantern at its end striking the side of Trote's head with a dull crack. The villager rears away. His eyes roll for an instant. Then he totters backwards and falls, his outspread arms dragging twigs from the bushes underneath him. The lantern sputters, most of its liquid spilling out and searing a path down the priest's leg. He stares at the fallen man in horror,

"Gabriel? It was an accident, I swear. Gabriel?"

Trote moans and rolls over, dragging himself onto his elbows.

"What did you do with her?" he asks, and something in his voice sounds viscous and wrong. "Where did she go?"

Renoir tries to answer. Before he can speak, laughter flows into the clearing from the dense shadows between two ancient trees.

"Silly Papa," says a voice both men recognise. "Here I am."

"Maria?" Trote rises, swaying wildly. "Maria!"

"No!" The priest lunges forward, reaching out one giant hand. But the younger man is already moving away from him.

"Maria?"

"Here I am, Papa. Here I am." The voice is full of joy, teasing, tickling. "Come on, Papa. Here I am."

Renoir drops to the damp forest floor. The lantern drops from his numb fingers. It rolls away, throwing crazy shadows around the clearing. Trote reaches the gap in the vegetation and pushes through, crying "Maria?" in his misshapen voice. The darkness swallows him, leaving the priest alone in the mottled light. The world pauses. A scream erupts from the shadows, madness choked off before reaching its crescendo, plunging the world back into silence.

"Poor Papa," says the naked girl who walks into the clearing from the direction of the scream. "I don't think he liked what he found."

"Maria?"

"You're certain?" the child looks down at herself and shrugs.

"How . . . He was your father. He didn't deserve . . . "

"Deserve? That's an odd word." She smiles, and Renoir fancies he can see red between her teeth. She steps closer, her soft, unbruised skin tattooed with tribal patterns by the light of the lantern. "We've been talking, your little girls and I."

"But . . . how . . . you . . . "

"There have been a lot of them, haven't there?" She stands with one hand on her hip, and begins counting names off on her fingers, turning so that Renoir sees the soft curve of her buttock. "Eloise, Michelle, that one in Toulon, barely out of her nappies . . . " As she counts, shapes form against the backdrop of shadows. Perhaps they resemble children, or forest creatures.

"No. Shut up. Be quiet." Renoir steps forward and raises a massive fist above his head. Maria laughs, and skips out of his reach.

"Even when you ran from France, you couldn't stop yourself, could you? Moving from town to town, each refuge smaller and more primitive, less and less of the world to tempt you . . . " she runs fingers across her nipples and strokes imaginary breasts, " . . . always so tempted."

"Shut up. You . . . you whore." Renoir's breath is heavy and sour. "You demon."

"Demon?" she laughs. "Demon indeed."

"Yes." Renoir draws himself up to his full height, ignoring how insignifcant he feels against the massive trees. "You *are* a demon. You cannot be . . . cannot be that sweet child whose skin you wear."

The beast barks, her head thrown back, her tiny groin thrust forward as if on display.

"Sweet? Sweet? That little slut? That little *animal*?" Quick as liquid she jumps under his grasp and rubs herself against his leg, then leaps back again. "They are like animals, are they not, children?"

She squats, spreading her thighs so her hairless labia squints at him. She begins to pee, the yellow stream splashing over her tiny hand. "Animals, every one." She flicks a spray of liquid at Renoir's face. He tastes the salt taste of her, and moans.

"Our Father, who art in Heaven . . . " He falls to his knees, raises hands in a private stance of prayer he has not used since childhood, " . . . hallowed be thy name . . . "

A twig bounces from his head, then something he hopes is a wet clod of mud. Laughter multiplies around him, new voices joining the Maria-Creature. Renoir bows further, refusing to let their image play against his imagination. "Thy Kingdom come, thy will be done . . . "

"You're praying to the wrong God, Father," she whispers into his ear. Moist lips and tongue caress the skin. "We come from older stock than that."

Renoir opens his eyes. Before him stand a dozen children or more: all naked, all lost beneath his flesh and his weakness over the course of many years.

"Eloise," he whispers, "Michelle, Jeanette . . . "

They giggle and wave as he names them, touch themselves with obscene fingers and too much knowledge.

"Poor Father," they sing in unison. "Poor, poor Father."

They slide over the uneven ground, skin alive and glowing with sweat in the lamplight. Renoir covers his face with massive hands, shielding his view from the approaching monsters, but it does no good. He cannot help himself. He has to peek through his fingers, has to watch their skin getting closer. The Maria-Creature picks up the lantern and opens its door. She smiles at him, and purses her lips in a mocking kiss. The girls gather round the fallen priest, crooning, and rubbing against him. Tiny hands begin to play with the fastenings of Renoir's clothes.

"What are you?" he sobs.

"Hungry," Maria says, and blows out the light.

AFTERWORD

Remember that nanna's writing group I mentioned earlier? Can you believe I read this to them one week? One lady quit in protest, and there were some long discussions held over my personal concept of right and wrong. Strangely, nobody seemed overtly concerned about the 'handful of wee' scene, and that's the point at which most seasoned readers of horror have their 'ick' moment when they read this piece. As to the writing, there was no real secret: I was just in the mood to be nasty, and address some of the issues that make my soul cringe.

THROUGH SOFT AIR

The first night, all he hears are screams.

What wakes him the next night, he can't say. One moment he lies in dreamless sleep, the next his eyes are open and trying to find focus in the darkness. For long moments he lies still, not daring to breath, searching for whatever it is that has brought him to this alertness. Nothing breaks the blackness. No movement or noise betrays the presence of the unfamiliar.

He sinks back toward oblivion. As his eyes close, he hears the sound that had registered itself upon his subconscious. He sits upright. His voice reaches out into the dark

"Who . . . who's there? What do you want?"

There is no answer.

Now he recognises the noise. The turning of pages. Someone is here, in his room, flipping through the pages of a book. The noise stops. A voice speaks from the air at the end of the bed, as if reciting words long held dear. A poem, written a lifetime ago by a young man not quite recovered from the horrors of the war that had engulfed him. He hears the book close.

"That's a nice one, Jeffy. Lets you know what it really feels like. Almost, anyway. It makes me wonder how you know. After all, you weren't with us at the end, were you Jeffy? Where exactly were you?"

Frozen muscles thaw. In a paroxysm of fear he lurches to one side, throws a hand out to the bedside light. Palsied fingers struggle with the switch. A burst of brightness and the lamp is on. Eyes gape towards the source of the voice.

The room is empty. A book lies open on the reading chair by the closed window. He doesn't have to see its cover to know that it is his first, the one published shortly after his return from the War.

It is only then that he recognizes the voice.

"But . . . that's impossible."

The old man sits in his bed, eyes glued to the book, until dawn creeps through the gaps in the curtain.

Too soon, the sounds of a bustling kitchen drive him out of his room and down the stairs to where the rest of the family has made his home their domain. He finds them gathered, dressed and in top gear already, racing through a day that has barely begun.

"Morning, Dad!" Elsie cries from the pantry, her thick waist and legs all that are visible as she rearranges his tins for her convenience.

"Afternoon, old timer," bellows her oaf of a husband from over a plate of bacon and eggs (*My* bacon and eggs, he thinks sulkily). His cheeriness grates against the old man's bones. "Decided to join us, eh?"

The oaf laughs that wheezing cough of his. Minute particles of food escape his maw and rain down on the plate.

"Where's Alec?" The old man speaks to his daughter's rump.

"Oh, out somewhere as usual."

The rest of her appears from the confines of the cupboard, plump arms full of cans that she dumps onto the wooden countertop. "You know what teenagers are like. Can't sit still for a moment if there's a corner they can mooch off into instead." She laughs a pale laugh.

"I don't know at all what teenagers are like these days," he wants to retort. "In my day teenagers lied about their age so they could fight a war." But he says nothing. He knows from long experience that such things are dismissed as the mutterings of a fool. These two are insensible to his memories. The only one who cares a whit is 'mooching in a corner somewhere'. He settles instead for a muttered "Hmmph" and shuffles towards the kitchen door.

"You don't want to go out there this morning, Dad. You'll catch your death."

"Let him go, love." The oaf gives a thickly-lidded wink. "He's tough as teak, aren't you, Geoff? Little cold won't bother you."

The old man ignores them. He spends the morning roaming the grounds, searching for his grandson, poetry book in hand. But it seems Elsie is correct. Whatever corner Alec is mooching in, he cannot find it.

Nothing has happened for a week. He's almost dismissed the events of that night as the product of too much imagination and coffee. Stop the caffeine, that's the trick. For the last few nights he's cut out that final cuppa before bedtime. Seems to have worked too, no more bad dreams altering the shape of the dark around him. Until tonight. Until moments ago, when he was woken by a whispered sound and saw the dead men standing at the end of his bed.

For an eternity he cannot move. Before he can find his voice, a hand is jammed over his mouth, stifling his shout of alarm. His struggles fail against the strength of men who appear to be in their twenties. Two of them press him back against the pillow, the skin of their hands cold against his face. It is only as they come into the circle of light cast by the lamp that he sees their features. Any fight within him dies.

"Yes, Jeffy. It's us."

The voice comes from nowhere and everywhere at once. Certainly not from the mouths of the dead men. The corpse (It must be a corpse; no living thing ever looked this way) at the end of the bed holds up a framed photograph in its three-fingered hand. He sees a picture filled with young men, their battle dress not yet crusted with French mud, their smiles not yet blasted away by the reality of the adventure they thought they were embarking upon. The voice speaks again.

"Have you ever asked yourself, Jeffy, what happened to us? Did you just assume we were dead and laid to rest, and you could live your life without fearing our memory? Look at us!"

He does. He really *looks*. He sees the missing digits, the open wounds that pepper their bodies like footprints across sand, knows why the flesh that holds him down is so cold and dry.

"Do we look like we've been resting?"

The dead men (He won't remember their names, he won't!) see the recognition in his eyes and let him go. He scrambles into a sitting position. Lips struggle to form a coherent question. The answer comes unbidden.

"We've been in Hell, Jeffy. While you've been living your fortunate life, we've been going over the top again, and again, and again. Each time remembering the pain. Each time being brought back to do it once more." One of the dead men approaches and reaches out to touch him. He flinches away as if stung.

"We've been in Hell sixty years, Jeffy. We went to war. We killed and were killed, and we're being punished for it. You're going there soon, but not to where we are. And we wanted you to see where you've left us, old friend!"

The dry cold hand touches him. The world fades away, and he rides a dead man's memories.

I've been at the front for three days. I've barely had the time to grind the teeth from my bayonet. Prisoners captured with a saw bayonet are shot, the corporal tells me. I'm not well read. The one book we had in the house was a Bible. I know the shape and nature of Hell. I've arrived here, well and truly. Six weeks ago I was a farmboy on a Hunter Valley selection, a summer of clearing ahead of me. Now all is mud and noise and rats that feast on the dead lying just beyond the barbed wire. Seventeen years old, the reasons I lied about my age burned away by the fear that overwhelms me with every breath. My spit has turned to bile. I'm never going to see my Mum again. I want so much to see her now: to hear her tell me that it's going to be all right; to lay my head against her clean, starched breast and cry.

I don't know how I get across No Man's Land. When the Captain's whistle blows, thoughts cease. All I know is the weight of the rifle held across my heart, and the dead feeling in my legs as they drive me forward, blocks of wood I pray will carry me somewhere safe, to that hole in the ground ahead where the worst thing to face will be other men I can kill, not this haze of smoke and fire and deadly unseen monsters that chatter and snap a thought-shattering 'crack' as they fly past me and make the chests and faces of my friends boil up and explode.

I reach the barbed wire. I see others caught upon it, bullets jerking them into unnatural dances. I alone, in my field of vision, squirm my way through and under, and drop into the slit trench in front of me.

Rifles are no good for trench fighting. Too long to move around in the enclosed space, too easy to grab and pull away from their owner, impossible to aim and fire. In a corridor less than three feet wide, any weapon you hold becomes a club, a pike to be swung with reckless abandon at the shocked faces of the men (Boys, my subconscious seems to register in-between frenzied blows) who surround me. I swing with desperate panic. I am alone in a tunnel of grasping hands, hate-filled faces, knives and fists, all with a single aim: murder me, end my life, trample my face into the mud that roils and sucks around my ankles.

How many do I kill? Any at all? I don't know. Time loses all meaning in the overwhelming urge to hit and hit again, to clear a little circle of safety where I can hold on and pray for someone to arrive and save me.

It can't last. Sheer weight of numbers was always going to overcome me. I feel in my bones, rather than as real pain, the 'thunk' of impact as something heavy crashes into the back of my head. I keel forward, the impact spinning me around. I see the trench club, a mess of barbed wire and rags wrapped around the handle of an entrenching shovel, as it is pulled away. Blood and flesh (My blood! My flesh!) sticks to its barbs. My legs lose their strength. My whole body goes numb. Two Hun grab me and hold me hard against the wall of the trench. I begin to sag, the full weight of shock and pain from my head washing over me. They use a shovel! Oh God! They hold me there, weak and crying, vomit rising in my throat, my eyes wide with shock and pain and fear.

A boy, oh a boy, no more than sixteen years old, his face distorted with hatred. He raises it above his head. I see the light glinting red from its sharpened edge. I scream "Dad!" before the shovel comes down. White agony slashes across the bridge of my nose for a millisecond...

He wakes with the pain still in him. The three dead men stand at the foot of the bed. Before he can focus enough to speak, he hears the voice again.

"This is how far you are from Hell."

The air behind the soldiers softens and flows, emptying to reveal a gap through which he can see and smell the inside of a trench. A whistle sounds above the thunder of artillery fire. The three corpses step through the gap and take up position at the foot of a ramshackle ladder leaning against the trench wall. The artillery stops. The whistle sounds once more. As the air closes behind them, the dead men begin to climb.

"That trunk there. No, under there. That one."

Alec lifts, and pulls, dragging an old trunk into the space in the middle of the attic floor. He runs his hand over the cracked wood and tarnished metal clasps.

"It looks ancient. What is it?"

"Oh, just some stuff," his grandfather smiles. He reaches into a dressing gown pocket and draws out a key. "I don't suppose you'd care to open it?"

The teenager smiles back. "You know I love this stuff." He takes the key from the old man and sets about the lock.

"I know, I know." Geoffrey sits back, happy at the sight of Alec's eagerness. He tries to ignore the dread at what the contents of the trunk will signify to him. Alec gives a small cry of triumph and lifts the lid, staring at the bundle of cloth revealed within.

"Pull it out then. Careful . . . careful." The khaki armful is drawn out until it lies in the dust. For a moment they stare at it, one in wonder, one in something resembling sorrow. With fumbling hands they unroll the cloth, revealing its treasure.

"It's . . . oh, wow!" The young man's voice is barely a whisper.

"My kit. Yes." Geoffrey looks down at the array of items before him, some innocuous, some deadly, all invested with the heavy weight of memory.

"What is all this stuff? Is that . . . ?"

"Yes, that's a rifle." He picks it up. "Short magazine Lee Enfield point three oh three calibre."

"This was your rifle?"

"You don't get them as going away presents, you know." He smiles wryly. Unconsciously his hands caress the burnished wood and metal, picking and pulling, beginning the ritual of dismantling and cleaning. "Hand me that cloth will you? No, this one I got later, after I left the hospital."

"The hospital?"

"I've never told you? I thought you'd have read it somewhere. Your mother should have said something. The war had finished by the time I was discharged, and they demobbed me pretty quickly after the first book came out. Not much of this stuff was mine to begin with. My mate was a Stores Sergeant. With thousands of things going through on a daily basis, he figured a few bits and pieces wouldn't be noticed, and well . . . " he smiles to himself.

Alec looks at the remainder of the assembled items.

"So what was yours?"

"Let's see. It's been so long since I've looked at any of this . . . the mess kit, the bayonet. Smuggled that out myself. That wooden stick, that's the handle of an entrenching tool. Don't think the head is in here at all. They came separately, you see. Oh, and this." He picks out a small, creased and crumpled book.

"What is it?"

"My paybook. Got all my service details, what I'd been paid and so on. If I'd been . . . well, killed, they would have used it to . . . identify me."

"Really? Can I have a look?"

The old man hands the book to his grandson. He gazes at it for long seconds as the boy turns it over in his hands, then swallows and looks down once more.

"Here's something a bit more interesting. You'll like this. My tunic. It's still got its badges. They gave me this as a bit of a gift."

For happy minutes they pore over the garment, discussing good conduct stripes and metal wound stripes (he had three, and happily told their stories), insignia and service chevrons. Finally they lapse into silence. The old man bends back to reassemble his rifle while Alec opens the front cover of the nearly-forgotten paybook.

"Grandad?"

"Yes?"

"Are you sure this is yours?"

"Of course. It's the one thing you never let out of your sight, even in hospital. Why?"

"There's someone else's name in it."

"What? Who?" Alec hands the book to him, opened at the offending page. He sees the name scrawled there, and feels his face blanch.

"What is it, grandad?" the young man asks, concern colouring his voice.

"This . . . name. It . . . one of the last . . . one of my unit. In France. I saw him last . . . "

"What happened to him? How did you get his paybook?"

"I don't . . . " He makes a conscious effort to gather his thoughts. "They died. All of them. On the Somme. When I was . . . injured. I didn't see him before the battle, didn't speak to him. He never gave me . . . listen, do you mind? I'm tired all of a sudden. Can we pack this up and take it down to my room? We'll look at it again later if you like, but I need a rest."

"Sure, grandad. Of course." In silence they re-pack the trunk and carry it from the attic, the old man grasping the paybook in one white-knuckled hand.

The night is so cold it covers the windows in a thin shell of frost, but he doesn't feel it. He sits in bed, blankets gathered about his waist; eyes focused upon the air a couple of feet beyond the bed. The strain of his effort is building a headache across his brow. The house is quiet. The absence of family noise reveals the cracks and grumbles of old wood at peace. The clock ticks mournfully, turning over the minutes towards 3:00 a.m. He cannot sleep in this room tonight, but neither can he move somewhere else and miss his unearthly visitors. So he sits, alert in spite of the hour, every nerve anticipating what is coming.

It does, soon enough. The air ripples and flows until before him stand a group of soldiers, the reek of their mud-spattered bodies filling the air. He drinks in their presence, eyes taking in the gaping, white-edged wounds where bullets have ploughed a path through bloodless flesh, the glint of shattered bone, the wracked and ruined visages that gaze upon him. They do not move or seem to speak yet he is assailed with voices, pummelled by questions that leave him no space for answer.

"Where were you, Jeffy? Why aren't you with us? How did you escape it? You belong with us. Why are you still alive, Jeffy? We're all dead. Why didn't you die with us? You should have died too, Jeffy."

All at once, as if following some signal, the voices cease. One of the soldiers moves towards him, measured tread approaching along the side of the bed. The dead man leans forward until they face each other nose to rotting nose. Every fibre in his body screams at him to scuttle away, run for the door, make his escape. His muscles refuse to answer the call to flight. He stares, lips refusing to name the man before him. Sixty years ago he knew him, knew all those gathered in the room. And while he has aged, the visage that commands his view is the same one that lives in his memory, the same youthful face that stares out from the photograph on his dresser.

Only now that face is ruined. It is missing an ear. A red furrow crosses the top of the head, bisecting hair and flesh and exposing the skull. Half the lower jaw is lost. Most terrible of all, however, is the life that shines from behind the single remaining eye, the judgement he finds there as he stares at the corpse that was his friend. They remain, eyes locked. He is stripped to the core by the dead man's gaze. His life is laid bare, his measure taken and found wanting. When the voice comes, it is soft and gentle.

"You were scared. You never thought it would be so loud, so thunderous. You just couldn't go over. It would kill you. The bullets would find you and cut you up. It would hurt so much and you'd be dead. You didn't want to die."

A sob escapes the old man's throat.

"You crouched in the trench, hid your head, hoping nobody would notice in the confusion. You splashed mud in your face and punched yourself in the ears until they were swollen and bleeding. When the medics came around they thought you'd been a near hit."

The tears stream down his cheeks. The memories he'd tried to lock away for seven decades are brought back to the surface, tender and bleeding, exposed to the cold air by that beautiful, deadly voice.

"You've never told anyone. Not during all the months in the hospital. Not after your poems were published and you were discharged. Not in the years since, with the books and awards piling up. It's all been hollow. You've carried the cowardice and shame, afraid to tell anyone in case they couldn't see that you were just a young, frightened boy thrust into something you had no hope of coping with. You've been afraid of them, the ones who applaud you. Afraid of the contempt and the hatred if they knew."

The dam is breached. He wails. The tears won't stop. He doesn't want them to stop.

"Yes, oh God, yes, all these years, I've missed you all so much. I was so young, so terribly, terribly frightened. I didn't want to . . . I didn't . . . oh I've missed you . . . "

"We've missed you too, Jeffy. Every time we've gone over. Every time we've been torn apart, and put back together, to go through it all again, we've asked ourselves where Jeffy is, and how we can let him know what he's missing." The corpse leans further forward. Only the merest whisper of air separates them. "The Devil grants wishes."

He tilts his head upwards, revealing the gaping hole in his throat. Geoffrey feels the kiss against his forehead, lips mingled with the jellied stickiness of open flesh pressed against his brow. He knows without doubt that this kiss is not curse, but absolution. He begins to scream. By the time his family burst in from their nests on the ground floor he has no voice left, and the room is empty.

The doctor shines a light in his eyes, taps his cheekbones, takes his temperature, prods and pokes him and asks him pointless questions. Finally, he shakes his head, replaces instruments in his bag, and smiles down at his patient.

"There's nothing physically wrong with you, so far as I can tell. You're quite healthy for a man of your age. In fact, if it wouldn't be unprofessional, I'd be jealous."

" I said you were wasting your time."

"Then what's the problem?"

"Hmmph. You're the physician. You've just said I'm fine."

"Yes, I have." The doctor sits on the edge of the bed. "But I've known Elsie all her life. She wouldn't drag me out here if she wasn't genuinely worried about you."

"It's nothing. I've had trouble sleeping, that's all."

"Maybe. I can give you something for that. But *I've* never had insomnia so bad I woke my whole family screaming. I've been your doctor for forty years and your friend a lot longer than that, Geoff. Something's wrong. What is it?"

"It's . . . David, do you remember when we first met?"

"During the war, yeah. Long time ago"

"Do you remember the hospital?"

"Sure."

"What do you remember?"

"Clean sheets. Cleaner nurses."

"No, no, I mean, do you remember *why* we were there?"

"I was injured in hand to hand combat with a Belgian whore, as I recall. Still can't stand the smell of gentian violet." David laughs at the memory. "You though, you'd been blown up, hadn't you? Couldn't hear a thing for a few days, bit of shellshock, that kind of thing, yes?"

"Yes. That was it."

"What then?"

"I . . . I just . . . I lost them, David."

"Lost them? Lost what?"

"All of them." He waves a hand towards the middle of the room. "They all went over, and I should have . . . but I just . . . I lost them."

"Geoff, you were blown up. They found you at the bottom of the trench with little cartoon stars floating around your head. You're seventy-nine years old. Isn't it a little late to be developing survivor's guilt? Or are you starting to consider your own mortality?"

"Dying? There isn't a day in the last seventy years I haven't thought about it. How can you live through all that death, all that slaughter, and *not* think about it?"

"You said it yourself. It was sixty years ago. Sixty years. You've lived a full life. God you've lived a life people *envy*. Why all this preoccupation with something that happened when we were Alec's age?"

"They're coming back, David. After all this time they're coming back for me. I'm scared."

"The memories? Oh, Geoff, at our age they're usually slipping away from us, not coming back." He rummages in his bag and pulls out a small jar of white pills. "These will help you sleep, and maybe come to terms with some of these memories that have you so worked up, all right? Give me a call in a day or two if nothing gets better." He gets up and moves towards the door. "If you want my opinion, as a friend, go out with your family, spend some of that big pile of money you have squirreled away under your mattress, and enjoy some of what you have in the present."

"David?"

"Yes?"

"How do you live with your memories?"

"I put them to rest a long, long time ago, old fellow." He laughs. "Except maybe that Belgian whore."

The old man sits at the end of his bed, head bowed, hands folded in his lap. His uniform itches, sagging against his hollow frame where once it fit snug against the taut muscles of youth. Beside him are arranged the accoutrements of his war: bandolier, webbing, slouch hat, rifle and bayonet both showing the benefit of an evenings arthritically applied oil. The pills were no help. It is not memory that haunts him. Now there is no escape. The clock ticks its doleful beat on the bedstand. The old man sits, lost in yesterdays, eyes staring through the backs of his hands.

It happens. The air in front of the bed begins to soften and flow. The old man rises and dons his webbing and hat. He stands at ragged parade rest, bayonet in one hand, rifle clutched in the other. Sixty years disappear. Once more the trenches of the Somme engulf his senses. He raises his eyes, looks straight at the dead friends before him. They stare back with the contempt of the young.

"I'm ready."

There is a moment of silence. Then laughter fills the air around him.

"You? Oh, Jeffy. You've got the wrong end of the stick. We don't want you."

"But . . . "

"You think we came for *you*? You're too old for war. What use is an old man in a fight? Can you swing a trench club? Can you run no-man's land?"

"But I left . . . You said . . . "

"We said you'd pay. And you will."

"Grandad?" The call comes from somewhere to his left. A teenager stumbles into view on the wrong side of the melted air, his face contorted in terror. The old man's throat fills with ice.

"Alec!"

"Grandad? What's going on? Help me, grandad!"

The air between them starts to fold in upon itself. The voice speaks out one last time, sardonic and cold. Each word strikes the old man like a German bullet.

"It's a young man's game, Jeffy. Did you think we'd only one way through? There's no place here for you, old man. Only the young go over the top. And he will. Again and again and again . . . "

A whistle sounds. Before the air shuts for the last time they drag his screaming grandson, crying to his grandfather to save him, towards the foot of the ramshackle ladder leaning against the trench wall. His final view is of Alec's face, terrified, overwhelmed with fear, disappearing behind the air's closing wound. Then the old man is staring into nowhere, bayonet and rifle forgotten at his feet, hands outstretched.

The only sound that breaks eternity is the ticking of the clock.

AFTERWORD

I started my career with three goals: *Writers of The Future*, *Aurealis*, and the Western Australian magazine *Eidolon*. *Eidolon* folded before I was able to submit to them, but the magazine that replaced it, *Borderlands*, accepted this story for their first issue, meaning I had achieve all three within my first year. Not a bad start. Another fascination for me: I don't believe anybody of my generation can really understand the experience of the WW1 trenches, and with so few survivors left, it's something that will pass from our social understanding too.

DARK AGES

I can't take my eyes from Sara. She waves to me from the back of her grandparents' car, blowing kisses with the wide-eyed joy that accompanies all the tricks she learns. I wave back, and tell her I love her. The car backs out of the driveway and into the street. I get a perfunctory gesture from Sara's grandmother, then I watch as they bear my daughter away. Every fourth weekend she leaves me, for two days of soft drink, sugar, staying up late, and all the other things they know I don't allow her to have at home.

Motherless grandchildren don't have rules.

As soon as the car is out of sight, I lock the front door and spend an hour wandering from room to room, absorbing the absence of laughter. I find myself taking mementoes from shelves and turning them over in my hands. With an effort I shake myself free from thoughts of the past. My will is on the kitchen table. Sara will be cared for. So many people can look after her better then me.

A six metre length of extension cord sits in a coil on top. I hang it over my shoulder, and take a dining chair out onto the patio. I lock the door behind me and place the house keys on the outdoor table, where they will be easily found. The extension cord unravels and I throw it over the beam, tying it off around the nearest upright. The chair goes underneath the loose end. I step up. I chose electrical cord because it is almost impossible to cut. It makes forming the noose difficult, but I have had more experience in tying nooses than I wish to remember. In no more than two minutes I take a last look at the home I have tried to make, nestle the simple knot behind my right ear, and kick the chair away.

I hang there for two days.

Niall finds me. I should have known it would be him. I've known Niall a lot longer than anybody else, an awful lot longer. I hear the scraping of the garden gate against the brick path, then a clatter as the stepladder he has come to return falls from his grasp.

"You stupid prick!"

I swing around to see him standing at my feet, annoyance coloring his features. Without speaking further he undoes the knotted cord, letting me crash to the patio floor.

He picks up the ladder and walks to the shed at the back of the garden. I hear the crash as he throws it inside. By the time he returns, I have managed to lever myself into a sitting position. I lean against the pole like a discarded puppet. The cord is still dug into my throat. It will be days before I can speak. I look up at him. I don't remember seeing him this angry. He is normally such a creature of movement. Right now he stands rigid, as if unable to trust himself not to put his hands around my neck and finish the job.

"I'm not going to do this again," he says in a cold, calm voice. "I'm not going to be responsible for you anymore, Declan."

He turns his back on me and walks to the gate.

"Who do you think would look after Sara?" he asks, just before he exits. "Who's going to teach her what she needs to know?"

Who indeed?

She was beautiful. So beautiful. I only had to look at her and the outside world would blur and darken, until all the light the sun had to offer became a single beam focused upon her, only her. We met at a rodeo, of all things, one of those semi-organized gatherings where the local rednecks converge from every corner of the surrounding countryside to tie ropes around the testicles of tomorrow night's dinner and prove their manhood by jumping on its back.

Niall had dragged me there to be wingman on yet another of his one-night stands. Emma played the same role for Niall's lucky partner. The program looked far too long, a procession of cattle forced into performing their limited range of tricks. Anyone semi-intelligent would lose interest by the time the national anthem had finished. By the time Niall came shuffling back from the bar after the third event, I was no longer in the mood to be mollified.

"I'll just sit here being bored until the end of the evening then, shall I?"

He gave the little half-shrug which has always meant he owed me another one.

"Oh, just go and get it over with."

He plastered an apologetic smile on his face and stood back up, his blonde friend on one arm. They backed into the aisle and made for the exit.

"Make the most of it," I called to the girlfriend. She glanced back at me with a quizzical expression, but Niall whispered something into her ear and she giggled, then laid her head against his bicep. Sometimes I forget just how big Niall is, until I see him side by side with whichever woman he has for the night.

"Well, that didn't take long." The voice behind me was warm and tinged with amusement. I twisted around in surprise. In my annoyance with Niall, I had completely forgotten about the girlfriend's chaperone. I shrugged.

"Guess he doesn't like her that much. Doesn't want to waste any more time talking to her."

"Ouch."

"I've known Niall for years. You get used to the signs."

She smiled a smile that told me she had known her friend for years too, and wasn't that surprised by the way the night had unfolded.

"I'm Emma."

"Declan."

We leaned forward and shook hands, then both laughed self-consciously at the silly formality of it. I sat back in my seat and studied her face.

"So what shall we do now? Cram into a corner of the bar and try to ignore the smell of sweat, or bring our warm beers back here and pretend we like the sound of moron hitting dirt?"

She laughed. "I take it you're not impressed." She nodded toward where a helmet-and-padding clad figure was being hurled to the floor. I pointed to the young bull trying to gore a lesson into his skin.

"If we were in Ancient Crete, he'd be living off scraps in the street with form like that."

She raised her eyebrows in enquiry. I indicated the arena, picturing the open blue sky and the heat haze shimmering off the white stone.

"Boys who reached their thirteenth summer would enter the arena. Naked. A full-grown bull faced them across the dirt. Those who'd learnt their lessons well could talk the bull into feeding from the handful of grain in their right hand. Those who hadn't . . . "

I shrugged, and looked at her eyes. They were a deep, deep blue, and right now they were fastened on mine. I blinked, and hurried on rather than find myself staring too long at her with my mouth agape. "When the bull charged, the boy would attempt to leap over it, grabbing a garland from its horns on the way through. They found their adult caste on that day. Their whole lives hung on how well they performed." I waved toward yet another falling redneck. "Compared to that, this is somewhat . . . lacking."

"Sure," she said, and took a bite from her hotdog, "But this is happening *now*."

She smiled, and despite all the lessons I have ever learnt, I fell in love again.

Two hundred years ago, surgeons wore their street clothes to operate. Most didn't even bother to wash their hands between patients. Anaesthesia was not yet in use. Even if the surgeon chose to perform a caesarean, rather than just smashing the skull of the unborn foetus in a craniotomy, septicemia and peritonitis ran rampant throughout the surgeries of Europe. Not a single Parisian woman survived a caesarean operation between 1787 and 1876.

I sit in the middle of Sara's new paddling pool and draw the blade across my wrists. According to the sticker on the inside of the plastic clam shell, the pool can hold 72 liters. A few hours ago, Sara had played here, splashing and laughing while I ignored her grandmother's disapproving lecture on all the dangers I expose her to by my negligence and inability to parent. Now the pool is empty of water, and Sara is bound to be eating her first bowl of ice-cream of the evening. That self-same guardian of her welfare will be pouring caffeine-laden cola into her sipper cup.

My wrists smile at me for a single heartbeat, before the blood finds the new-made exit. I turn my hands over, and watch the first red drops fall and roll down the sides toward my ankles. It takes my body a little over six hours to manufacture enough blood to fill the half-shell. By the time Sara would be heading to bed it is beginning to spill over the edges of the pool, and I haven't suffered so much as a slight headache. I sigh, and step out of the pool. Leaving red footprints behind me, I go inside to have a shower and bandage my wrists.

Niall pulled at the collar of his tuxedo and eyed me.

"Have you told her yet?"

"How many have *you* told?" I whispered back, my eyes fixed on the door at the far end of the church. I didn't need to see my friend to feel his guilt.

"Only Blodwyn."

"And you remember how well that turned out?"

"I . . . " He laid his hand upon my arm, and leaned further toward my ear. "Declan . . . "

"For better or for worse," I cut through his warning. His grip tightened, then fell away. I kept my eyes on the door. He took a long step backward, leaving me exposed and alone on the dais. Too late, it occurred to me that I was now alone in a room full of strangers.

I could have turned to him, and appeased his fears. But at that moment Emma appeared through the doorway, and my eyes could no longer move from the sight of her.

It was like making love again, watching her come toward me down the aisle. Our eyes kissed, and promised never to let each other go. Nobody else existed in those moments. Not while we said our vows, not while we feasted and danced, not when we left the revelers behind and drove to the hotel to lie naked under cool sheets and consummate physically what we had sang in our souls all day.

Nobody else existed, and I would give all the years I have left for that one fragile day of perfection.

Five hundred years ago, after his wife had undergone several days of agonized labour, and a dozen midwives and barbers had failed to bring the delivery to any sort of conclusion, a German sow gelder named Jacob Nufer used a razor blade to open his wife and bring the child into the world. The authorities had refused him permission to perform the operation. He did it anyway. Mrs Nufer not only survived, she had more children. There had been several centuries of recorded caesarean sections. She was the first mother to survive one. It would be 1794 before another wholly successful caesarean was recorded.

I lean on the pestle, grinding into the mortar until the pills are nothing more than a fine white powder. Take one per day with food, the label on the box orders. I look at six months of medication and wonder if it is enough. The drink is salty, and powdery, and when I finish there is a thick layer of sediment at the bottom of the glass. I refill, and drink again, and again, until the glass is empty of residue. I make my way to the too-large bed and lie down on my half, letting one hand fall into the empty space beside me. I close my eyes.

I wake two hours later, refreshed and alert. I walk to the bathroom and stare at myself in the mirror, waiting for the tears to stop.

It took two attempts to get the epidural in. During the operation, the anaesthetist was called upon to lean over the canvas screen they erected so we couldn't see anything. He pushed down on the top of Emma's stomach: once, twice, again. It's okay, they told us. It happens all the time. The baby looked healthy and normal when it was at last delivered. A girl. My heart stopped, just for a moment, but it did stop. My daughter cried out, her little face screwed up around her eyes. I heard the tiny squawk she made, and my eyes blurred and watered in response. I wondered if Niall could hear her out in the corridor, or Emma's parents in the house they had refused to leave to be at the birth.

Emma squeezed my hand, and I remembered my task. I followed the nurse as she took the baby away to be cleaned and weighed, dogging her footsteps in my duty of making sure our precious child was not swapped for some demon child in the two minutes she was away from us. I ghosted along behind her as our daughter was wrapped in a baby blanket, returned to the surgery, and held against her mother's chest. I sat down again, placed one hand on my daughter's head, and the other on my wife's sweaty neck.

"Who is she, then?" I asked.

"Sara," she replied. "Definitely Sara."

Sara was not with us, three days later, when it all went wrong. She was asleep in her crib in the neonatal room when her mother was rushed to the ICU of a larger hospital. The infection the maternity ward staff failed to notice had taken hold, and there were grave fears. Three days, and the caesarean was still cutting into her, getting deeper and deeper beyond my reach.

I signed the forms allowing the doctors to perform an emergency hysterectomy, should the need arise.

"Just a precaution," the consulting surgeon said with a smile, as he folded the form and put it in the chest pocket of the street clothes he wore to the consult. "A quick look, clean out any infected material. It'll be fine."

The last words I said to her, as they wheeled her into the surgery, were simple and only half wrong.

"I love you. I'll see you when you wake up."

A thousand years ago, Trotula of Salerno performed a caesarean to save a child's life whilst Constantine the African stood by amazed. A thousand years ago, she wrote 'Concerning The Suffering of Women', advocating the use of opiates to help women overcome the pain of labour. A thousand years ago, Trotula died. Less than a hundred years later, Henry IV sacked the city. The Church, which preached that women should suffer unrelenting pain in childbirth, stood by and watched as her teachings were scattered and lost. Then it banned women from the surgeries. Those with practical healing skills and herbal knowledge were persecuted as witches. Unlike Trotula of Salerno, the Church is eternal. It can afford to wait.

I take the gun from my mouth and lay it on the table. I will taste the bitter tang of the muzzle against my fillings for days. Besides, I'm not convinced it can do the job I need it to do, and I'm afraid of what things will be like if it doesn't. I look over at the picture of Emma I keep on the bookcase. She still smiles at me, but it no longer illuminates the air between us. I feel very old, and cold, and dark.

"What then?" I ask her. "What?"

She makes no answer. I look at her picture, and my mind slips free of the restraints I place upon it. Sara is in bed. The world is locked outside, where it belongs. The phone is off the hook. It is safe to remember.

Two and a half thousand years ago, I stand in front of a barrow at the town of Vix and watch as the villagers carry my love into her tomb. They have adorned her with gold, and placed such treasures inside her hole in the ground that she will reach the next world a princess, a priestess, a queen.

Two and a half thousand years ago, I watch my peasant love disappear into the dark and know she will never emerge. There are storm clouds overhead, and the wind that strikes my chest is cold and angry. I gaze toward the town and realize I will not be walking back with the rest of the mourners. I wish I had brought a cloak with me. As if he knows my mind, Niall reaches out and presses heavy fabric into my hand. I put it on, and look at him. He has brought two packs with him, and two walking staves. I remember the words I say to him then, as the townsfolk finish sealing the barrow and turn back to their lives.

"Never again. Never again."

And now I sit in my house in the present, with my ghosts around me, and let tears adorn a face that has known woad, and powder, and three thousand years of fashion. There has been an 'again', and this time I cannot simply walk away and begin over.

As if on cue, Sara cries out. I go to her room and look down at her, curled up in the safety of her cot. How much effort would it take to fetch a pillow, bring it back, and place it over her face? How long would I have to hold it there before her chest stopped moving? I reach down. Such a small act. Such an easy thing. But what would I do if her chest didn't stop, if it continued to rise and fall no matter how hard I pushed, or how long the pillow stopped her breath reaching the outside air? Which side of the family does she take after? I brush a fingertip against the skin of her cheek. She wriggles, and says a single word amidst her restless crying.

"Daddy."

I find the pacifier at the end of its chain and place it back in her mouth. She settles immediately, snuggling into herself and drawing comfort from the rubber nipple.

I sit in the dark, stroking her hair until dawn.

AFTERWORD

A story that relates directly to the death of my first wife, a few days after the birth of our child. Each of the little factoids are true, as far as my research can tell. My distrust of, and repulsion towards, the hospital system in Australia has never left me, despite several stories written with a cathartic end in mind. When my beautiful second wife Lyn went into hospital in late 2004 to have our first child, it was the end point of nine months of mental torture for me. No matter the odds, I *know* what happens to pregnant women in hospital. I never looked down at my daughter and asked the questions the narrator in this story asked, but then, I always had the option of killing myself. Go back and read the dedication at the front of the book . . .

TALES OF NIREYM

Some time ago, no more than four years since leaving my mother's village, I found myself in a hinter-town at the northern edge of what was then the Single Dominion. Like many Edgetowns of the time it was a ramshackle affair, raised by men with intentions of staying only as long as it took to hunt, or fell the forests that covered the borders. And like many towns it had been reinforced and added to as the forest refused to empty, and the seasons had lengthened into generations. Tracks became muddy streets, shacks became buildings, and itinerants became mayors, landowners and businessmen. Before they quite knew it, the town had a name, and stories began tumbling down onto the plains and into the Golden City. Dominions are built this way. When thought becomes fact, scribes are dispatched, to collect information for the Dominus. Soon the map that dominates the ruler's war room wears another pin, marking the new town as forever his property.

I had walked among more than a few such towns, and I had yet to lose my awe at their differences. I was still years away from seeing the similarities that lie below the glamours of somewhere new, and becoming bored by them. Being young, and still obsessive about my chosen trade, I spent weeks talking to the men of the town and recording their stories, sending them back towards the Golden City with the solitary courier who paddled his pirogue along this stretch of the river.

Eventually, having run out of specimens to interview, I spent a night drinking at the smallest and most comfortable of the Lodge Huts.

I saw an old man there, silent, brooding, sitting in the dark of the farthest corner, looking like a gargoyle or house demon carved out of the wall. Each night I had seen him, but he neither moved nor acknowledged the presence of any other in the hut, so I had let him be. But this was my last night in the town, and I had enjoyed my ale enough so that some small measure of bravery had entered me, so I sent a tankard over to him and raised my writing tablet in answer to his stare.

He watched me for a minute then nodded once. I gathered up my bag and drink and walked quickly to his table before either of us could change our minds.

Up close, I could see that he was larger than he appeared—not brutish, but with a solidity as if he were built from rock or wood. There was a density about him that swallowed the light from the sconces above, making this corner of the room darker than it might otherwise have been. He sat with one knotted hand resting on the table. Even though we were inside and it was warm, he still wore a cloak about his shoulders, and his other arm remained hidden beneath it. In all the time we talked he never once moved that arm, or brought that hand to join its brother.

"Took you long enough," he growled in the guttural accent of the south.

"Most people come to *me* when they see I'm a scribe." I gave him what I hoped was my most open smile.

"You thought I had no story, then?"

"No, no." I opened my tablet, counted the pages I had left, then lifted the stylus from its niche. "Everyone has a story. It's the sharing that is the important element. And that's voluntary."

"Everyone." The old man took a drink from his stein. "Collect many from the women?"

I frowned. "Women don't have stories the Dominus needs."

"Humph. And what is it you do with your stories for the Dominus?"

I shrugged, smirking. Everyone knows what happens with the tales a scribe collects. "They join the library at the palace, and the Dominus calls on them when his mind turns to whatever part of the Dominion they come from. As long as they are true, and suit his needs. Have you never been scribed before?" I had not met a man who hadn't been scribed, and most had done so more than once. Many villages elect councils based on the number of scribings they contribute to the library. As long as they are true.

The old man barked, a short sound that could have been a laugh.

I blinked, than asked, "You do have a story you wish to tell?"

He looked me up and down, measuring me with a gaze that seemed uncommonly sharp. A corner of his mouth twitched and he said, "Oh yes. I have one you'll like."

"As long as it's true." I held my stylus over the top of the first page. The old man took a long draught from his stein, placed it on the table, and began.

"There was a girl, and her name was Nireym. She was born in a small village high in the Collness Mountains. In the years before her birth the village had been an outpost for the Dominus, but he had died, and the five pretenders still fought over the throne. The town was far from the Golden City, isolated both by distance and harsh terrain, and so it had lain ignored and forgotten for years. Nireym's mother had died giving birth, and it was left to her father to raise the child alone. He had been an acolyte, and now served as a teacher or elder, not a practical man. Nireym's upbringing was not . . . proper, at least as the customs of the time dictated. By the time she was ten, the girl could stand against any boy of the village, and compete at the various challenges boys find important. If not the strongest fighter, or the fastest runner, she could at least hold her own. At tasks requiring concentration or clarity of thought, such as poetry or archery, she had no equal her own age. If she knew nothing of the thirty domestic tasks or the proprietary of motherhood, and if the mothers and daughters of the village sniffed in disdain and turned their backs, well, father and daughter simply laughed and continued in their ways. For the father valued intelligence and independence above all things, and Nireym had both in abundance. Between them they lived a happy enough life, and prosperous, isolated as they were from the dictates that would have made Nireym as other women, and her father a heretic."

"But?"

The old man smiled a small, cold smile. "Yes, but. When Nireym was sixteen she and her father had an argument. It doesn't matter what it was about. Something small and pointless. Such things always are, and avoided unless both sides are pig headed enough to hold firm. Anyway, when he rose the next morning, the father found Nireym gone and her possessions missing. And one other thing. She had taken a parchment from his library. A dangerous parchment, for it was written by the poet Germaine, and was a forbidden text in the wider world."

"Germaine? I don't know him."

The old man looked at me for a long moment, then lowered his eyes and continued.

"Germaine was a woman, a concubine of the Dominus Ephrazim. When the Dominus was at court, which was often, she would dress as a man and live a poet's existence in the artist's quarter of the Golden City. She wrote her observations of life there in a series of scrolls called 'the Femminile'. In time she was discovered. The Dominus had her put to death. Her writings were suppressed and destroyed. Many believe that much of the low status of women in the Dominion dates from this time, and the rage of Ephrazim at Germaine's actions."

"But if they were destroyed . . . ?"

"Oh, you can destroy parchments, but not ideas. Some copies were kept hidden, or escaped notice, lost or forgotten or kept in corners too dark and dusty to warrant discovery. The father had been an acolyte, and had come into possession of one such copy."

"Which one?"

"It was called 'On Differences'. It listed seventeen ways in which a woman could be distinguished from a man: by smell; by movement; by attitude; and so forth. Germaine had put these things into practice, and had lived successfully as a man. You can see why such knowledge might be considered dangerous in a Dominion such as ours. And Nireym had been fortunate to grow up in a place where she was allowed to be an equal amongst boys. Her father understood what she intended. He also knew that the world outside the village walls was a much different place, and that Nireym would profit from distance and shelter."

"Women were possessions, if I recall."

"Possessions, yes, but there was a deeper level of degradation than that. How old are you?"

"Twenty. Twenty-one next circus month."

"You've grown up in less restrictive times."

"You don't find these times restrictive, Master?" I asked, relying on politeness to cover my impudence. The old man was not fooled. His finger thumped the tabletop in counterpoint to his speech.

"Women can show their faces in the street. They can work in fields. They can touch money without their husband or a notary present. Things weren't always so. In the time that this story occurred women were less than chattels. They were nothing. Literally nothing. They had no status at all. They had less legal rights than cattle, less market value than water. Laws concerning what he may or may not do to a slave governed a man, but no such laws existed regarding women. They were, well . . . it was not a time for a girl to be intelligent, or independent, or to walk the world without knowing the forms and rituals of submission." He sat back and looked at me. "Nireym had left her home, without a chattel slip or notary or a notice of servitude, unaccompanied and unowned. This alone was enough to have her put to death. If she was discovered with the parchment on her . . . it was not an enlightened time."

"Some might say it is still not an enlightened time."

The old man held up his hand. "We could discuss that for a month. It might be bad now, but it was worse then. Do you want to hear the story?"

I glanced down at the notes before me. "Yes."

"Nireym had run away, bearing a parchment that would mean death for a man, worse for her. Her father loved her dearly. She was all the joy he had in the world, the only thing he viewed with pleasure or pride. He packed his belongings and began his pursuit that same morning."

The old man drew a last draught from his stein and stood it upside-down on the table. He raised his eyebrows at me. I sighed and signalled the barkeep for another. We sat in silence until it arrived.

"Well?"

"The father searched for over a year, but he never found her. He returned to his house a broken and sorrowful man, and lived from then on with neither hope nor joy."

"That's it?"

"Should there be more?"

"Yes!" I threw my hands open in frustration. "What happened to Nireym? What about the parchment? Her teachings?"

"Did I mention teachings?"

"Well . . . I . . . it follows. Surely."

"Humph." He tapped the fingers of his visible hand on the table, hard flesh against equally hard wood. "Teachings." He gazed past me. A fireplace was set into the counter of the room. His gaze travelled to the flames and stopped. When he spoke again his voice had a different timbre: older, deader. It was as if he recited the facts of a trail long cold.

"The next that was heard of Nireym, *maybe*, came a year after her father returned to his home. A village at the far end of the Collness Mountains." He doodled in the ring left on the table by his mug, and I saw a map form under his touch. "A young man, a stranger, had taken part in the village games. He acquitted himself well in most things, winning the archery competition, and placing high in poetry. He retired early each evening, abstaining from the festivities."

"But?"

"There was a young lady with him, thought by many to be his sister. She entered the women's hut at the ordered time. She spoke to the young females of the village, talking of freedoms that could be achieved by subterfuge and the power of women to live more than one life. Many of the girls spoke in agreement there in the darkness of the hut, listening as the men walked through the night and caroused."

I grimaced. "I shouldn't expect a happy ending to this, I suppose."

He grinned in response, and I resisted the urge to shudder. "The mothers of the village knew their place. Word reached the elders. They visited the stranger's rooms with plans to roust him over his sister's heresy. They found it empty. The pair had disappeared." He drank from his mug, and replaced it on the table with a satisfied belch. "And that probably would have been all, except that three girls from the village ran away over the course of the next week, never to return."

"Three girls? That hardly seems conclusive."

"Taken on its own, no. But there are similar stories from across most of the province, scattered across the following few years. Each tale finishes with daughters lost, families abandoned by obedient and proper girls, who were never heard from again."

"What happened to them?"

"How should I know? They were never heard from again, or if they were it doesn't matter to the story." He drained the last of his drink and this time did not wait for me to order another. I summoned the barkeep anyway.

"It might have ended there," he continued, "and no link be found, except for a soldier. One night, in a lodge like this, he told me a story. He'd come from the south, where he'd been in service to the southern pretender . . . "

"The Dominus"

"Now he's Dominus, yes, but then he was still just one of five little warlords fighting over the corpse of the real ruler."

I raised my eyebrows. "That's treason."

He snorted. "I've done worse. Anyway, this soldier was a mercenary from out of the K'Tarkin provinces. He and a friend deserted because of lack of food and pay. After all, what else is a mercenary fighting for? They abandoned their posts one night, passing through lines unfamiliar to them, hoping they would be viewed as running errands and ignored. They snuck around a company stationed right at the outer flank of the pretender's phalanxes, and there they found . . . "

His fresh mug arrived and he paused to take a long series of swallows.

"What?"

"What do you think? The troop was very small, only about twenty or so, as far as the soldiers could tell, and the outer edge seemed a strange place to station such an insignificant force. It was enough to pique their interest. The two men thought they'd stumbled upon some sort of special company, or even infiltrators. Instead they found women."

"What?"

"A troop of women, right there amongst the pretender's army, to all intents and purposes fighting men like any other. But inside their tents, away from all but the hidden eyes of the mercenary pair, undeniably, unmistakably . . . female." The old man smiled into his mug. "Oh, he had no proof of course, nothing but his word, and what good is the word of a mercenary? He claimed his friend had snuck into a nearby tent and stolen a parchment, a parchment that told how a woman might live as a man. It also gave instructions on how to find and educate those who might be taught."

"What happened to it?"

"The men were discovered. His friend was killed and he barely escaped with his life."

"And the parchment?"

"Lost, reclaimed by the one they had thieved it from. He and his friend were deserters, and now his friend was dead. He didn't stay to argue."

"You think it was Nireym?"

"Doubtful. She was the daughter of an acolyte, and in her own way she had taken on the role of teacher. More likely it was a group of her adherents, living the way they chose to live." He smiled a thin, sharp smile. "Assuming it was even true."

"You don't think it was." My writing hand was aching, and I took the opportunity to shake some life into it. The old man saw the movement and frowned.

"I've seen nothing in my years of wandering to suggest that a woman has less right to choose the course of her life than a man. And nothing to suggest that a drunken soldier has anything trustworthy to say."

"Treason again."

"I've done worse."

I picked up my stylus once more.

"So is that it? Her message reached people, that's good. For her, I mean." I coughed into my hand. "Did she ever see her father again? Was she ever found?"

The old man wiped his hand across his eyes, then reached below the table and scratched at the hidden part of his other arm.

"There is one more story, one I heard while I was slaved to the Dominus' service. It might be connected, or it might not."

"Yes?"

He stared hard into the fire. "One day, about a decade after Nireym had run away from her home, a rider appeared in her father's village. He was tall, slim of build, with hair worn long and braided in the manner of the barbarians of the northern peninsular. He wore a longbow across his back, carved and white, as if made from whalebone or winter mahogany. The southern pretender had crossed the Collness Mountains on his final push to the Golden City two years previous. The town had been plundered and razed. Only a handful of people remained to scratch out survival from amongst the ruins. The horseman rode through the empty streets, looking neither right nor left, until he reached the house where Nireym and her father had lived. The house was no longer there. He tied his horse to a solitary standing beam and walked amongst the ruins as if he knew them, stopping here and there with a short exclamation or a cry, as if in pain. In the wreckage of what had been the library, he stooped, and drew from the ashes a blackened object. It was a hand, twisted and charred almost beyond recognition."

"But why did . . . "

"The stranger used the edge of his cloak to rub ashes away from a ring that still circled the hand's thumb, though it was warped and melted by the fire. He pulled the ring off, and placed it upon his own hand, which was smaller and more delicate than the remains of the one he held. He laid the hand back amongst the ruins and regained his mount. Looking neither right nor left, he rode out of the village and towards the north. He was never seen again."

The old man lapsed into silence, still staring into the fire. After a few long moments his eyes closed, and his chin dropped toward his chest. Sensing the end of the tale, I placed the stylus back into its niche and closed the tablet.

"Thank you for your story," I said. "It was entertaining, even if its truth cannot be verified."

I started to rise, and the old man sprung to life. Before I cleared my chair he reached out, bunching his fist into my tunic and pulling me half over the table towards him.

"Reach into my bag," he hissed.

I stared at him in sudden terror. "What?"

"Reach into my bag." His eyes darted to the left. Mine followed. A bag lay in the corner of the booth, its top unclasped.

"But I . . . "

"Fool. I can't do it for you." He shrugged his right shoulder, and the cape fell away. I saw his arm fully for the first time, down to the stump where his hand should have been. My own hand scrabbled for the bag's top and reached inside. I found a roll of paper and drew it out. I looked up at the old man's face, saw pain and fury mixed in equal parts. He spat words at me through closed teeth. "Seven years a slave to the Dominus and thirteen escaped. I've searched every face I've seen, every person who moved around me, looking for her, searching for her. I've doubled the rules Germaine formulated. There *are* women out there, and there are many better at it than you."

He let go of me with a push, grabbed the empty bag in one movement and made for the door. I watched him leave, my hands smoothing my clothes back into place, making sure my disguise lay perfect around me. I unrolled the scroll and spent half a minute reading the observations recorded upon it. Then I re-rolled it and tucked it into my tunic, until it nestled against the parchment I keep hidden there.

I rose from my seat, paid my bill, and followed the old man into the darkness of the night. I looked up at the stars, my mind wandering back to that night four years earlier, when I had made my monthly climb into the fetid enclosure of the Red Hut, raised on stilts so that not even the ground would have to bear the contamination of my bleeding. I remembered peering into the gloom at the woman who sat there and the conversation we had. I could still feel her hand, hard and calloused, as she pressed a small scrap of parchment into my grip, just before she climbed down into the pre-dawn gloom. As I walked back to my lodgings I rubbed my hands together, feeling the rough, hard skin, remembering her voice.

"Teach as many as you find," she had said. "It won't always take place in shadows and dark. When men start to learn, then the change will take place."

I gathered my belongings from my rooms and walked away from the town, heading north.

AFTERWORD

A story about my fears when it comes to parenting my daughter: read 'Nireym' backwards, and my daughter's name is there. One of the reasons I love my wife Lyn so deeply is that she saved me from all the mistakes I saw myself making as a single parent. I think it touched the same chord in a few people: it garnered favourable reviews when it came out, and was short listed for the 2005 Aurealis Award for Fantasy, totally buggering my public anti-phantasy stand! There's a novel in this story, somewhere: some day soon, I know, I'll have to deal with the father finding his daughter, and what that means for both of them.

FATHER MUERTE & THE RAIN

It was the second sunrise of the day. Benito D'Amico and I sat on the patio of his café, watching the crowds who gathered to ooh, aah, and take photographs that would fail to develop when they returned to the real world. That's one of the wonderful things about Costa Satanas. Everybody sees it differently. Everybody imprints their own desires upon the town's psyche. And just like most desires, people wake up back in reality holding only a hazy memory of what it was they wanted at the time.

Still, if people want something badly enough, the accumulated need can force the town into concrete modes of behaviour. Over the years a second sunrise has become the norm here, without my help.

People stood hand in hand on the beach, watching the waves of the bay turn red and gold then dim to a deep royal blue. The sky seemed to pause, before the sun peeked out from its hiding place as if seeking applause for an encore.

"Bellissimo," Benito said over the rim of his wine glass. "Each time more beautiful, Father."

I smiled into my coffee. Benito was an actor in a former life. His theatrical mannerisms remind me of happier times. I was just about to reply when his face fell into a craggy frown.

"What is it?"

He pointed toward the rising sun.

"You have better eyes than I, Father. What is that?"

I followed his gaze. "I'm not sure. A storm cloud?"

"Here?"

My frown now matched his. Benito was right, of course. It doesn't rain in Costa Satanas unless I wish it. Besides, this cloud moved too fast.

"I think we'd better head down to the beach."

The cloud reached us before we could get that far. There was a sound like several hundred people slapping each other, and objects began falling toward us. Silver, wriggling objects that landed here and there across the beach without striking a single one of the gathered tourists. Benito picked one up, laughing.

"Fish!" he cried. "A storm of fish!"

I took it from him and examined the armoured head, the rudimentary fins and tail.

"Not just any fish." I said in wonder.

"Ugly fish."

"Coelacanths." His look demanded an explanation. "Prehistoric fish. Dead for millions of years, apart from my own collection." I gave the dying fish a puzzled glance. One or two had escaped their private harbour over the years, but none since the nineteen thirties, and never in such numbers. The mass of silver shapes on the beach numbered over a hundred.

"Another thing." Benito pointed to the crowd. "Look."

Down on the beach the tourists were trying to pick the fish up and failing, much to their amusement. Several were trying to catch them as they fell from the sky, howling with laughter as the animals passed through their hands, arms, and bodies. Benito and I stared at each other, then at the creature I still held.

"How . . . ?"

"I have no idea." I dropped my fish and picked up another, then another. Beside me, Benito did the same.

"Hello, fellows. Smile!" Arms full of ancient animals, we looked up into the grinning face of Henri Anglomarre, local photographer and owner of the strangest camera I'd ever seen. There was a flash of light. Benito and I dropped our bundles and covered our eyes.

"Henri!" we cried in unison.

"Don't worry," was his reply, "it's just an automatic." He held up the offending machine. "The special one is at home. I'm making some alterations."

"What kind of alterations?" Henri and I had met when I discovered his camera was capturing the soul of its subject, not just their image. The thought he might be tampering with it did not fill me with joy.

"Oh nothing much. Just some tweaking. Hey, weird fish." He put the camera down and bent to pick up a nearby coelacanth. His hand passed straight through it. "Woah."

Benito and I exchanged glances.

"Try that one." I said, pointing to another. He did, with the same result.

"Okay, that's officially weird. Father?"

"Why is it that every time something unusual happens in this town people think I know what's going on?" I saw their raised eyebrows. "All right, but not this time."

"Well, at least they've stopped falling." Benito indicated the beach, where the crowd was dispersing now the novelty was beginning to wear off. All except one elderly couple. As I watched, the man picked up a coelacanth and tried to hand it to the woman. It fell through her outstretched hands. They tried again, and again only the man was able to grasp the creature. I felt a tickling at the back of my mind.

"Henri, what adjustments are you making to your camera?"

"Oh, nothing much." He looked proud. "Just an idea I had. If I'm correct I should be able to take pictures of a person's soul, instead of capturing it. You know, like auras. It's a bit like Kurlian photography, see, it's just a matter of rerouting the soul fluid through the capture filaments instead of . . . "

"Would you mind fetching it for me?"

"Huh? Uh, okay, of course." He ran off toward his nearby studio. Benito looked sideways at me.

"An idea, Father?"

"Perhaps. Might I order another coffee? Dark as the devil . . . "

" . . . and twice as sweet. I know." He moved away, taking the hint with a grace uncommon to him. I walked down onto the beach and approached the couple, picking up a fish as I went.

"Good morning." the woman greeted me.

"Odd morning." I replied, hefting my silver burden. "Not our usual way of fishing."

They laughed in reply. "You don't go fishing for ghosts, Father?" the woman replied.

"Ghosts?"

"Sure, why not? Why else this?" She tried to take the coelacanth from my grasp. Her hand passed through it before touching my own.

"Then why can I hold it, and your husband?"

"Don't know. Maybe you're just more spiritual than the rest of us." She indicated my jacket and hat. "You are a priest aren't you? Only you . . . "

"In a manner of speaking. Although at the moment I find myself unaffiliated. But what about you, sir? Are you . . . ?"

"Not a bit. I'm a psychiatrist. Retired." He held out his hand. "Jim Prendergast. My wife Anna." I shook their hands. "I've no idea why I get to hold these fine fish and nobody else does. Still, makes a good story to tell the friends back home."

I nodded. At that moment Henri returned with his camera, a bulky affair wrapped in leather and steel.

"Henri, would you do me a favor? Would you take a picture of my friends the Prendergasts? With your permission, of course," I asked them.

"Sure."

"Thank you. Bring it to Benito's, if you please. Oh, and put the fish in the photo as well, could you?"

"The butterfly effect."

"Sorry?" I sipped my coffee and looked up into Benito's excited, sweaty grin.

"I've been trying to remember what it is that causes rainstorms to drop fish."

"There's a name for it?"

"Well, not for the fish dropping, so much." He thudded into the chair opposite, oblivious to the breakfast crowd at the other tables. I saw Maria, his only waitress, glance in our direction and throw her hands up before moving to take orders. I made a mental note to give her a perfect dream tonight, then turned back to the fat restaurateur.

"Then what is it?"

"A theory of weather. If a butterfly flaps its wings in South America it will cause a storm in Europe. Maybe a butterfly flapped its wings in prehistoric times and dropped fish in a rainstorm today." He smiled in triumph.

I stared at him over my cup, tying to decide between acknowledging that stranger things have happened in my lifetime and poking holes in his theory. Henri saved me the decision by slouching into the café and dropping a photo onto the table in front of me. I picked it up.

"Damn thing's broken," he said. "Or at least it's still not right."

"Why's that?" Benito asked. He signalled Maria to get the young man a drink. Maria responded with a hand signal I didn't think girls like her knew and stormed off into the kitchen. Benito looked at us apologetically.

"Excuse me, gentleman." He rose and followed her, ignoring the numerous calls for his attention.

"You see?" Henri pointed to the photo. Indeed, I could. Anna Prendergast shone, her soul a cascade of iridescence. But that was where the colour ended. Her husband and the coelacanth were no more than grey smudges, indistinct and cold next to her furious warmth. I looked up at Henri. The tickle at the back of my mind grew more insistent.

"Have you heard of the butterfly effect?"

"It's a Moonspell album, isn't it?"

"No. Tell me, if butterflies can cause fish to fall out of the sky, what would you say made the ghosts of fish fall?"

He laughed. "I don't know. A ghost butterfly?" His smile stopped. "Why are you looking at me like that?"

"Come on," I stood up. "We have to go somewhere."

The voices in the kitchen were joined by the sound of smashing crockery. We moved out of the door and into the morning.

Albrecht Wunderkammer opened the carved door of his emporium before I had the chance to knock. Alone of all my citizens, he possessed the uncanny knack of anticipating my approach. He knew it annoyed me, and always took pleasure from the knowledge. His smile was both genuine and taunting.

"Ah, Father, what a pleasant surprise. And young Henry, isn't it?"

"Henri." The younger man replied in anger. I looked at him in surprise. Like many of us, Albrecht has not always been what he is now. Some of those things have been less than beneficial for a person of Henri's background. Not even Albrecht was aware. Many of those with past lives have no recollection of what came before. For some it is the only way they can continue to function. I shook my head. Perhaps Henri simply didn't like having his name mispronounced. Wunderkammer ushered us into his store and closed the door.

"What can I do for you, gentlemen? A curio perhaps, or a special gift? Something for a lady?" He raised an eyebrow at Henri, who turned his head and examined the shop's cluttered interior.

"What is this place?"

"A shop," I replied, wandering from exhibit to exhibit, touching Peruvian funerary masks, brushing a finger across a lotus blossom of a type only grown in the private gardens of the Japanese Emperor. "A nexus. Curios and falderal, gewgaws and artifacts, from all corners of the globe. Isn't that right, Albrecht?"

"That it is, Father. Couldn't have put it better myself. Rarities from places the ordinary simply cannot reach, for a price the ordinary can reach with ease."

"Yes, places." I stopped before the display case that had been my objective. Small gilded cages stood upon the shelves. Each one contained a butterfly of great and distinct beauty, small bursts of colour trapped behind bars. I heard Henri suck in air behind me.

"Some people would cage rainbows," he said, and his voice bore such anger that it made me blink. "Something is in pain in this shop."

I drew my eyes away from the young man, and focussed again on the reason for my being here.

"All manner of places, Albrecht," I said, drawing a cage down from the shelf. "And times?" I turned an inquisitive look upon the shopkeeper, and saw him blanch.

"Oh no, no, no, Father. Not I. I wouldn't do that again."

I felt Henri's questioning gaze as I stalked towards Wunderkammer, cage held before me like a lantern.

"Costa Satanas folds in upon itself Henri, like a tessaract. Sometimes pockets of time and place get caught up in the folds, pockets I do my best to protect from poachers and tourists. And unscrupulous shopkeepers. Don't I, Albrecht?"

"No, Father. I mean, yes." The old man backed into the counter and uttered a cry of shock. "I didn't do it. I didn't, I swear!"

I leaned over him, held the cage in his face so it filled his vision.

"There was a rain of fish this morning, Albrecht—ancient fish, brought on by the butterfly you sold. There will be other things next, from other times, unless we get it back to where it belongs. Things that won't entertain the people I protect, Albrecht, things that will hunt them and tear them to pieces."

"Please, Father . . . "

"Will you be there when the smilodon roam my streets, Wunderkammer? Will you stand against Vercingetorix's warriors? Where is it, Albrecht? Who did you sell it to?"

"I didn't . . . "

"Who?" I shouted, using a voice I haven't drawn upon in longer than Albrecht has been alive. A rain of dust fell from the ceiling. Some of the larger animals in the rear of the shop began to whine. A trickle of blood began the journey from Wunderkammer's nostrils to his top lip. He slumped on the counter, and answered in a voice not much more than a whisper.

"A boy. His name . . . the receipt book. Tourist."

Henri moved behind the counter and drew out a leather-bound ledger. He flipped through the pages, muttering obscenities at the entries while Wunderkammer and I held our positions.

"Got it," he said, tearing a page out and handing it to me. I looked down at the scrawled entry.

"This boy has left us. He flew out two weeks ago, back to the world. Do you know what that means?"

"No!"

"A piece of us has entered the world, Albrecht. The last time it happened we almost lost ourselves." I put it in my jacket pocket and laid the cage on the countertop. "Pray it takes a smaller gift than last time to recover the butterfly. Pray very hard. The shape of your future depends upon it."

Albrecht hung his head in fear. Then Henri surprised me once more. He rounded the counter and came between the old man and I. He leaned into Albrecht's face and hissed in a dangerous voice.

"Let them all go. Don't be here when I come back."

"He won't be," I said as Henri stalked toward the door. I made to join him, looking back over my shoulder at the defeated shopkeeper.

"You know what I promised last time."

He nodded. As I closed the door behind me I saw him move toward the cages at the back of the shop.

Benito caught up with us as we reached my house.

"You forgot your . . . what's the matter with him?" he asked, as Henri brushed past and pushed open the front door.

"I'm not sure," I replied. "I think someone's opened a memory he'd rather have left alone. Anyhow, I'm glad you're here." I laid a hand on his shoulder and steered him inside. "How do you feel about taking a little trip?"

"I still don't know why you can't just go yourself."

Benito perched on a stool in my kitchen. I looked through the window at Henri, sitting with head bowed in my back garden. The garden is not always the safest place for the uninitiated. There are paths there I keep close to my attention for a reason.

"Because you will need to leave Costa Satanas, and I cannot. Call it fear of falling, if you like."

"Fear of flying?"

I thought back to my arrival in this place: the pain of the fire, the shuddering impact, the knowledge of just how isolated from home and family I had become. I shook my head. "However you like. Just accept that you must go in my place, hmm?"

"If you insist. What do I have to do?"

Out in the garden, a furred head appeared amongst the grass, striped and broad across as a man's chest. I opened my mouth to shout a warning but before I could utter a sound the tiger bounded across to Henri and laid its head in his lap. Without looking up he wrapped his arms around its neck and buried his face in its fur.

"Father?"

"Huh? Oh, yes." I turned from the window. "You have skills in this matter that I lack. I know nothing of lepidoptery and your expertise will be vital."

Benito laughed. "I don't know anything about . . . what you said."

I held out the cup of liquid I had been stirring. "You did once. Drink this."

"Go to the Baron. Give him my marker. He'll fly you there." Benito took the token from my hand.

"It's thousands of miles."

I smiled. "The sky has holes, old friend. The Baron knows them all."

"He doesn't have an aeroplane."

My smile grew broader. "You know the biplane on the tavern's roof? It's not just for show."

"But . . . " his round face broke into a sweat.

"The roof goes for longer than is visible." I laughed "It's quite a ride.

You'll love it." Before he could protest further I turned to a shelf and drew down a small butterfly made of brass and studded with jewels.

"A long time ago," I said, staring into its emerald eye, "the third most beautiful woman in all of history took a lover. She was a noblewoman in the ancient city of Alexandria. Her lover, well, he wasn't noble at all. But he *was* in love with her. As a mark of his devotion he commissioned the famous inventor Heron to produce this toy."

I held it up to the light, turning it this way and that, so Benito could see the exquisite craftsmanship. "Her name has long been forgotten. Her husband, who was an important man, discovered the tryst. The beautiful woman was flogged and broken in the public square, then banished to some filthy little dunghill away from the civilised world, where her beauty soon faded into madness and indignity. The lover was driven through the streets while each citizen took his turn to make a single cut with knives the nobleman had forged for the occasion. They drove him, bleeding and insensate, to the cliffs outside the city, where he was thrown onto the rocks below. His possessions were destroyed, his name erased from the city records."

I flicked a small switch on the butterfly's rear, and it flew across the room and landed on Benito's outstretched hand. "It took me a very long time to track this piece down, and a greater fortune than I shall ever see again to purchase it."

He found the switch and turned it off. I passed him a box and he laid the butterfly inside, then turned to leave.

"Benito?"

"Yes, Father?"

"It is the boy's, understand?"

He paused with his back to me. "Yes, Father."

He tucked the box under his arm and exited into the street. I watched him walk toward the town quarter containing the Baron's tavern.

"Forgive me, lady," I whispered to the air, "but the need is great." Old scars itching, I turned to other tasks.

"Henri?"

At my voice the animals around him scattered and ran for cover. Henri watched them go.

"My Dad," he said, without looking at me, "was the most superstitious creature God could have created. Cameroonian *and* a football manager." He smiled sadly. "Do you know that in Cameroon they still believe in curses? They work, of course. They work if you believe. They bury chickens at the corner posts to curse opposition teams. Dad would make me walk around the pitch before each game. Every time I started crying, they'd dig." He sniffed at the tears sliding down his cheeks. "Never missed a chicken."

"What happened?"

"The most superstitious people on Earth. They came for me one night. I was six. I felt the dogs three streets away." He looked up into a sky years behind us. "A boy who can sense animals, but who doesn't think to wake his parents."

He bowed his head again. "The old man on the beach. He's dead, isn't he? That's why you wanted the photo with the fish. My camera's not broken, I just didn't read the photo right."

I sat down next to him. "Yes, I think so. I'm not sure quite how yet, but he is."

"Someone will have to tell him."

"Yes. Otherwise, when they leave . . . "

Costa Satanas is a special place, with its own special powers. But all powers are defined by borders. Once past them, few people can resist the natural order. Henri looked up at me.

"Where's Benito?"

"I sent him to get the butterfly's ghost."

"Benito?"

I explained why I had sent the restaurateur, and the past life I had reawakened within him. Henri listened in silence.

"As long as he gets back in time, there should be no problems."

"In time for what?"

"The life I've reawakened. In that life he did some . . . unpleasant things. Those memories will return as well, sooner or later. He should get back before they resurface, and I can dispense with the recall."

"What kind of unpleasant things?"

I told him.

"And you would risk him knowing, just for . . . " He stood and walked toward the door.

"Where are you going?"

"To see the old man. To try to explain."

"But . . . "

"Forgive me, Father," he said without looking at me, "but if you can do that to a friend . . . for a priest, empathy is perhaps not your greatest gift."

"I'm not a . . . " I began, but he had already left.

With nothing left to do I went to the tavern to await Benito's return. There are any numbers of ways to change your perception of time. Over my life I've learnt spells and incantations designed to speed or slow the clock at will. This time, I decided to stick with alcohol. Spells may be able to alter time, but a bout of drinking can do that *and* lessen the pain of a friend's truly spoken words. I spent a few hours wishing the stuff could make me drunk as well. Unfortunately, I no longer speak to the one who pours the wine that can accomplish that task. Still, the rum I was imbibing served its purpose. It didn't seem so long before a gloved hand fell on my shoulder.

"Father?"

"Baron."

"*Guten Tag*. I believe this is yours?"

He placed a small gilded cage on the bar before me. Inside its bars shivered a coloured butterfly. It was beautiful, but alien, like a less refined version of a modern butterfly. I opened the cage door and cupped the insect inside my hand.

"Here," I said, offering it to the Baron. He held out his hand and I dropped the butterfly into it. The insect dived straight through the centre of his palm before taking wing and flying through the open door and into the sun.

"He'll find his way home," I answered his astonished stare. "Whenever that was." I looked around. "Where's Benito?"

"He said something about needing to get to Church."

"Benito?"

"*Ja*. He seemed shaken, almost ill."

"Oh, no. No." I ran to the door.

"Father?" the Baron's question followed me into the street. "Why would Benito wish to suffer penance?"

I found Henri coming out of the Hotel Quixote.

"Have you seen Benito?"

"They're fine, thanks. They're in pain, and struggling with denial, but I think they'll come to terms with things."

"Sorry?"

"The Prendergasts." He gestured toward the hotel. The sound of crying came from inside. I looked through the open doorway into the lobby. The old couple sat on a lounge chair holding each other. Mama Casson was with them, gripping their hands and attempting to get them to drink from two steaming bowls.

"What's she feeding them?"

"A combination of things. But that doesn't concern you, right? You've solved your mystery, got your butterfly back? You don't need to worry about their little problem, their hurt and confusion and need to understand."

"Henri." I stood helpless in the face of his restrained anger. "Some of us . . . it is not always natural for me. I try to learn. Please. Benito?"

He looked over his shoulder at Mama Casson, who nodded.

"I've not seen him."

"The Baron said he was going to Church, that he was going to suffer penance."

"Aw, hell."

We set off for the Avenue of The Artists. As we ran, I asked, "So how did it happen?"

"What?"

"Mister Prendergast."

"On the ferry. As it crossed into the bay. Says he remembers a tightness in his chest, blurred vision, not being able to breathe. Then they passed the headland and everything cleared up. He thought it was just an angina attack. He's been on pills."

"But he'd died."

"Right on the cusp between here and there. One in a million shot."

We ran on.

"You're a good man, Henri."

"I'm trying, Father, I'm trying. What the hell?"

We came to a stop outside the twin churches of Costa Satanas' patrons, Saint Genesius and Saint Michael of Tolentino. Or more accurately, where they had been. Only the multi-coloured confusion that was the Church of Saint Genesius faced us. Of the smaller, dour grey Church of St Michael there was no sign.

"Oh, no." I breathed.

"Where is it?"

"He's gone in. We're too late."

"But where is it?"

"It's gone."

"Gone?"

"Moved. Gone." I kneeled, and began patting my jacket pockets, emptying them onto the ground in front of me. "The churches have been battling for centuries, feeding on the faith of supplicants and staking out new territories. It could have moved anywhere. Damn it!" I swept aside the pile and began building another from my pocket's contents.

"What is it?"

"I need a token. A lost cause."

"What?"

"Saint Michael of Tolentino is patron saint of lost causes. If we have a token, we can use it to track him, but I can't bloody find one."

"How many pockets do you have in that thing anyway?" Henri asked, eyeing the growing piles of refuse.

"As many as I need. See?" I held up a red felt bobble nose. "If it were Genesius, I could have just used this."

"Clowns and lost causes," Henri muttered. "That ought to be a clue." He reached up to the multitude of chains around his neck and pulled one over his head.

"Here."

"What is it?" I took the chain and looked at the round brass medallion hanging from it. A stylised image of a tree was embossed upon one side.

"Nottingham Forest Supporter's Club. Trust me, no cause is more hopeless."

"Right. If you say so."

I took the medallion from the chain and placed it on the ground between us. Rummaging through the pile of pocket discards, I found a vial of Dead Man's Water, a small jar of powdered honeysuckle, and a mouse pelt. I plucked a few hairs from the rodent's back and placed them on the medallion, then sprinkled the herb and water over it, muttering words I learned during a short, unhappy stint with a cabal in what would have passed for my youth were I to measure time that way.

"What was all that about?" Henri asked as I finished the chant and began stuffing objects back into my jacket.

"Homing spell. See?" I pointed to the medallion, which now stood on its edge. In a way neither of us could quite quantify, it seemed to be waiting for us to get ready so it could be off. "Go on then," I said, and it began rolling at a slow but steady speed down the street. I picked up the last of the items and smiled.

"Ha, I'd forgotten I had these."

I held out the battered paper bag to Henri and did my best Tom Baker. "Jelly baby?"

"Uh, no. Thanks." With another dubious look Henri started to move away from me and after the medallion. "Shouldn't we be following that?"

"I suppose so." I sighed, popping a sweet into my mouth. One day, I swear, I'll introduce this town to Doctor Who. For now, however, I had other duties to attend to. I set off after Henri and the rolling medallion. As we followed it, the token rolled faster and faster, until we had to run to keep up.

"It's getting closer." I gasped as it led us up a hill close to the outskirts of town. "The nearer it gets to its objective, the faster it goes."

"I hope it's as close as it's going to get." Henri struggled to get the words out. "Maurice Green I'm not."

"Who?"

He looked at me sideways. "I'm going to have to introduce you to the Olympics one day, I swear."

I'd competed in the Olympic Games when all you ran for was glory and a laurel of smelly leaves, but I chose not to mention that to my young companion. At that moment the medallion turned a corner. We rounded in its wake and stopped in our tracks.

"Is it just me," Henri asked, "Or is this street slightly, uh, *different*?"

It wasn't him. Costa Satanas is, usually, a vibrant melange of noise and movement. It is the very soul of what a tropical holiday spot should be, or at least a tropical holiday spot viewed through the dreams of an uncritical tourist. The street we now stood upon was leached of colour. Gray and brown buildings slumped along either side of the ill-formed cobbles. No sounds reached us, no signs assailed our sight with coloured promises, no unfurled umbrellas cast shade under a sun that hung lifeless and dim above.

"Oh, no," I groaned. "It's in the soft streets."

"Soft streets?"

"You know Costa Satanas conforms to the imaginations of those who come here?"

"Uh, yeah?"

"Well, what do you think happens to the streets no-one visits?"

He shrugged. "I don't know. I didn't think a small town like this would have such streets."

"This place is bigger than it looks, Henri, in all directions and times. And towns evolve. They travel. Slowly, but they do travel. Spaces get left behind." I grabbed his arm. "You'll have to go in first."

"Me? Why? It's not dangerous is it?"

"Listen." I turned him to face me. "The soft streets are a blank template, waiting to be formed by the people who walk them. If I go in first . . . "

"Oh, please." He laughed. "You're a priest. What can you create that's so fearsome?"

"I keep telling you, I'm not a . . . "

"I know, I know. But still." He patted my shoulder and pushed me ahead of him. "Come on, we're wasting time."

"Henri . . . " The eyes, surprisingly, really *are* the windows to the soul. Like all windows, some of us hang heavy curtains to ward off those who would peek inside. I looked into Henri's gaze. I opened my curtains, just enough to give him a glimpse of what lay behind. When I closed them again, and looked onto the normal world, he lay curled up in the road crying. I leant down to help him up. He scuttled away from my touch.

"My God, what are you?"

I sighed. "You know more than anyone living, my friend."

He rose, and made a determined effort to gather himself.

"I'll lead. You'll close your eyes then?"

"It's a little more complex than that. The streets respond to a person's desires, whether they be conscious or otherwise." I began to subvocalise a hypnotic mantra I learned more lives ago than I care to count. "I can't give them anything to latch onto. You're going to have to . . . "

Consciousness left me and I fell to the cobbled street.

I woke to voices shouting my name, and a muted grey light that found the spaces behind my eyes and poked them until they watered. Henri stood above me. A small, morose man with an expression of pious misery carved into his face peered over his shoulder. Henri was shaking my shoulders.

"Okay," I croaked, removing his hands and sitting upright, "I'm up. You don't have to shout."

"I'm not shouting," he replied, his voice booming a path through my skull. The man beside him scowled at me.

"He cannot come here. I told you." His words thundered through me as well. Then I realised where I was. Churches always find a way to cause me pain.

"Michael . . . " I began.

"Do not speak to me!" he cried. "I know what you are! *Vene sancte spiritus . . .* " He backed away, raising a cross and chanting. I looked to Henri.

"Do you know what he's saying?"

"You don't know?"

"I've never got the hang of normal Latin." I levered myself out of the pew and stood up.

"I thought all priests . . . "

"I'm not a priest. Neither is he. He's the physical embodiment of the church. Like a golem, just more annoying. Have you found . . . Benito!"

I saw the figure hunched in the front row. I pushed past the grey saint's simulacra and ran to the restaurateur. He was praying, eyes squeezed shut, bent over clasped hands and mumbling Italian in a heartbroken monotone. Begging forgiveness. Begging release from the burden of his monstrosity. Begging absolution for crimes for which he had already suffered penance in between lives. The crimes I had revisited upon him.

I kneeled before him and placed my hands upon his.

"Benito."

"Why, Father?" he asked without opening his eyes. "Why?"

"I . . . I could think of no other way. It was necessary."

"No." He shook his head. "No. It was easy."

I looked at his tear-riven face. "I can make you forget."

He raised his eyes then, and gave me such a look that I was forced to turn away.

"Tell me I did not do those things."

"It was another life, Benito. Another you. You paid for those sins."

"And you gave them back to me!" He tore his hand from mine, raised it as if to strike me, then lowered it to his side. I kept my head averted, allowing him the blow.

"You paid for them. Giving them back was the sin. Benito, it was *my* sin."

"You're damn right it was!" A hand fell upon my shoulder and pushed me away from Benito's slumped form. I looked up in shock. I allow few people to touch me, and none so dismissively.

"Mister Prendergast! What are you doing here?"

"Who do you think helped drag you in here?" he responded. "He won't touch you." He nodded towards the angrily quivering Michael. "You're too damn heavy for one person to lug all the way up the street. What do you keep in that jacket anyway, rocks?"

I fingered my pockets. "Mister Prendergast, you don't understand . . ."

"Oh, I understand, more than you think, Father. I've worked with past life therapy before. Only *I'm* qualified." His sniff spoke volumes for his opinion of clergy who dabble in psychological fields. I decided not to correct him on either count. He leant over and spoke to Benito.

"Son, if you need to talk you can come and see me any time. I've found some offices . . ."

"You're staying here?"

He looked at me with scorn. "Doesn't seem I have many choices, if what your young friend tells me is true."

"It is. I'm sorry."

"Are you just. Well, *his* word I trust." He leant back to Benito once more, dismissal in every angle of his body. I stepped backwards and bumped into Henri and Mrs. Prendergast.

"Don't worry," she said. "Tom's very good, and we've found cheap office space in an old curio shop. Henri found it for us, didn't you, love?"

Henri blushed.

"Besides," she continued, "we've no family, and I wasn't really looking forward to going back to the retirement home. Winters there are so cold, and Henri tells me it's hardly ever winter here."

"But . . . "

"You're young," she said. "At least in the ways that matter. One day you'll know what we know." She nodded toward where her husband was helping Benito to his feet and walking toward us. "A lifetime together is better than any time at all apart."

She took her husband's hand. I turned to Benito.

"Are you . . . ?"

"I don't need forgetfulness. Or absolution." He tilted his head toward Michael. "I need to understand, to deal with it in my own way. I think . . . I think I can do that."

"If you're sure."

"I am."

He moved away, then stopped and with his back to me spoke words that broke my heart.

"It's all right, Father. I forgive you."

I stood on the steps of the church and watched thunderclouds build over the town, layering and sculpting them to mirror my guilt and shame. The street around me lay dark and stony, no longer soft now it had been trodden by souls human enough to give them shape. Henri stood beside me and watched Benito and the Prendergasts walk away.

"You're not perfect."

"I know."

"But?"

"But." The others turned a corner and disappeared without a backward glance. "My . . . family . . . haunt me, Henri. At any time I find myself a single step away from lapsing. It takes a constant will, constant memory. Each time I forget, for even the slightest moment . . . "

I gestured toward the space Benito had moved through. Henri considered me for a moment, then reached into the air before him and waved his fingers. A small scrap of colour fell from the sky and into his grasp. He turned to me and placed it on my palm.

"Here," he said. "To remind you."

He gripped my shoulder briefly, and walked away. I looked down at the butterfly on my hand and felt tears I had held back for centuries scald my cheeks.

AFTERWORD

After pontificating to anyone who'd listen that I hate sequels, I don't do sequels, I'll never do a sequel... when Keith Stevenson, editor of *Aurealis*, wrote to me and said "When the hell am I going to get a sequel to Father Muerte?" I replied "Six weeks", then spent five of them staring at a blank page. This story made it to Keith in time for his last issue as Aurealis editor, and procured me my first cover. The good Father has seen the light in two more stories after this one, plus there's a novel on the way, so it seems to be an idea that won't go away.

PATER FAMILIAS

The formal lounge room is cold enough to raise goose bumps. The visitor perches on the edge of his armchair and views the fireplace with fierce longing. His host pours tea. Steam rises in swirls of heat.

"I apologise for the atmosphere," the old man says as he hands over a cup. "It's essential for my work, and my daughters prefer these conditions."

His guest takes a sip, grateful for the infusion of warmth. "Your work?"

"Is private, and not why you're here. You wanted to discuss my previous career?"

"I did." The visitor places his cup onto a small side table and lifts a notebook and pen. "The association has been reviewing your case histories. They've asked me to seek clarification over some anomalies. Particularly in light of . . . "

"In light of the circumstances surrounding my retirement. What is it you wish to know?"

"Several of your terminations. The mothers reported that no information was given them regarding disposal of their children. Nothing has been recorded in the case notes."

"May I see?" His host holds out a liver-spotted hand and the book is placed into it. The old man reads the notes in silence. "They wanted their babies killed, rather than face the thought of losing their own life. I felt no obligation to tell them. They had forfeited the right to care."

"It's not a matter of care, sir. The association requires complete records."

The surgeon stares at his visitor for long seconds, then passes back the notebook.

"Do you know what takes place during a craniotomy?"

"The association prefers caesarean sections, now that such procedures guarantee some chance of survival for both mother and child."

"I'm sure they do. But these operations took place more than twenty years ago. And all were craniotomies."

"How do you know? That isn't in my notes."

"I remember. Answer the question."

"Well, it involves cracking the skull of the unborn infant, doesn't it?"

"It involves more than that." The old man leans forward, illustrating his words with pecks of his withered hands. "You reach up inside the mother and strike the child's skull with a hammer until it crushes like an egg. Then, while the woman is still pushing against her contractions, you pull the corpse out and dispose of the remains. How is your tea?"

"Um." The young investigator picks up his cup with a shaking hand and takes a long swallow. "It's fine, thank you."

"You seem shaken at my description." The surgeon looks at him with a cold, calm gaze.

"It sounds . . . barbaric."

"It is necessary. The cranium of the child is too large to allow passage. A caesarean will kill the mother. Doing nothing will kill them both. This way, she lives to bear a child again. Unlike the alternative."

"But recent advances . . . "

"Are only recent. Not a single woman survived a caesarean in Paris for over a hundred years. Did you know that? It was only in 1794 that they recorded a successful case, less than a decade ago. I was operating under *those* circumstances, not the new age your association trumpets."

Sounds from the adjoining room intrude upon the two men. The surgeon tilts his head.

"Dinner is about to be served. You'll stay with us?"

"I'd be honoured."

"Good, good. Are you married?"

"Uh, no, I'm not. Why do you ask?"

The old man smiles. "My daughters are reaching that age. A father likes to take an interest."

"I'm sure I shall enjoy their company, sir."

"I'm sure you will." The surgeon smiles again, although whether at his visitor's discomfort or at some private joke, it is impossible to tell.

The investigator coughs, and looks around at the masculine decorations adorning the lounge room. His gaze falls upon a box within a display cabinet, opened to show a variety of small, silver-plated tools. He spies a shining hammer among them, and turns away.

"You have children. Is there no Mrs . . . ?"

"She died. In childbirth. Our first child, a caesarean. They both died. The surgeon was inexperienced and chose to proceed without consulting me first." A bell sounds, and the doctor rises. "Shall we go through?"

"But you said you had daughters?"

His host opens the door to the dining room and steps through. The young man follows. The host's offspring have gathered round the far end of the table, surrounding a solitary chair. The investigator smiles in greeting, his lips freezing into a rictus at the sight of their misshapen heads, their shattered and twisted bodies hidden beneath cotton shifts, their faces destroyed beyond recognition by the pounding of tiny silver hammers. He turns in sudden panic, but the old man's bulk is blocking the only escape. The surgeon moves into the room, closing and locking the door behind him.

"Any fool can kill," the old man says, and the investigator recoils at the love in his voice. "The real joy comes when you keep them alive."

AFTERWORD

This is the monster at the end of the book. As a writer, there are some concepts that grab your imagination by the throat and won't let go. I'd discovered craniotomies a couple of years before this story was written, and couldn't get the idea out of my head. The barbarism of it appalled and fascinated me, and having lost my first wife to the tender mercies of obstetric medicine, I have long since fallen out of love with the medical fraternity. At the time of writing, the story's been short listed for the 2006 Aurealis Award for Horror, and it's a story that seems to split readers: at least one recent reviewer made the mistake of thinking the poor grown-up daughters are the monsters.

PUBLICATION HISTORY

Father Muerte & the Theft first appeared in *Aurealis* 29, June 2002

Silk first appeared in *All-Star Zeppelin Adventure Stories*, Wheatland Press, October 2004

Carrying The God first appeared in *L Ron Hubbard Presents Writers of the Future Vol. 18*, Galaxy Publishing, August 2002

Pass The Parcel first appeared in *The Australian Woman's Day*, November 2001

Through The Window Merrilee Dances first appeared in *Andromeda Spaceways Inflight Magazine* 16, December 2004

The Divergence Tree first appeared in *Orb* 3/4, June 2002

The Hobbyist first appeared in *Andromeda Spaceways Inflight Magazine* 10, December 2003

Letters To Josie first appeared in *Borderlands* 3, April 2004

A Stone To Mark My Passing first appeared in *Elsewhere*, CSFH Publishing, October 2003

Vortle first appeared in *Encounters*, CSFG Publishing, August 2004

Ecdysis first appeared in *Andromeda Spaceways Inflight Magazine* 11, March 2004

A Very Good Lawyer first appeared in *Glimpses*, Vision Publishing, October 2003

continued

Stalag Hollywood was winner in the *Katharine Susannah Prichard Writer's Centre SF&F Competition 2003*, and appears for the first time in print.

Brillig first appeared in *EOTU*, June 2002

Through Soft Air first appeared in *Borderlands 1*, April 2003

Tales of Nireym first appeared in *Orb Issue 6*, June 2004

Father Muerte & The Rain first appeared in *Aurealis 33/34/35*, December 2004

Pater Familias first appeared in *Shadowed Realms* 3, January 2005

Made in the USA
Lexington, KY
05 June 2012